T0305009

ISOLATION ISLAND

LOUISE MINCHIN

ISOLATION ISLAND

HEADLINE

First published in Great Britain in 2024 by
HEADLINE PUBLISHING GROUP

1

Cataloguing in Publication Data is available from the British Library

Hardback ISBN 978 1 0354 0746 0
Trade paperback ISBN 978 1 0354 0747 7

Typeset in 12.76/16.82pt Adobe Garamond Pro by Jouve (UK), Milton Keynes

Printed and bound in Great Britain by Clays Ltd, Elcograf S.p.A.

MIX
Paper | Supporting
responsible forestry
FSC® C104740

Headline's policy is to use papers that are natural, renewable and recyclable
products and made from wood grown in well-managed forests and other
controlled sources. The logging and manufacturing processes are expected to
conform to the environmental regulations of the country of origin.

HEADLINE PUBLISHING GROUP
An Hachette UK Company
Carmelite House
50 Victoria Embankment
London EC4Y 0DZ

www.headline.co.uk
www.hachette.co.uk

*To David, thank you for always being my rock
when I find myself in a hard place.*

Prologue

Dusk is falling when she finds it.

Above her, the clouds have taken on the colours of an ageing bruise – grey, mauve and purple – and the air holds a strange, almost greenish, light. It is a lull. The lichened stones are slippery from the rainfall, and debris is strewn across the graveyard. Long grasses are flattened against the headstones, and among the yew trees that flank the monastery walls she sees a scar, vivid orange in the murky light, where the storm has sheared a branch from the twisted body of an ancient trunk.

She guesses, from the dark smudges on the horizon, that it will not be long until the rain comes again. But, for now, she is relieved simply to be outside, breathing in solitude and fresh air. Flashes of lightning are sparking from the banked-up clouds in the distance, and she can hear the wind begin to moan. Time to go back.

She turns for what, strangely, feels like home.

At the end of the path stands the ruined west end of the ancient chapel, a stage-set of stone columns and crumbling arches, dominated by the tall square belfry. Heading towards it, she passes under the shadows of the trees. Here she hesitates: surely, she doesn't need to go in there? But when she sees the heavy oak door is slightly open, the latch hanging, she ignores her better instincts.

It scrapes against its lintel so that she has to put her shoulder to it to push it inwards, a wedge of pale fading light falling on to the flags and merging the dark interior into disjointed angles. Stepping inside, she feels her body tense in the cool of the space, the hairs on the back of her neck rising as though being pulled up into the emptiness above her head. It's the smell, she thinks, the distinctive dank mix of ancient stone and dust. The smell of centuries. The smell of time.

'Hello?' she calls, her voice echoing up the cantilevered stone stair-case and into the void.

But the creaking she hears in return is indeterminate, nothing more than the wind whistling through the open windows above.

'Hello?' she calls again, girding herself to climb the stairs, an unwelcome prospect in the shadowed dimness, with not even the torch on her phone to light her way.

She takes the first flight as quickly as she can, the sound of her steps on each stair magnified. Instinctively, she moves towards the wall, searching out its solid reassurance with her trembling fingers. As the stair turns, she finds herself clinging to the corner, alarmed by the height of the drop to her right. It is then that she sees it. Behind the door she has just come through there is a darkened mass wedged against it, a distorted shadow.

As she flies back down the stairs, she knows what lies below, what she has found. When she reaches the misshapen heap, she gasps for air and scrabbles at the rough cloth, desperate for a response. There is none. Only cold flesh and a lifeless hand, with no reassuring pulse.

Sitting back on her heels in despair, she reaches out to pull back the hood that hides the face. Her mind fractures with shock and confusion, two conflicting thoughts running through her head: It can't be true, and, Yes, it is. Because what lies in front of her is both impossible to believe and all too real. Outside the tower, the wind screeches as if in warning. She suddenly feels the enormity of how alone and vulnerable she is, crouched at the foot of an ancient stair, holding a cold, unmoving hand in her own.

Chapter One

A piercing scream evaporates into the ether. At first it seems formless, an animal howl fragmented by the buffeting wind and spray. Until it drops off into a moan: 'Not again! No . . . no . . . Make it stop. Please . . .'

For the fifth time in a row, the sleek black speedboat slams into a wave, its bow leaping almost vertically into the air. Water pours off its flanks, shiny and slick as an orca, breaching high out of the dark waters of the freezing sea loch and landing once more with a bone-shaking bang. For a moment it is as though it has lost its momentum and will stall here, stranded amidst the swells and valleys of the gunmetal-grey water. Then the two massive engines gain purchase under the surface and the launch surges forward again, the churn of its propellers forcing a furious white froth to the surface in its wake.

Hunched against the side of the boat, her ribs crushing with the weight of the g-force, Lauren hears the howl only dimly. She is fighting to keep herself focused on one thing only: her own breath, rising and falling, restricted by the tight embrace of her lifejacket. The salty ozone taste of the in-breath, the steaming puff of the out-breath. As long as she can keep her mind fixed solely on that rhythm, she can fight the nausea that is threatening to overwhelm her. Everything else – the harness uncomfortably buckled at her chest, the camera drone hovering dangerously close – is blocked out as she fights the constriction in her throat, sickness rising as the boat lurches. She wishes she were at the helm: that is always where she feels best when she is out on the water, but then this sea is unusually rough, even for an experienced sailor like her.

A part of her registers that the begging voice is coming from the brawny man beside her. The one that earlier looked at her pityingly as she checked and rechecked her harness, trying to find faith in its clanky clasps and sodden webbing. Now, his huge bulk is bent into a crouch, and his legs are so long they are pressing two perfectly symmetrical knee-shaped dents into the blue faux leather of the seat in front of him. His face is waxy and sallow under the dripping spray, his eyes closed.

Strange that this is the same man, Aidan 'Mac' Macdonald, whose photos have emblazoned the sports pages of newspapers for most of the last decade. That iconic image – both arms raised, rugby ball aloft, his face tilted in triumph towards the banks of fans at Murrayfield as the Saltire unfurls behind him – was taken only a couple of years ago, at his triumphant, miraculous farewell match against England. It's difficult to reconcile that heroic image with the hunched figure moaning beside her.

Lauren raises a wry eyebrow both at him and at herself. Who is she to talk? Lauren Brooks, investigative journalist, who has always prided herself on her ability to throw herself in at the deep end, tough it out, while her mind files impressions and critical details even under the most trying of circumstances. Who, over decades, has honed her ability to persuade people to share their deepest secrets and manoeuvred herself both into and out of some truly hair-raising situations. But here she is, reduced to nothing but sodden breath and overwhelming nausea. And by what? An inflatable RIB full of celebrities, and some rough seas.

If she is completely honest, however, it's not only the boat that's making her feel like this. There has been an uneasy shifting in her stomach for weeks now.

The first flutters of nerves started as soon as she finally told Steph, her agent, to say yes to what had seemed at first a laughable request: an invitation to appear on *Isolation Island*, the epic new reality show set to launch in the autumn.

The first approach had been an email: would she like to be one of the 'carefully selected' (read: willing to endure almost anything) famous faces braving the monastery on Eilean Manach, a.k.a. Monk Island, the derelict medieval abbey that would be the location for the grittiest of gritty reality TV series?

Pitching itself as the gothic antithesis to the sunshine-and-bikini shows, this is, the proposal claimed, going to be a major event. The contestants will be marooned, in the depths of the Scottish winter, on a deserted island known both for its isolation and the rigours of monastic life at the edge of civilisation. They will be completely alone, relying only on themselves and each other, no matter what the island throws at them.

And it will throw a lot, because Production has rigged it with challenges and pitfalls that will be controlled remotely from a base back at the mainland. Just as the medieval monks had to obey the abbots, the contestants will have to submit to whatever instructions the programme's directors give them. Their continued existence there is entirely at the whim of the producers – who will decide who 'lives' and who 'dies'. They will never know quite what is in store for them. The cameras will be trained on them twenty-four hours a day, seven days a week, and the programme will air twice daily – morning and night – to reach both the crucial breakfast audience and the lucrative prime-time viewers, going live in each slot to check on the progress of the contestants.

The twist? The last man or woman standing will win the prize of their dreams, worth over a million pounds and tailored specifically to them. 'Answered Prayers', the producers are calling it. 'Aim high,' the production company said as they put her own unique prize together. Tell us what it is you fantasise about: the never-never project you have always dreamed of fulfilling, the chance to get that record deal, that TV show, or that one-time massive sponsorship deal. Whatever you most want, we can make it happen. The incentive they are now dangling in front of Lauren is a mouth-watering one: her own flagship investigations series in the most prestigious slot on the network, post-watershed and pre-news, at 9 p.m. If it happens, it will be an unimaginable turnaround for her.

What the others are being offered, she has no idea. There is a strict ban on them discussing their potential prizes with anyone, and everyone else's prize will remain a mystery, to her and to the audience, until the very end. There can be only one winner.

Lauren's first response was an automatic no, even though she loves reality TV and all the psychological drama that comes with it – the unexpected friendships, the bubbles of raw emotion, the silly moments of childish conflict that go on to dominate the national conversation. But she loves them as a viewer, not as a participant. For a start, she doesn't think of herself as a celebrity. Fame is not something she wants or has ever sought. It is a sometimes irritating, occasionally useful by-product of her particular kind of journalism. Secondly, deep in her heart, she never wants to be the story. She is the reporter, not the subject. So why would she allow the eyes of the nation to be trained on her every move?

She let the email fall to the bottom of her inbox, embarrassed by the faint ruffle of satisfaction she felt that she was even in the running for such a huge show, and added it to the list of things to mention to her agent on their next call. Lauren could already hear the laughter – 'God, if they're asking me, the casting agents must be really scraping the bottom of the barrel. Can you imagine? Stuck with a whole load of celebrities, cameras recording my every move?'

But Steph didn't react like that at all. When they talked, her voice took on a slightly desperate edge. 'Are you sure, Lauren? It's a big show. And with . . . things as they are at the moment . . .'

Lauren said she would think about it, denying to herself that she knew what Steph meant: that she might need something like this, because her successful career was on hold right now, quite possibly for ever.

Things changed for her when the whispers began to swirl about who else would be on the island. She knew better than to trust the rumour mill – most of it put out by ambitious agents or the TV network to whet the public appetite – but this was different. It was too early, they were still finalising the details of the show itself, not yet ready for the public push. And the tip-off didn't come from the usual gossipy UK media circles. It came from an American contact from her time in LA making an undercover documentary about a doomsday cult. This was someone she trusted. So, when they talked, she listened.

The big fish the production company was on the verge of netting, apparently, was true Hollywood royalty. A real star, as close as you could get to the classic silver-screen icon. So far, so predictable. Celebrity fixers were always after the impossible when it came to these shows, and her sources liked to big themselves up by insinuating they knew more than they did.

But when she heard the name, she was astounded. What were the chances of that being true? The sceptical reporter in her told her the rumour was far-fetched – why would a star of that calibre do a show like this, halfway across the world? But then she heard the reasons why he might accept the gig. That he was desperate to get some positive headlines to deflect from his private life, especially as the Hollywood actors' strike had put any other projects on hold. In the light of what she knew about him, it began to sound like not just a remote possibility, but likely.

That was when her reporter's mind began to tick away in earnest. This might be the opportunity she had been chasing for over a year. If he really was in the show, he would be separated from his army of protectors: the lawyers, the agents, the managers, publicists, PAs and stylists that formed a thick layer of security and sycophancy between him and the real world. And if she were part of the cast, she might have a chance to get close to him, to get the evidence she desperately needed to expose him for what he really was. If she played it right, she might finally, after her endless attempts to unmask him, get some sort of justice. It was an outlandish and unlikely prospect, but if it happened it would be a one-off opportunity she couldn't afford to miss.

The night before the deadline to sign up, she slipped in and out of restless dreams in which a dozen fantastical scenarios played out against a menacing background of stone and sky, until she woke with a fragile, four-o'clock-in-the-morning decision. One that she half thought she'd take back before dawn but didn't. She would do it. She would risk it, even if he was a no-show. She had nothing to lose, no more cards to play.

She was in.

Chapter Two

Right now, hands tightly gripping the handle of the seat in front of her, trying in vain to keep herself upright, Lauren is seriously questioning that decision.

Months ago, back in the safety of her flat, when she signed her fifty-page contract, it all seemed to make so much sense. Even as she endured the exhausting series of medical and psychological checks to make sure she was fit to take part in the programme, she reasoned it was the right thing to do. But as the tiny smudge of rocks ahead of her grows on the horizon and reveals its dramatic shape, her confidence slips, replaced by dread in the pit of her stomach.

Perched precariously above a jagged, geometric tumble of high cliffs is the forbidding silhouette of the monastery, etched against the sky. A tall circular watchtower dominates the scene, like an exclamation mark, a stark warning to anyone who approaches that they are being observed at all times. It dwarfs the belfry, which still stands defiant next to the derelict remains of the chapel, destroyed in a fire decades ago.

Here and there the walls are pulled apart entirely, torn down by merciless gales that have sent masonry smashing into pieces on the rocks below. Everything about it is foreboding, a place to scare you away, not welcome you in. In Lauren's endless hours researching the history and geography of Eilean Manach, nothing has prepared her for the starkness of its wind-torn reality.

As she takes in her new home, the boat steadies. It has entered the lee of the island, and the sea is no longer choppy; the rolling waves have dispersed. For the first time, Lauren begins to take serious notice of her fellow passengers. She needs to start thinking of them as contestants, competitors, not just a ragtag bunch of semi-famous faces. All of them are in motion, talking feverishly amongst themselves.

Beside her, Mac straightens from his crouch at last. She watches him as his eyes fix on the monastery. For a moment, his face holds a curious blankness – no fear, no excitement, no enthusiasm. It is as though he is looking inward, not outwards at the forbidding sight ahead. Then he blinks and becomes the brash hearty sportsman she has seen in so many interviews and on numerous quiz shows.

'Jesus, would you look at that?' he says. 'I don't reckon it's going to be a five-star stay. By the state of the place, my money is on some of us not even surviving a couple of days.'

On the other side of him, a strident voice cuts through the rumble of the engine. Jude Wright. It was the sight of Jude, disembarking from an identical brand-new black Land Rover Defender this morning, that had made things real for Lauren. She was dying to see another face after the long the journey north from London, but her spirits sank on seeing the infamous severe ash-grey bob emerge from the first 4x4 to pull up after hers.

Jude is famous for three things: making an absolute fortune by turning her family's failing brewery into one of the biggest employers in the north of England; the stint she did as an angel-investor on a TV series in which she spent a week living with a family before deciding whether or not to put her money into their business; and her no-nonsense, sleeves-rolled-up attitude. What was her catchphrase again? 'What are you doing to earn my time?'

She is going to be formidable company.

Right now, she is deploying a soothing tone on Mac. 'Don't you worry,' she says. 'You're going to be fine. They'll have chosen the location so it looks worse on camera than it really is. Trust me, there's no way they'll put us through anything too terrible. I'm sure of it. For a start, I wouldn't stand for it.'

Lauren catches a hint of Stockport in her vowels, though so muted she must have made an effort to soften it over time. Her maternal tone makes it sound as if she has been telling Mac what to do for years, though Lauren knows for a fact that they only met this morning. Lauren remembers that part of Jude's TV persona is to assume the role of the tough-talking but tender-hearted matriarch of whatever situation she is put in.

Jude's hair, which is cut to an immaculately straight line, with an equally straight fringe, is somehow still in place as she leans over and puts her hand on one of Mac's powerful thighs in reassurance.

How does she do that, thinks Lauren, conscious of the fact that her own hair is sodden, her fringe plastered to her forehead. Jude might be scrubbed clean of her signature red lipstick, and the lifejacket-and-waterproofs combo is a world away from her usual attire, but Lauren gets the feeling that she is pretty used to being camera ready. Certainly, as they sat down in the boat, she saw Jude's eyes give a professional flick towards where the on-board camera was positioned, choosing her seat accordingly.

'Thanks, hen,' says Mac, but he doesn't look reassured.

Sitting at the stern of the launch are the final pair of the contestants so far. Directly behind Lauren is a small girl, not much more than twenty. She is slight but strong, and there's something deliberate and glossed up about her, on a perfect miniature scale. She has managed to come through the last half-hour looking pretty immaculate too, Lauren thinks, as she twists round to look behind her. Yes, her hair is dripping wet, but it has stayed where it was when she embarked, held back by a perfectly placed turquoise bandana. She appears to be fully, if lightly, made up, something that seems impossible until Lauren realises it is an illusion created by carefully laminated eyebrows and tinted eyelashes. Even the spray from the boat has given her a healthy glow.

There was a confused shuffling among the older contestants this morning when she pulled back her hood to reveal her shining, blonde plaited hair and perfect smile. Lauren recognised her immediately as Taisie, one half of the staggeringly successful social media phenomenon Hollie and Taisie. She only knows who they are because Daisy, her seventeen-year-old niece, is a massive fan of theirs. She, like millions of other young girls worldwide, avidly watches their online channel where they give advice on everything from how best to style your make-up to how to split up with a boyfriend.

Their enthusiasm and their friendship are infectious, and what apparently started as a playful hobby has grown exponentially. They are now selling their own lines of make-up and skincare – incredibly glossy formulations and packaging that they claim they created from their kitchen counter – and in the last two years they have gone stratospheric. Lauren knows that, between them, Hollie and Taisie probably generate more clicks and make more money than most of the rest of the passengers on this launch, possibly even Jude, who is at the height of her powers.

Taisie is the only passenger on board who has remained quiet as the boat bounces from wave to wave, her eyes fixed on the horizon, composure pretty much intact throughout. Some 'ooh's and 'wowee's came out of her camera-perfect smile as they took their places, but mostly she has stayed watchful, guarded. The only thing she has muttered is how she can't believe she doesn't have a phone to record the moment. From what Lauren knows of her, there isn't anything Taisie does that isn't filmed and broadcast. Every minute of her life is streamed on social media.

Lauren can't work out if it's her age or being in the company of these well-known faces that has silenced her, or perhaps just being among strangers at all. She can't picture the life of a young influencer, but it strikes her that it is probably intense, lonely and claustrophobic, however flattering the glow of the ring light.

Towering over Taisie in the seat next to her is a tall, striking young man. He too started the day impeccably turned out: the perfect amount of stubble covering his taut jawline, eyebrows exquisitely arched, a carefully styled shock of peroxide-white hair contrasting stunningly with his deep tan. This is Nico, runner up on a top-rated Saturday night TV talent show a couple of years ago, when he charmed the country with his raw musical talent and humour. He was always the one smiling, making a joke out of things and comforting the other singers when they needed a shoulder to sob on.

He was set to win until twenty-four hours before the final vote, when it emerged that he had previously been part of a struggling duo. In an emotional video, which predictably went viral, his former bandmate Xavier claimed Nico had unceremoniously ditched him, leaving him with a mountain of debt. Nico strenuously denied all the allegations, insisting their parting was amicable and that he owed no money. He even pleaded his case in tears live on television while holding his mother's hand, but the damage was done.

When the votes were counted, he lost out to a far less talented singer-songwriter who, up until that point, would have been lucky to have come third. Since then, Nico hasn't quite been cancelled, but he has definitely been paused. He has appeared on some TV quizzes and daytime shows, but his music career has, for the moment, hit a brick wall.

Earlier today, Nico greeted each of his fellow competitors with a joyful burst of chatter, an almost permanent grin lighting up his face. Lauren noticed that he had a pertinent word for each of them, greeting Taisie with puppyish enthusiasm and the rest of them with a smiling kind of deference. As the boat got underway, he made them laugh with his ever-wilder predictions of what might lie ahead. But now he's been quiet for at least half an hour, and he's looking nauseous as he bumps around the back of the boat. His signature hair is drenched and colourless. He shoots Lauren a quick 'we're all in this together' wink, but it looks like he is hanging on by a thread.

As she smiles in response, Lauren wonders where everyone else is. The rumour mill told her there would be ten of them on the island, but there is no sign yet of the other five. Her throat is becoming tight at the thought that the person she hoped to be here, the only reason she signed up in the first place, might not be coming at all. But as they approach the tiny jetty jutting out from the beach, Nico whoops and points behind them. Five specks of red are bobbing up and down, tiny against the expanse of sky and sea, each one trailed by a drone. 'Look, look, over there. Canoes!' he shouts.

'Kayaks, actually,' says Jude. 'I recently did an episode with a small business who were doing an adventure start-up in Wales. Think I managed to steer them in the right direction,' she laughs. No one acknowledges the joke, and she carries on: 'Though I didn't invest in the end. Anyway, taught me all sorts about kayaking!'

Five more chances, thinks Lauren. It's impossible to tell who is in the kayaks. The figures are no more than silhouettes battling through the spray and the wind, and each one wears a bright red all-in-one, topped by a balaclava. They straggle out in a line across the cresting waves. The first two, who look like a man and a woman, are well out in front, powering through the water with fast efficient strokes.

Behind them is a smaller shape, another woman, surely? She is keeping up a decent pace, though without the grace of the leading pair. Some way behind these three are two broader silhouettes, paddles bashing out an uneven rhythm, the last one in particular struggling to keep in reasonable contact with the line of boats, the prow of the kayak lurching drunkenly across the waves.

Each figure could be anybody, literally anybody, thinks Lauren, mentally scrolling through images of all the celebrities she can think of, as if flicking down a tabloid sidebar of shame. And landing, each time, on one particular, familiar face. She can't stop herself trying to superimpose the well-known physique, usually dressed in deliberately distressed designer chic, on to each of the approaching figures. The knot in her stomach tightens. Could it be him? She is suddenly hyperaware of the camera on her face, as though her innermost thoughts are being printed across her forehead. Stop it, she thinks to herself. Don't give yourself away. You'll find out soon enough.

The sight of the others has broken the ice. Everyone on the power boat is babbling, each one of them proffering a theory or a rumour they have heard. 'Is it . . .?', 'Could that be . . .?' Nico's levels of excitement have completely transformed his features; he is jiggling up and down, pointing.

'I bet that's him off of that gameshow . . . Looks like him . . . ooh, what if they're royalty? That would be amazing. That one in the middle could be . . . Oh, no, I think it's a girl.'

Lauren can hear the whirr of the camera refocus from face to face, harvesting their reactions, which may be why Jude seems loath to give too much away. Mac is still too green about the gills to work up much energy for the guessing game. But as Lauren turns round to get a better look at the boats, it is the expression on Taisie's face that catches her attention. There's a small knowing smile at the corners of her perfect lips, at strange odds with the intensity with which she is scrutinising each person in turn. What on earth could be going through her mind? Lauren finds the younger woman hard to read.

Turning back towards the shore, the contestants are shocked to realise they have reached the jetty. In the abrupt silence when the engine cuts out, the five of them pause, look at each other and, fuelled by adrenaline, they burst out laughing. They have made it; the first test is over.

The boat rocks, unsteady on the water as they climb out. Up close, the ladder is worn and rickety, and a layer of ochre rust stains Lauren's palms as she climbs. The boards of the jetty are green with algae and slippery underfoot, the odd jagged-edged hole punctuating the planks. The only thing that looks as if it belongs in the twenty-first century is the fluorescent orange life ring hanging on a post. Thinking of the shiny Soho production offices where she went for her pre-show interview, she registers a small shock at how dilapidated everything feels. It's all about the atmosphere, she tries to reassure herself. They must want it to look rough and ready for the telly.

Lauren sways as the ground seems to move beneath her feet, and she sheds her heavy lifejacket with a sense of relief, which is cut through with a small shot of alarm as a click and a whirr alerts her to another lens tracking her. She looks up and clocks one, two, no, three different cameras all pointing towards the group from different angles. The cameras are well camouflaged, blending into the surroundings so perfectly you wouldn't see them if you were watching on television, and they are trained on her.

It's a show, it's a show, she reminds herself, the realisation dawning that there is no gesture, no expression, no action that will not be caught and broadcast from this point on. Even with her years of TV experience it is unnerving, and she thinks how she might look to her family, her beloved mum and dad, watching fretfully at home. So as not to worry them, she forces to her lips a smile she doesn't feel.

A shout rings out across the beach. 'There, over there!' It's Nico again, waving out to sea.

As the five from the boat have been disembarking, the other team have made enough headway to be nearly at the water's edge. In excitement they run towards them, reaching the shoreline just as the first of the kayakers pulls up with a crunch of sand, and lifts himself elegantly out of the seat. The unidentifiable tall and lithe figure plants his paddle into the ground with some drama, before standing with his back to the water and pulling off his balaclava with a flourish.

To her surprise, Lauren finds herself cheering with the rest of them. The grinning face that emerges is Jackson Powell, who only months ago had heroically become Olympic champion in both the 800 metres and the 1500 metres. There's almost a touch of parody to the way he looks – six foot two of perfect honed Olympian, the epitome of sporting prowess and sportsmanship. He carries himself as though those two gold medals are still hung around his neck, and Lauren notices that shaved into his close-cropped dark curly hair, just above his right ear, are the five Olympic rings. His eyes flicker from face to face, and he laughs out loud.

'Hey, guys!' he says. 'I guess you took the easy way here, did you?'

There follows a flurry of bear-hugging, backslaps and high fives. It's hard to tell, thinks Lauren, whether any of the people here actually know Jackson already. It's something she's used to watching from the sidelines, this showbiz familiarity, as if you're all part of the same family, or best friends, even though you've never met. She takes a moment to remember that this time she is part of all this, and that she too has to join in with the fake camaraderie. As she rearranges her expression, she notices that Nico grins widely as Jackson pulls him into a hug. And is that a faint blush she sees on Taisie's face as she stretches up to double-kiss the Olympian's cheeks?

The greetings are interrupted by the arrival of the second kayak, pulling up next to Jackson's. This one is steered by a woman, and, eschewing the theatrics that accompanied his arrival, she has pulled off her balaclava almost before they have turned to notice her.

Again, the face and tangle of long auburn hair is familiar to anyone who has followed the recent summer of sport. Kez Jones, one of the most successful Paralympians of all time. Her record in the pool is unmatched – she has swum her way to five golds and three silvers in consecutive Games. There's a determination on her features as she emerges from the kayak, managing the awkward transition on to the shore with gracefulness despite the prosthetic below the knee of her right leg.

The waiting celebrities are impressed, though the greetings are a touch more muted this time round, Kez lacking Jackson's electric charm. Almost as soon as she is on dry land, they are scanning the water for the next arrival.

'Who else is coming?' someone asks.

'No idea,' says Jackson. 'They dropped us off at separate spots – we didn't get a chance to meet each other. And they told us not to speak till we arrived on the island. Followed us, filming all the way.' He nods up at the drone that was trailing him.

Taisie is already jumping up and down and squealing before the next kayak pulls up: 'OMG, Hollie! Holl, Holl, Holl, you made it!'

'Oh my God, that was insane!'

The figure in the kayak scrambles out, launches herself at Taisie and pulls off her hood to reveal a tumble of wavy brown hair, sparkling green eyes and a wide infectious smile. It is Hollie, the other half of the famous double act. Seeing them on the beach together, Lauren thinks that despite the differences in their features they look like cardboard cut-outs of each other: the exact same height and build.

The two girls are leaping up and down in each other's arms, oblivious for the moment to the circle of celebrities, lost in a world of their own. Eventually, just as it gets awkward for everyone else, they break away from each other and indiscriminately bestow a whirlwind of embraces.

Lauren is mesmerised. The quiet, circumspect Taisie that she observed on the boat is completely transformed, vivacious and effusive. The social media phenomenon begins to make sense; they are the perfect double act. It's as though Taisie is drawing strength from her counterpart, as though a light has been turned on. Without Hollie by her side, Taisie is a shadow.

There are two remaining contestants left on the water. The one in front seems to hang back a bit, letting the other, by now flagging badly and lurching sideways, draw ahead. As he does so, chest heaving and paddle slipping in his hand, the figure in front pulls off his headgear, seemingly too impatient to wait for the shoreline. Spluttering, puce, with sweat and brine dripping from his chin, the face is nevertheless as familiar to most people as their own families: the balding head and smiling eyes of Frank Stubbs.

For thirty years, ever since he was a teenager, Frank has played Jimmy Black, the happy-go-lucky stalwart of the country's longest-running soap. Lauren has watched his character fall in and out of love, seen his businesses go bankrupt, witnessed his trial for fraud, his subsequent time spent in prison, and enjoyed his sage advice as he morphed into the deeply flawed but charismatic lynchpin of the show. His beer belly and the laughter creases on his face are part of the national wallpaper. He's the person you think you know, even if you've never met him. The familiarity of his presence, incongruous on this lonely beach, gives Lauren a shot of optimism, which she sees reflected in the faces of her fellow contestants.

She laughs along with the others as he clambers and staggers out of the kayak. But her attention is elsewhere. One more left to arrive: this is her last chance. She watches as the final vessel circles round and pulls up in the dead centre of the row of scarlet boats. The rower leans back, taking a moment to scan the shoreline.

One by one, the celebrities fall silent, eyes turned towards him. Flinging the paddle down, he spreads his arms wide, stretching up to the sky in a gesture that should look ridiculous but is somehow commanding. Even the gulls, whose eerie cries have been echoing around the high cliffs, seem to fall silent. The only sound to be heard is the hum of the various cameras zooming in, half of them focused on the kayak, half on the waiting faces.

Lauren feels her pounding heartbeat as the hands come down, crossing at the wrists to remove his headgear. Her breath stops, just for a moment, and then catches in an inward gasp. He pulls the balaclava deftly over his head to unveil a square jaw, salt-and-pepper stubble, Californian tan and a thick shock of tousled pewter-grey hair, still miraculously dry. That famous pair of slate-blue eyes, the irises ringed by charcoal, framed by deep laughter lines. The gamble of her career has paid off.

It's him, Nate Stirling.

He's here.

Chapter Three

'Oh. My. GOD.' Nico is the first to react, theatrically falling to his knees on the sand. 'Ohmygod ohmygod ohmygod. No WAY! My mum is going to die when she sees me with you!'

Everyone else seems to have lost the power of speech, starstruck. It seems utterly unbelievable that standing on the sand in front of them is five feet ten inches of bona fide Hollywood royalty, turning his mega-watt smile on them.

Nate Stirling has been famous for as long as most people can remember. He is the Oscar-winning star of a long list of award-winning films, from thoughtful indie dramas to massive commercial blockbusters. To the younger generation, he is Todd Hunter, action hero personified, central character in the box-office-busting *Hunted* franchise. The older ones in the group probably remember him better for his wild days, when he made headlines for his boisterous escapades and his endless string of glamorous girlfriends.

He has changed since then. Eventually settling down with fellow A-lister Jennifer Wrey, he reinvented himself as a devoted husband and philanthropist, working hard to rehabilitate his reputation. Rumour has it there's trouble in paradise, but Nate's image is squeaky clean now, and he is almost as famous for his charity work as he is for his acting. And here he is, exuding the kind of sheen that only contentment and a multi-million-pound income can bring. It's as though the beach has been transformed into a film backdrop, and the glowing figure of the hero has stepped out of the screen to join them.

'Guys,' he is saying, as he reaches out to shake Mac's hand first. 'This is pretty awesome, isn't it? Great to see you all.'

Lauren would love to take in the individual reactions to this bombshell, but adrenaline is coursing through her body so fast she can barely focus. The film she is watching is light years from what everyone else is seeing.

To the others, Nate is the all-star leading man. But she sees someone hiding his real nature behind a smiling mask. What looks to everyone else like a genial smile appears to her like the flash of shark's teeth. Those famous eyes, resting first on Kez and then on Taisie and Hollie, seem to her not warm but calculating, the trademark quizzical lift of his eyebrow a warning.

It gives a nightmarish quality to the scene. Lauren feels the disconnection that has accompanied her over the last few months building to a head. How lonely it is to look at the same thing as everybody else but to see something that is hidden from their view.

For over a year, she has dedicated herself to revealing the truth that lies behind Nate Stirling's burnished image, risking everything on this investigation, and she has been stymied at every turn. The Big Boss's words ring in her ears: 'This is *not* a story, Brooks. You don't have the evidence, and we don't have the lawyers or the fire power to protect you. Leave it!'

But she is sure it *is* a story. And she will do anything to follow it up. Her quest to expose the real Nate Stirling is what has brought her to this island, to this strange moment with this group of famous faces, but she barely knows how to react. Something in her hadn't allowed herself to believe he would really be here, and now that he is, she has to catch herself, realising that her reactions are out of step with everyone else's.

The others have breached the force field of extreme fame that surrounds Nate and have reached the hugging and back-slapping stage. Jude is smiling broadly, Jackson has his arm round Nate's shoulders, and the two girls are flushed with the aura of people who have been blessed with kisses from on high. Lauren is the only one who is hanging back. Flicking her gaze quickly at the camera drone to the right of her, she arranges her face into the broadest grin she can manage, and steps forward.

'Hi,' she says, determined to sound confident, 'I'm Lauren. Lauren Brooks. I'm a journalist over here. On *Inside Investigations*, usually.'

She's trying to read his expression for a flicker of recognition. She has never been sure whether her attempts to expose him, her endless inquiries about his behaviour, have reached his ears or whether they have all been dealt with by his 'people' before they got to him. All she knows is that everyone she has spoken to who has a bad word to say about his reputation has been threatened with legal action by his lawyers.

It's impossible to tell if he knows who she is; his smile doesn't miss a beat as he takes her outstretched hand and pulls her immediately into an embrace. Despite what she knows about him she manages to resist the instinct to move away.

'Great to meet you, Lauren. Really great. Wow, what an awesome bunch of people.' He looks around him. 'Man, would you look at this place!'

Nico, who is standing as close as he can get to Nate, grinning from ear to ear, is desperate to find out what has brought such a huge star into their midst. He can hardly get his words out. 'So, oh my God. Are you a reality TV fan like me? What kinds of shows do you watch in the States? Is that what's brought you here?'

Good question, thinks Lauren, taking stock, watching Nate as he responds.

'I wish I could say it was. Actually, I'm kind of a rookie with these shows. For me, it was more about the location. You know what I mean? When they told me we were going to be totally alone – and in Scotland, in a monastery – I thought it was a perfect opportunity to do something different—'

'Same here!' interrupts Nico.

'Not only that, but I have Scottish ancestry,' says Nate.

Lauren clocks Mac's eyebrows raising slightly at this, but before anyone can ask Nate more, they are interrupted by a piercing blast. It's the captain of the launch, who is blowing hard on a small silver whistle. The celebrities giggle, but his expression is serious, and within seconds they are focused on what he's saying.

'Contestants. Here are your first instructions. You are to place your lifejackets in the RIB. Once you have done that, find the kitbag with your name on it,' he points a short stubby finger down the beach, to a pile that is lying on the sand, 'and change out of your civvies into the clothes you will find inside. Place everything else you have brought with you back inside the bag. And I mean *everything*.'

The last word is said with a barking force. This is not a request; it is an order.

Jackson reaches the misshapen pile of hessian sacks first. He hands out the bags in turn, matching each contestant to the name printed in large chalk capitals on the side.

Nate is first to tip out the contents, and groans as he does so.

'They cannot be serious!'

'OMG. What even *is* this?' says Hollie. She is holding out what appears to be a length of sacking in a muddy shade of brown, turning it this way and that until it resolves into a long garment with wide sleeves and an enormous floppy hood.

'Oh my God! No way. Taisie, we can't be seen in these!'

Taisie turns her bag upside down. A length of rope falls on to the sand, followed by a pair of leather slippers lined with fur, a pair of socks, and a smaller bag made of rough undyed cotton. She picks each item up by the tips of her fingers and slowly inspects them.

'Is this meant to be a belt? It's huge! And these sandal things. What's inside them? That better not be real fur. We would NEVER wear that, would we, Hollie? And they're going to be way too big for me!'

'Mine are going to be way too small.' Mac has already put on his rudimentary footwear, and his heels are falling off the back.

Lauren is peering into her smaller cotton bag, and sees that Hollie is doing the same, inspecting its contents. She was assured repeatedly by Steph that everything she needs will be provided on the island. Absolutely everything. So apart from what she is wearing, she should not under any circumstances bring anything else. No food, no cosmetics, no extra clothes, and, most crucially, no mobile phone. She feels bereft without it – it is like an extension of herself, her constant companion – and this is the first time she has been parted from it for years.

Still, though, it is a relief when she sees some of the provisions: five pairs of knickers, two bras (which look like they're the right size), a wooden toothbrush (thank God), a small wooden comb, and two plain glass bottles filled with unidentified liquids.

Hollie opens hers and sniffs them.

'Some kind of shampooey stuff, I think. Is this actually moisturiser? Taise, what do you reckon?'

Taisie dabs in a forefinger. 'Yeah. Bit gross. But I think we can do something with it.'

Kez is the one who looks most worried.

'Has anyone seen another bag with my name on it? I can't find a few of my things.'

'Nah. Not over here.'

'Nope, sorry.'

Any further answers or attempts to search for her missing things are halted by the captain, issuing their next instruction in clipped military tones.

'Form a line over here so I can fit you with your mic packs.'

The celebrities jostle into place, automatically ceding the head of the queue to Nate. One by one, the captain shows them how to tuck the square black battery case on to the back of their waistband and sling the mic loosely around their necks. As they do so, he reminds each of them sternly that their mics are to be switched on at all times.

'You have ten minutes to put on your habits, then place everything you came with into the large sack with your name on and hand it over. Put everything in! Anyone who doesn't obey to the letter comes back with me to the mainland. Game over, no discussion.'

Despite bubbling groans of complaint, everyone does what he says. As quickly as they can, and hopping comically from one foot to another, they start to pull off their damp clothes and strip down to their matching dark blue thermals, which they had been told to wear under their other clothes.

It is hardest for the kayakers, who are inhibited by their tight-fitting dry suits, and there is a moment of hilarity when Nico and Jackson try to assist Frank, who is struggling to get his legs out of the rubberised cuffs. They pull at his arms so hard that he loses his balance, topples backwards and lands sprawled on the sand, laughing along with the rest as Mac gives him a hand up and a pat on the back.

Ten minutes later, they are all transformed. Ten brown figures, all dressed exactly the same in matching hooded monks' habits, stripped of the trappings that marked out their individuality. As they stuff their own clothes back into their sacks, the air is full of laughter and good-natured mockery.

'Never played a monk before. This could be a right laugh,' Frank quips, clearly having recovered his humour after the exertion of the kayak trip. 'What about you, Nate?'

'No, I played a priest once, a while back. But a monk? No.'

'Good job too! Don't imagine you'd like anyone messing with that fancy barnet of yours, would you?'

The gentle jibe is met with giggles from the girls and a hearty low chuckle from Mac, but confusion crosses Nate's brow. He clearly doesn't get the joke and, judging by his frown, doesn't seem to like Frank making one at his expense.

'Barnet?'

'He means your hair,' Jude steps in.

Nate is about to say something else but is stopped by an order from the captain.

'That's it, time's up. Hand over your belongings.'

They pass the now-bulging sacks to the captain. Lauren assumes he will throw them back in the boat but instead he chucks them into a heap just above the waterline. It is only then that she registers what he is carrying in his left hand: a rusty green jerry can.

'Stand well away, everyone!' he shouts, and in one quick movement empties the entire contents of the can on to the pile. The chemical smell of petrol is acrid in the fresh air.

'No! No way!'

'What the hell . . .? Those are my things!'

'This is not acceptable!'

'Hey, you can't do that! Stop him!'

'For God's sake, man . . . stop!'

Their protestations fall on deaf ears. It is too dangerous to do anything else but stand back and watch. With a flourish, the captain takes an old-fashioned Zippo out of his top pocket, flicks it twice before it ignites, and hurls it skywards.

For a moment, as it somersaults through the air, Lauren breathes out in relief, thinking the flame has been extinguished. When it lands there is a millisecond of silence. Then there is a swoosh as the air is sucked away from them, followed by a loud *whoomph* that reverberates around the high cliffs and thumps in their chests and ears.

They watch in abject horror as everything they brought with them goes up in flames.

At first the shock renders them speechless, and for a brief moment they watch in silence as their possessions twist and turn in the crackling pyre. Then the reality hits for those who had tried to smuggle in contraband.

'God damn it,' says Mac. 'My chewing gum . . . I hate not having any. Had a few packs inside my pockets.'

'Well, it's worse for me. That's my cigs up in smoke,' says Frank.

'My lipstick . . . I can't believe they've done that!' Jude is apoplectic.

Lauren stays silent. Cursing. The small burner phone she sewed into the inside of her jacket just in case of emergencies is no use to her now. It is a lifeline gone.

'What about my sunglasses? They cost me a fortune.' Nico is showing every sign of having a meltdown, until they realise that Taisie's perfect face has crumpled into real, distressed tears. Hollie reaches out to pull her into a hug.

'My photo! Hollie, that's my photo in there . . . I know you said not to bring it, in case it got lost. But I just needed it near me . . . and now it's gone.'

Hollie strokes Taisie's hair and looks up at the row of puzzled faces. 'It's a picture of her mum. She died not long ago.'

A distant memory stirs in Lauren: her niece telling her how distraught she, and all Taisie's fans, were for her when she revealed her loss.

A murmur of sympathy goes up, and Hollie speaks louder, into Taisie's ear. 'Taise, come on now. It's fine. You know you've got copies of that photo. It's your screensaver.' And then, a little more sharply, 'Taisie, don't do this. It's fine, you are going to be fine.'

Taisie sniffs, and her face emerges from Hollie's shoulder. She gulps a few times, then gives a weak smile. 'Sorry. So sorry. That was just silly of me. I just wanted to feel like she was here with me. Sorry, Holls. You were right.'

The others cluster for a group hug. The cynical side of Lauren wonders how much of their display is genuine empathy and how much is for the watching cameras, but there's no doubt Taisie looks more cheerful when she emerges.

The metallic double cough of a motor starting breaks them apart. Without a final word, the captain has returned to the RIB and is readying it for the return journey. They fall silent. Lauren has an overwhelming impulse to leave. To run down the beach, throw off the ill-fitting gown and jump on board, letting herself be carried back to her home, back to normality. It is only the thought of what she came to try to do that keeps her feet planted in the sand.

As the boat casts off from the jetty Lauren looks around and sees that the sense of dislocation she feels is mirrored in the others' faces. It manifests like a physical weight, a shift in gravity, not just on her but on everyone else as well. Some have sunk down on to the sand, enveloped in the unfamiliar folds of their habits. Others seem diminished, their shoulders slumped, eyes fixed on the stern of the boat, which is now getting smaller and smaller as it heads away from them, back to the security and safety of the mainland. They look distraught, desperate, as if they are silently praying for it to turn round and come back to rescue them.

Lauren can imagine the way the burning fire, the disappearing speedboat and their horrified expressions will be intercut and edited.

There'll be music playing, no doubt. Probably strings, possibly even bagpipes, given their location, carefully designed to underscore the drama of their situation. But she knows that what is broadcast on screens in millions of homes has no hope of conveying quite how unsettling it is to be trapped in this strange new reality. What on earth is she doing here, standing at the shoreline in the middle of nowhere with nine strangers?

They watch the fire die down into greasy embers, none of them knowing quite what to say. Not even Nate, confident and ostentatious minutes before, has anything to add. Nor the previously jovial Frank. Without the rousing soundtrack, the solitude of the island buzzes in Lauren's ears. As the sound of the boat fades, all she can hear is the shush of the waves, stretching for miles all around them. They are alone. Isolated.

But not, of course, completely. Because above their heads a camera drone is fighting to keep its place against the wind, the mosquito whine audible whenever it swoops close. Every now and then a mechanical click or whirr breaks through the quiet as yet another hidden camera refocuses. With a kind of vertigo, Lauren realises that although they feel as if they have been dropped off the edge of the planet, the world is still with them, watching.

Already, she knows, they are being assigned their roles by the public: the ditsy girls, the ferocious businesswoman, the action hero. Actors waiting for the curtain to rise. The scenes have been laid out for them. The lines will be their own. Time for the drama to start.

'What's next, then?' Nate says, as if hearing her thoughts.

In response, they all turn their heads towards the high walls that loom above the cliffs. That must be where food and shelter lie. Which makes the first challenge pretty clear: how will they reach it?

Chapter Four

They seem to be entirely trapped on the beach. The perfect semi-circle is surrounded by sheer stony cliffs, their steep sides impregnable. There is no obvious route out, no way to reach the monastery.

'Surely there must be a path? We can't be stranded here, can we?' Jude is asking Jackson, who has his back to the water and is standing purposefully, hands on his hips, gazing skywards.

'I reckon I could climb it, find a way up for us. Get some rope or something and throw it down.'

'You can't do that! It would be far too dangerous. There must be a path!' Jude sounds outraged.

'We're going to need to get a move on to find it if we want to be out of here before dark,' Mac says ominously.

'Dark? What are you talking about? It can only be just after two. We have hours to work it out.' Nate is incredulous.

'Nah, pal, afraid to say you're wrong. This is Scotland, in late November. It gets dark early here this time of year. We have a couple of hours at the most.'

'He's right, the light is already fading, and I don't think staying here is going to be safe.' Lauren is trying to keep rising concern out of her voice, but it must be showing, as her words galvanise them all to move off in different directions and start searching the foot of the cliffs.

It is Frank who eventually solves the puzzle.

'Wherever the entrance is, the director is going to want a good shot of us, so best get looking for the cameras – then we'll find it.'

Nico, Taisie and Hollie have given up their investigations and are huddled together by the embers of the fire by the time Frank finally discovers it, by following a line of lenses hidden among tussocks of wiry grass and wedged between stones.

'Hey, come on, you lot. I think it's here.'

But their ordeal is far from over. All Frank has found is an old chain tucked into a crevice. Jackson is the first to grab it and scrabbles his way up to a ledge.

'Yo, Frank. Great work. I can see the path now. Up there to my left.'

It's like a magic eye. As soon as Jackson waves at it, they can all see exactly where they should be going, but that doesn't make it any less alarming. The steep path is cut into the rocks, skirting beneath the cliff face, and then winding back on itself to the tussocks of spiky grass above.

The cold metal chain squeals as they pull it, their steps tentative on the slippery stone in their cumbersome slippers. Their voluminous robes drag against their calves, inhibiting their movement. It is only together, the stronger hoisting the weaker up the first few feet, that they manage to do it. As Mac helps her, Kez's face is set with grim determination, her mobility hampered by her prosthetic leg. When it comes to Nate's turn, he refuses Mac's hand and uses his own strength to clamber upwards.

The rest of the track is equally perilous: narrow, wet and slippery. With the moan and crash of the sea as their soundtrack they all press themselves against the sides, away from the ever-increasing drop.

'This can't be right. This can't be right. Not for a gameshow,'

Lauren can hear Jude muttering ahead of her. 'It's too dangerous. This is ridiculous.'

When they finally make it over the brow of the cliff, they are greeted by a welcome carpet of soft purple heather. One by one they drop on to it, lying on their backs, taking a moment to breathe while they wait for the stragglers.

In this moment of respite, Lauren assesses her companions. Sprawled on the ground the ten of them look a million miles from the beaming publicity photographs that are probably being used to trail the series even as they lie there. They are all soaked with sweat from the climb and most of them have pulled their floppy hoods over their heads against the sea breeze, peering out from under them with streaming eyes. Frank is struggling. He is panting heavily, mouth open, chest heaving, and his face has turned a mottled bluish purple.

'I'll be all right . . . just catch me breath,' he says. 'Probably best they burned my smokes. My lungs feel like they've glass in 'em.'

'Take a breather, pal. Just let your heart rate come down. You'll be OK.'

Frank does what Mac says, and immediately looks better.

The monastery lies ahead of them, and it is no less forbidding from this angle. Its high defensive walls, built against the weather and the threat of Viking raids, look impassable. The main entrance, flanked by two small turrets, is resolutely shut, boarded over by what looks like a raised drawbridge. Mac and Jackson, full of macho energy, make a foray towards it and disappear down into the empty moat. They come back, after what must be nearly twenty minutes, disappointed.

'No luck,' says Mac. 'We can't see how to get in. It's already too dark. There is no way in and no way around; it's blocked by a massive metal fence. Looks like all the TV kit is behind it – a huge satellite dish and aerials and stuff, like you have with outside broadcast teams at matches. There's no way we can climb over it. It's too dangerous.'

LOUISE MINCHIN

The mood has plummeted, light years from the giddiness that accompanied their arrival on the beach. It's the hunger that is getting to most of them. So far there is no sign of even a scrap of food. Nico is particularly vocal about that.

'I couldn't eat a thing this morning. Too nervous. Think I'm going to pass out if I don't get something to eat soon.'

Clearly, they had all imagined that they would be inside by this time, warm and fed. Now all they can do is have circular discussions about what they should do next. And the more they talk, the worse the situation gets as darkness falls.

Lauren is beginning to shiver, the damp seeping into her bones from the heather she is sitting on. Kez has clicked a button on her leg to remove her prosthesis and has placed it carefully on her robes in an effort to keep it off the wet ground. She rubs the skin below the knee, saying to nobody in particular, 'I really need another sock.'

'You can have one of mine,' says Hollie.

'Oh, no. Thank you, but I didn't really mean that kind of sock. I have special medical ones that go over my stump. It kind of shrinks during the day and rubs when I do something out of the ordinary, something strenuous, like climb that cliff. They've promised me I'll have a store of them while I'm here and I could really do with a fresh one right now. That's what I was looking for in our bags on the beach.'

Mac turns his attention to Kez. 'I'll take a look, if you like,' he says. 'I'm a paramedic by training. Did that alongside the rugby until I went professional. One reason why they wanted me on the programme, I think. D'you want to let me have a wee peek?'

He bends over Kez's leg, while Lauren wonders at the way people can surprise you. She had no idea Mac was a paramedic and, judging from Kez's profuse thanks, he's a good one.

Lauren lets the others bicker about what to do. She is quiet, watching and listening. Even though she can see Nate Stirling sitting right in

36

front of her, an animated participant in the discussions, she is still utterly astonished that he's actually here, on this island, with her. She has an extraordinary opportunity to get close to him, and with it comes an enormous responsibility to get it right, not to overplay her hand. She must not let down the people who have trusted her with their secrets.

The others are just coming to the conclusion that another party should try to find a way in when the crackle of a loudspeaker rings out from inside the walls.

'Novices!' it says, in a deep tone that reverberates in the still air. 'Novices, you will be live on air in one minute. Do not swear. I repeat, do not swear.'

'Jesus Christ!' says Mac. 'I'd forgotten about the bloody lives.'

'Mac, shush! How are they even going to see us properly?' says Jude. 'It's practically pitch black.'

But before they can answer her, the loudspeaker is counting down. 'Live on air in five . . . four . . . three . . . two . . . one!'

As the countdown comes to an end, a loud creaking comes from the monastery walls. They turn to locate the noise and jump in fright at the sudden flash and boom of two large flames igniting. A pair of torches hung on the wall illuminate the space between them, which is slowly being revealed as the drawbridge lowers into place on its groaning ropes. The shock of unexpected brightness in the dark landscape is reflected in ten pairs of eyes, the sudden flare transforming ten exhausted faces into smiles and laughter.

'Wow!' says Nico, as they start towards the bridge, swept up in excited chatter.

Lauren is running by the time she finds herself at the edge of the moat, and the drawbridge clunks into position at her feet. Ahead of them are two wooden doors – huge and forbiddingly closed. The crisscross bars of a heavy iron portcullis hang across the top of the archway above them, glinting like giant teeth in an open jaw. Lauren shivers, with cold and with anticipation, and steps on to the bridge at the same time as Nate. Just as she does so there is another muffled roar, and behind them, on the bank of the moat, two large braziers filled with firewood roar into flame simultaneously, throwing tendrils of heat into the night air.

'That is so cool,' says Nico.

'I love it, I LOVE it,' says either Taisie or Hollie; they sound so similar Lauren can't decide which.

Seeing the dancing flames, part of Lauren agrees, but there is something sinister about it too. The sophisticated pyrotechnics remind her that, although they are alone on the island, they are being controlled from afar by unseen hands.

It is then that an eerie sound starts to roll out from behind the monastery walls. Quiet at first, and then louder, haunting and plaintive. It is unmistakably the solemn chanting of monks.

Everyone freezes. Every rational part of Lauren knows that all of this is nothing more than technological tricks, but she can't help imagining the chorus in her mind, picturing a host of hooded figures lined up to meet them on the other side of the door, cowls shadowing their faces. The notes rise up into the sky, to a collective shudder from all the contestants. The younger ones look downright terrified, and even the older ones seem a little spooked as the chanting rises to a pitch and then stops, the last notes fading into the distance.

They look at each other, wide eyed, and then, without discussion, move forward across the bridge, a camera drone's red and green night lights flickering just above them. Nate is the first to reach the reinforced doors, the others coming to a halt one pace behind him. He has cast back the hood of his habit, and Lauren cannot help wondering if he has deliberately swept a hand through his wavy grey hair to make sure he looks more like his action hero persona, Todd Hunter, the one everyone watching at home will doubtless be thinking of. Then he cuts the tension of the moment with a wide smile and trademark arch of his left eyebrow.

'Well, time for Open Sesame,' he says, reaching towards the doors and trying to lift the giant latch that stretches almost a metre wide across them. There's a comic fumble when it doesn't budge. Lauren, who is next to him, moves to help but he imperiously holds up a hand to stop her. 'I've got this.'

Dismissed out of hand, Lauren swallows hard to cover her flash of irritation.

Nate tries again, rattling it furiously. The latch judders but doesn't rise.

'Stuck,' he says shortly, impatience getting the better of his command of the situation. He leans his back against the door to catch a moment's breath, fuming.

Suddenly there's a metallic grinding noise from above, and Lauren sees a chain set into the side of the door start to move quickly, links rattling as they shoot upwards. With no thought in her head other than an instinctive sense of danger, she reaches out her hand, grabs Nate's habit, and pulls him hard.

Rocked off balance, Nate lurches forwards, falling on top of her. She's aware of their limbs tangled up together, a shooting pain when her elbow hits the hard deck of the drawbridge and a gasp of indrawn breath from the others. And then, a split second later, a deafening metallic clang, a sickening thud, which reverberates through her body, and the shaky rattle of chains slowing into silence.

And then nothing but screaming, a repeating note of, 'Oh my God. Oh my God! The gate!'

Shifting Nate's weight off herself, Lauren raises her head and looks down the length of her prone body, to see that just where he was standing seconds before, a row of thick pointed metal bars, heavy with decorative ironwork, has crashed on to the stone flag below. The portcullis.

Turning her head to the right, she's met by the eyes of one of the most famous men in the world inches from her own, pupils dilated in shock.

'That *thing*,' he says, all the theatrical reverberation wiped from his voice. 'It nearly killed me!'

And then both Lauren and the watching cameras are rewarded by the sight of a Hollywood legend pulling himself on to his knees beneath the flickering light of the torches and retching into the moat below.

The loudspeaker crackles back to life. 'We are off air,' it says shortly, and subsides into the night.

Chapter Five

'It *couldn't* be on purpose. There's no *way* that was meant to happen!'

'Oh my God, it was so close!'

'No. It wasn't meant to happen like *that*. Something must have gone wrong.'

'Just imagine. Imagine if he was still standing there. I just can't believe it. I mean, just *imagine . . .*'

'I know. I mean, thank God. Thank God.'

'But it's not the point, is it? Who cares what was *meant* to happen? The point is, it's not *safe*.'

The voices swirl around Lauren, and for the moment she lets their words slide past her. Her elbows are smarting from where she hit the wooden planks of the drawbridge, and her heartbeat is only just beginning to settle. They have all retreated to the far bank of the moat, their first instinct being to get as far away from the dark shadows of the portcullis bars as they could. They have arranged themselves in a ragged group around one of the braziers, Nate and Lauren in the middle. The others have unconsciously formed a protective circle round them. The first few minutes were spent checking them both over, and thanking Lauren again and again for her lightning-fast instincts.

'Thank God, you grabbed him.'

'You were amazing!'

'How did you *know*?'

She hasn't answered, and in truth, she doesn't know herself. It was nothing more than a sixth sense of impending danger, one that has saved her in life-threatening situations before.

For Nate's part, he has been sitting cross-legged, head in hands, largely in silence. Having established that both he and Lauren are physically fine, the others are now playing out their shock by trying to work out what happened and why.

'Well, I'm not standing for it. It shouldn't have fallen like that,' says Jude, puffed up in her outrage. 'I mean, someone could have been *killed*.'

'Someone nearly was.'

'And live on air!'

At this, one of the girls – it sounds like Taisie – lets out a nervous giggle. 'Can you imagine the headlines? If they had actually killed someone? Especially Nate. Can you imagine the trouble they'd be in . . .?' She trails off, realising how inappropriate she sounds.

'Taisie!' says Hollie sharply. 'That is literally not OK.'

'What kind of a programme is this?' says Jude. 'Wasn't there a risk assessment? What about Health and Safety? We're stuck out here, starving and freezing. And how are we ever going to get inside now that the gate has fallen? Why haven't they fixed it? We haven't even spent a night here and one of us has nearly been killed.' She's on her high horse now, on a roll, and in response there are nods and murmurs of agreement from the others.

I bet they cut this bit out of the edit, thinks Lauren. In front of her, Nate is still unmoving, head low between his knees. Outrage swirls around Lauren from all sides, but for the moment, after that intense unexpected rush of terror, she is still assessing what just happened and why.

'. . . In fact,' it's Jude's voice again, 'I think they're going to have to stop this show altogether. How can they carry on after that? I think we should *make* them stop it. I think we should *leave*. All of us. Now!'

Silence. Where before, people were murmuring in assent, Lauren notices a sudden shift in the atmosphere.

'I mean . . . yeah,' says Nico cautiously. 'But at the end of the day Nate's fine, really, I guess. Aren't you, Nate?'

'It was, like, really, really scary,' says Hollie, 'but if it was just an accident?' Her voice rises at the end; hard to tell if it's a question or just her natural uplift.

'But it's not just the gate thing, is it? insists Jude. 'I mean, what are we meant to do now? I'm freezing. It's dark. We have no food. Kez doesn't have her things. We're locked out. Look at the state of us. Look at Frank.'

They all turn to look at Frank, who hasn't said a word. He looks pale, even in the orange light from the fire, and is intermittently racked with violent shivers.

There's a pause. How interesting, thinks Lauren, journalistic antennae buzzing. However scared everyone is, they all want to keep going. Why is that? What have each of them been promised? Why are *they* here?

'It just feels kind of stupid to stop now, just because of one thing,' says Jackson. 'We don't want to look like a bunch of losers, do we?'

'Exactly. We don't even know if anyone was *really* in danger.' It's Nico again. 'They have cameras on us all the time. It was live and everything. It was probably deliberate. For the drama, you know. They probably dropped that thing when they saw Nate was out of the way, part of the show . . . and it's not like he's actually hurt . . .'

He tails off, and each one of them turns towards Nate, the epicentre of their strange circle. He is the one who has control over their fate. Slowly he raises his head. His face is solemn at first, and then he breaks into a wry smile that lifts only one side of his mouth and doesn't reach his eyes. His eyebrow lifts again; he is back in character.

'Oh, come on,' he says, exaggerating his accent into a Southern burr. 'I couldn't ask you to call off the whole show just because of me. It's not the first time some stupid stunt has nearly killed me. Probably not the last either.'

There's a half-laugh at this; Nate is famous for doing his own increasingly dangerous action shots.

He continues, his voice rising in volume a little with each sentence. 'What's a little cold? What's a little dark? What's a little danger?' More laughter. 'We're made of tougher stuff than this. Come on! I bet in the morning we'll be inside, and warm and dry, and laughing. Let's not let the fact they nearly killed some damn movie star stop us! Let's give ourselves a chance to show them what we're made of.'

By the time he's finished he's in full movie declamation mode. And it works. As well as laughter there are the beginnings of applause. Jackson lets out a whoop, and somehow even Jude looks mollified.

Well played, thinks Lauren. And she has to admit she feels a little more energised than she did a few minutes ago. But why? Why is Nate so keen for them to stick it out, keen enough to give a full-scale oration, however ironic? The juddering of the chain and the resounding clang of the portcullis falling is still reverberating through her bones. Nate felt the same whistle of air brush his face as she did. He must know as well as she does that that was no stunt, that it was a massive failure of health and safety, a dangerous accident.

So why does he want to stay and put himself through the clear perils of the show? Is it really because he wants to have a chance of winning his own secret unassailable prize? No. In her gut she knows

44

it's more than that. If what she has been told is true, he is running from something. Hiding in plain sight.

The irony of her situation – saving the one person she came here to expose – dawns on her as he focuses on her across the brazier, flames dancing in his slate-grey eyes.

'Thank you,' he mouths at her silently, and smiles a wide, genuine smile. And for a fleeting moment, in spite of herself, she finds she is smiling back.

Chapter Six

The group resolve is back stronger than ever. And yet, where does that get them? At least the wall sconces and braziers are giving them some light, but otherwise they are stuck. It's pretty clear to Lauren that something has gone wrong, that the portcullis should have opened, and they should now be inside, safely ensconced in their temporary home away from home.

Knowing that they have been told, repeatedly, that there will be nobody else on the island, that they have to rely entirely on themselves, she joins Nate, Mac and Jackson as they try to lift the portcullis. Even with their combined strength straining every muscle, fingers scrabbling on the rusty metal, the thick bars won't budge.

Jude and Nico work together, yelling into their microphones, asking for help, but to no avail. There is no answer.

'Right,' says Nate, who seems to have placed himself at the helm of all decision-making. 'We need to make a plan.'

He divides them into groups, including one person to sit with Frank, who clearly is in no state to do anything other than keep warm. Lauren smiles as she sees how quickly Jude volunteers for that duty. Nate nominates Lauren and Kez to scout around for firewood or any fuel to shore up the fires, and then asks for volunteers to have a go at climbing the walls to find a way in. Hollie and Taisie raise their hands, and Nate lifts one of the heavy torches out of its bracket, handing it to Hollie to help light the way.

When she shines it on the high walls Nico notices a sign, clearly freshly written in a gothic script on a blackboard:

These walls are sacred. Do not climb.

He points it out to the others: 'Look at that; doesn't help us much!'

'Yeah? Given what's just happened to me, I think we can ignore that, can't we?' Nate says. 'Go on, someone give it a go. What about you, Jackson?' he suggests, despite the girls' offer only moments before.

'Sure, I can try,' Jackson replies. As he does so, Lauren is pretty sure she catches Hollie subtly rolling her eyes at Taisie and Taisie's small grimace in response.

Despite Nate's dismissal of them, Hollie holds the torch up higher for Jackson to see. In the flickering light the walls look slick and smooth, difficult to get a grip on, but the mortar has crumbled away between some of the stones, which could work as footholds.

'Mac, give me a leg up, bro. I'm betting I can reach that ledge – it looks like there might be a gap in the wall above it. Maybe I can squeeze my way in.'

Does Lauren like their chances? They are two élite sportsmen, after all, so they should make it, and she is pretty convinced she could too, but she's not sure how some of the others will fare. Frank is still huddled by the fireside, clearly struggling. In his current state there is no way that he is going to be able to make the climb.

Kez, too, is shaking her head. 'I don't think I can do it, I'm afraid.' She hunches down, rubbing her knee and staring miserably at the ground.

'It doesn't matter,' says Jackson. 'I'll get up there with as many people as can make it, and then we'll work out a way to raise that gate thing from the inside so we can get the rest of you in.'

As he is saying this, he and Mac are already manoeuvring into position. He uses Mac like a climbing frame, balancing himself on his broad shoulders, and stretches up, steadying himself against the wall and grabbing on to the ledge with his fingertips. Using his arms as levers, he raises himself so he is level with the ledge, swings himself on to it and disappears through what must be a hole in the wall.

There is the longest of pauses, and then his head pops out and he is grinning. 'It's tight, but I made it!' he says. 'Pass me up the torch, and then you can start coming up.'

As the group discuss who should go next, Lauren keeps an eye on Nate, who is quiet, clearly weighing his options. For his age he is fit, muscles toned by years of working out, and Lauren reckons with help he could probably make it, so why is he hesitating?

But then she thinks of Jackson's spectacular strength, how his athletic grace would contrast with a man in his fifties, scrabbling for a handhold, then being heaved up like an ungainly sack of potatoes. It would be a long way from the well-choreographed action sequences Nate has built his reputation on, so it's not a surprise to her when he decides to stay behind.

'Great work, guys. Tell you what: I'll stay here – keep Frank company. Looks like he needs it. You go ahead and find a way to let us in.'

This leaves Lauren with a dilemma. She knows she's strong enough to scrabble up the wall, and the thought of being warm and inside is tempting. But her instinct is telling her to stick with Nate. They have no idea how long it will take the others to let them in – it might be just the perfect way to get close to him. She opts to stay.

In the end, five of their number disappear through the gap. Nico and the girls make it look relatively easy. It is Mac himself who has the worst of it – there's nobody strong enough to give him a boost. Both Nate and Lauren brace themselves against the wall, giving him a leg to balance on, and he makes a great leap, catching hold of Jackson's out-stretched hands. Muscles straining on both sets of arms, Mac heaves himself up the wall, and the remaining contestants share a grin as they see his slippers flapping about above while he tries to squeeze himself through the small space. When he finally does so, they hear him shout.

'As soon as we work out how, we'll be right back to fetch you. Take care of yourselves.'

'Sure thing. See ya,' is Nate's response.

Left alone together, he pauses for a second, as if he is assessing Lauren, then nods his head and conspiratorially gestures for her to come closer.

When she does, he leans towards her and says in a hushed voice, 'Didn't want to worry the others, especially the girls and Jude. She's already wound up about it not being safe here. But we both know that was way too close. Without you that gate falling could have been a whole different story.'

'I know. I can't believe they let that happen. What do you think went wrong?'

'I'm guessing someone was a bit trigger happy with the release button. Probably over excited by the show being live, maybe me being here. Whoever it was, you can bet they'll be finding a way to make up for it right now. My manager sure won't be happy. I'm pretty pissed myself.'

'Don't blame you. What are you going to do?' Lauren asks, hoping to God he's not planning on leaving, even after his inspiring speech.

'Nothing. I know he'll sort it. Plus, I want to be here, part of this show, so I'll let it slide. For the moment, anyway.'

'Yeah, well, fingers crossed it was a freak one-off. And let me know if I can do anything to help after the show, if you need me to say how close it was, back you up or anything.' Lauren suppresses a shudder as she attempts to suck up to a man she despises.

'Thanks, Lauren. That's good of you. I could sure do with getting inside there now, though. What the hell is taking them so long?'

Since they heaved Mac up the wall there hasn't been the slightest sign of the others.

'I can't hear them,' says Lauren. 'If the portcullis is stuck it could take them a while to find another way. Shall we wait it out by the fire? At least we can stay warm.'

Nate nods and follows her back to where Frank, Jude and Kez have taken shelter in the lee of the drawbridge, next to the flickering flames. They gather round, forming a makeshift camp, sitting on their haunches. Everyone looks miserable in the shadows, especially Frank. It is Nate who breaks the ice.

'Jesus, you guys, I am so jet-lagged. What time do you think it is? I'm kinda finding it hard to tell.'

'No idea. Late, but not like midnight late,' is Kez's best guess.

'I've been trying to work it out myself. I reckon they'd have gone live on air around half nine, maybe ten or so. Must've been an hour or so since then,' Frank adds.

'Man, I could do with some shut-eye.'

Long minutes stretch in front of them while they wait. With no way of telling the time – no watches, no phones – it seems endless. They make repeated forays back towards the cliff path to gather armfuls of heather, stoking the fire for lack of anything else to do. The conversation revolves around how long the others are taking to get back to them and then returns again and again to what happened to Nate, what a close call it was, and how unacceptable it is that any of them should have been put in this position.

Gradually, the conversation peters out and they sit in silence for a while. Lauren looks round at the oddness of her surroundings. On one side, there is Frank, the nation's favourite roguish uncle, who is as close as he can get to the warming flames. He has stopped shivering and the mottled tone has retreated from his face, but his trademark joviality has been extinguished.

Beyond her, one of the most photographed men in the world is resting his face in his hands and staring morosely ahead of him. Jude is the only one who looks vaguely happy to be where she is, sandwiched between the two of them.

Nate looks up and catches Lauren's eye.

'It's Lauren Brooks, right? Your name seems kinda familiar. Have we met before?'

A *frisson* of fright goes through her. Is she just being paranoid or is there the tiniest hint of menace in his voice? The last thing she needs is for him to realise who she is or have an inkling about what she's been up to, especially when she's just started making in-roads with him. When they first met on the beach, he didn't flinch. She was almost a hundred-per-cent sure there wasn't the slightest hint of recognition. But he is an actor, after all, and an Oscar-winning one at that. Lauren forces a laugh and tries to brush his comment off.

'Great chat-up line, Nate! Original. No, we haven't met before. I think I would remember.'

Frank guffaws, laughter shaking his whole body.

'Course she would! Big-time actor like you. Not likely she'd have forgotten meeting you, even if you'd forgotten her!'

'She's quite famous here in the UK. Aren't you, Lauren?' Jude butts in. 'She does these fantastic documentaries, really hard-hitting stuff. That one you did about the sex-trafficking through nail salons – that was excellent, so well researched. They had to change the law because of it. So was the one about corruption in grass-roots football. Brilliant. I don't watch much telly, but I always watch what you're up to.'

'Thanks, Jude. Appreciated,' Lauren mumbles, frowning in the darkness. She's flattered, but the less information Nate has about her and her investigative journalism career, the better. Before Jude can give any more away Lauren deftly turns the line of questioning in the opposite direction.

'Anyway, Jude, enough about me, what have you been up to recently? What businesses have you saved?'

Thankfully she takes the bait and starts wittering away about her latest passion project. Nate visibly tunes out soon after, as does Frank, and it's not long before the three older contestants have dozed off, slumped over each other in an awkward huddle.

Lauren feels uncomfortably awake. Nate's question has unsettled her. That, combined with the cold and the adrenaline still lingering after the near miss with the portcullis, make for a heady cocktail. Kez is also awake, massaging her stump.

'Are you OK?' Lauren whispers.

'Yeah, it's just a bit painful. But it's been much worse.'

Lauren thinks back to what she knows about Kez. Famously, she had been a prominent young swimmer before she lost her leg in an accident caused by a reckless driver.

'I guess you're used to toughing things out. Probably better prepared for whatever they've got in store than the rest of us.' She gestures towards the monastery walls.

'Maybe. I'm used to things being physically hard. But I'm not so good with the idea of cameras on me all the time. It's already feeling weird. I think some people in here are just a bit more used to it than others. They almost *like* playing up to the audience. But I only really do publicity for specific things, such as part of a sponsorship deal or something. Never done anything like this before. It's making me really self-conscious.'

Lauren nods in agreement, admiring her honesty, and wondering what they can have promised Kez to lure her on to the show. The urge to ask her is strong, but she remembers the underlined black print on her contract and bites the question back. If they talk about the prizes, they will forfeit their own and, even if she can't see them, there are likely to be cameras locked on her face right now, recording their hushed conversation.

She looks up and around. Their little patch of ground is warm and dry. They have a bank to rest on, and the light from the flames. Above them, she realises, the clouds have retreated, and the sky is a high canvas of midnight black, scattered with more stars than she can ever remember seeing. The reassuring half-moon has emerged from the horizon and sheds a peaceful light.

She feels her eyes closing and sinks into a fitful sleep.

Chapter Seven

Lauren wakes to the tolling of a bell, a mournful, distant sound that seems to be conjured out of the layers of the past.

Heart thudding, she opens her eyes, sensations tumbling through her brain in search of logic. The bank of a moat. A dying fire. Stiffness in her joints. The darkness, lightened faintly at one horizon. Bodies stirring beside her.

In this silent place, so far from anywhere, each note strikes an eeriness into the landscape. And then, as the tolling fades away, she hears a voice, so deep and disembodied it feels like the spirit of the monastery itself.

'The bells toll. Novices, wake up! Arise!'

Lauren looks around. All five of them are sitting upright now, straining to catch every syllable of that disembodied voice.

'It is time to enter. But hear this, in the monastery on Eilean Manach, your actions have consequences. You are being watched. You are being judged.' The timbre of the Voice rises, booming out of the darkness. 'In this place, your transgressions will be punished. Prepare to face the consequences. Prepare for justice.'

It is so over the top it should be funny. But it isn't. As the last echoes of the pronouncement fade away into the leaden cold, Lauren begins to see the faces of the others in the pale light of dawn. Kez looks determined, Frank is rubbing his eyes, Jude is open mouthed. And Nate? Nate is dead still. His eyes are wide, his mouth half-open. She finds herself unable to look away, trying to pinpoint exactly what it is she sees in his expression.

Until one word flashes across her mind. *Dread.*

As they shake off their slumbers there is still no sign of the others, but then a small door at the side of the portcullis slowly opens.

'Ridiculous. The producers could have let us in last night. Totally unnecessary, leaving us out here in the cold,' grumbles Jude as they stiffly make their way towards it. Kez is limping slightly, listing to one side.

'Probably thought it would make better TV to leave us out there, make us suffer a bit. Make it look like they *meant* for the gate to fall, like it was part of the game. Clever way of covering it up, I reckon,' Frank chuckles darkly, and Lauren is glad to see both his spirits and his colour have recovered despite his uncomfortable night.

As they step over the threshold into the monastery itself, Lauren gasps at the sight that greets them.

It is like stepping through a portal and being transported hundreds of years into the past. They are in an enclosed cloister, with curved stone arches held up by twin columns, carved with angelic figures, which delineate the space between the covered walkways and the open sky.

In the centre of the quadrangle, out in the open, there is a well, its low surrounding wall sculpted by the centuries of monks drawing their water there. On the far side is what must be their new home: a long stone building punctuated by tall narrow windows. The pale pink light is just beginning to creep across it, bringing out the rose colour in the stone. Everything from the ancient flagstones to the cherubs watching over them speaks of ancient tradition.

This is it: home for the next two weeks.

Lauren and the others gravitate towards the well, peering over the edge to see themselves reflected in the surface, glinting back at them in the winter sunlight. For a moment, the lack of food, the cameras and the general strangeness of the situation all fade into the background as Lauren lets the sense of tranquillity wash over her.

The quiet doesn't last long. It is broken by a whoop from Jackson.

'Hey, you made it!'

'Yeah, after a night frozen under the stars. What the hell happened to you lot?' Nate says, unable to hide his irritation. 'So much for you coming back to get us!'

'Sorry, mate, there was no way of getting the gate open from the inside. We looked everywhere. It probably wasn't much better in here, to be honest.'

The others appear, shaking themselves out of a corner of the cloisters where they've clearly been sheltering. By the looks of it, their audacious climb didn't earn them a comfortable night either.

'OMG, we had to sleep out here! It was *freezing*. How are all of you?' Rumpled concern is written on Hollie's face. She goes straight over to Frank and gives him a hug. Taisie follows suit. 'I've been worried – are you OK?' Hollie asks.

Frank grunts, 'I'm fine, lass, cheers for asking.'

Out of nowhere, the Voice booms out across the courtyard.

'Novices, welcome! You are now inside the gates of Eilean Manach. I hope your stay will be a fruitful one. You have many penances ahead of you. Some of you will triumph, some of you will fail. Only one of you will have your prayer answered. Within these walls, obedience is everything. Pay attention to what I tell you and heed my instructions closely.'

There's a pause while they take this in.

'Flippin' heck, not sure how I feel about taking orders from someone I can't see,' whispers Frank. 'Who do they think they are, the Voice of God?'

'Guess it means we can't argue with them,' Lauren whispers back.

The Voice of God is speaking again. 'Already, some of you have broken monastery rules. Last night, five of you ignored the warning signs and climbed the sacred walls. For that, there will be consequences: you will be punished. It is decreed those of you who obeyed the rules are Saints. Those of you who transgressed are Sinners.'

A chorus of protests meets this pronouncement, but the Voice ignores them: 'Now, step inside, into the great hall.'

At these words, the doors to the long building begin to swing open on noiseless hinges. The realisation that they are going inside for the first time in twenty-four hours hits Lauren, and she is overcome by a wish for this all to be over.

The contestants rush towards the opening door, jostling through the entrance. Inside, they find themselves in a white, cavernous, sparsely furnished room, with rough-edged beams high above them and flagstones underfoot. At one end there is an enormous fireplace, piled with logs but unlit. Better yet is what's in front of it: a long but narrow trestle table running down the length of the hall, one half piled high with food. It is only then that Lauren realises quite how hungry she is.

Without speaking, they take a step towards it. Only to be stopped, immediately, by a curt order.

'Novices, halt!' it says, and it is extraordinary how quickly they obey. 'You *shall* break your fast. But first, I have a task for you all. You are bidden to gather in the chapter house.'

Dragging her mind off her aching hunger, Lauren files with the others through a doorway marked with a wooden sign, into a smaller, octagonal room where stone columns frame tall stained-glass windows and vault above them into a domed roof. Ten tall wooden monks' desks line the walls, and in the centre stands an empty lectern. Lauren notices that Frank sidles in after the rest of them. He grins at her, showing her a hunk of stolen bread clutched in his fist. She smiles and shakes her head just as the Voice booms out again.

'Before you sate your hunger,' it says, 'I need to know the answers to two questions. You are commanded each to take a desk, and to respond according to what is in your heart.'

There are a couple of giggles at this, and an attempt by Frank at a knowing comment, which comes out too muffled for comprehension because of the mouthful of bread he is trying to swallow. But there is something about the Voice and the surroundings that compels most of them into silence as they take their desks. On each, an inkwell, a quill, and a scroll of parchment. Unrolling it, Lauren reads the following words:

Which of your fellow Novices do you believe is most fit to lead you during your time in Eilean Manach?
Which of your fellow Novices is most in need of beneficence?

'Beneficence? What the hell is that?' says Nico, articulating what they are all thinking.

An argument breaks out as to what the scroll is asking. The first question is pretty clear: they are being asked to vote for their leader. But the second? The consensus is that they need to vote for the person who most needs some extra comfort. An excited chatter breaks out about what that might be. An extra comfortable bed, perhaps? Some special treat to eat? There's more giggling as they each take the unwieldy quills and dip them in the inkwells.

Lauren looks down at the paper. For their leader, her first instinct is Jackson. He's easy-going, with a warm natural authority, and everyone seems happy to follow him. But just as she starts to write his name, she stops herself. What if their choices are made public? If she is to get closer to Nate, he needs to think she's on his side. She's pretty sure most votes will go to him anyway, so what difference will it make? She changes the J to an N.

She hesitates over the other name. It's hard to choose without knowing what exactly is at stake, but Kez has put up with so much more than the others. The awkward climb from the beach on her prosthetic leg, barely complaining about her missing things, even as the others bitched and moaned. Picturing her in a warm comfortable bed, Lauren deliberates for a moment and then writes Kez's name.

'Stand up from your desks, and post your answers, open, into the box beneath the lectern.'

Lauren complies, guessing that a camera inside the box is registering what they've written.

'Now, gather at the centre of the room,' says the Voice.

There is an agonising pause. It's partly filled with some nervous laughter, a bit of chitchat about what the reward might be, and how the Voice is going to read their different handwriting.

Lauren tries hard to picture the Voice as she knows it really must be – a veteran actor cast specifically for the ominous timbre of his voice, reading words fed to him by a bunch of twentysomethings slurping coffee in a production office. No doubt they're laughing at the hoops they're making the contestants jump through.

But, in spite of her rational thoughts, for Lauren, the Voice is taking on its own personality. In her imagination it belongs to a hulk of a man, toweringly tall, with wild hair and an untamed beard, features sculpted by exposure to harsh Scottish winters. She imagines him slowly and invisibly circulating among them, breathing down their necks and judging their every move. She shudders at the thought of it.

It speaks again. 'Novices, in one minute you will be live on television. What you do in the following five minutes will be broadcast to the nation. I remind you, do NOT swear. Any transgressions will be noted and acted upon. Do not look directly at the cameras.'

'Shit,' says Nico, 'not again!' He is frantically brushing his blond quiff upwards. In fact, every single one of them has started tending to their hair. Only the girls and Nate seem to have much success. The rest of them look, accurately, as though they have spent the night outside.

The Voice begins counting down, the sequence of numbers sounding anachronistic in the vaulted stone space.

'Novices, you have spoken,' says the Voice. 'You have nominated your Abbot. They will have the privilege of sleeping in the Abbot's quarters. They will allocate the daily tasks among those in the ranks of the Saints and Sinners and will be my second in command. They, like me, must be obeyed at all times.'

They all try to stand upright and look natural under the suddenly heavy gaze of the cameras. An image of her mum and dad watching anxiously at home makes Lauren stand a little taller and hold her shoulders back. Silence falls. Interminable seconds pass. When she is watching from the safety of her sofa at home, Lauren always loves these moments, but it feels downright silly to be standing here stock-still, the only sound the low hum as the cameras zoom in to take close-ups. They shuffle awkwardly, trying not to catch each other's eyes and to hold in the bubbling giggles, but none of them says a word while they wait for the result to be delivered.

'So, Novices, until further notice you must defer . . . to . . .' Here the pause becomes so agonising that Lauren struggles to keep her face composed, '. . . Nate!'

Whoops reverberate around the room. Mac and Jackson pat him amiably on the back and he high fives Hollie and Taisie. Even though she voted for him herself, Lauren feels a short sharp stab of irritation that Nate's influence will become official.

She focuses on listening to what the Voice is saying now.

'Novices, we asked you also to consider which among you deserved special consideration. Which one of you needed to be shown some mercy after the difficulty of the last day? Which one of you struggled most with the rigours of your journey?'

Another long pause, the rising hysteria worse this time. Lauren notices how many of them are shooting reassuring grins in Kez's direction. Sure enough, when the Voice speaks again, the words are predictable. 'The answer you have given . . . is . . . Kez!'

Once again there is a mini outbreak of celebration. Taisie and Hollie, who are standing next to Kez, exclaim on her behalf and hold up their hands for high fives. She smiles but hesitantly, before tuning in to what the Voice is saying.

'We have taken into account your wish to show mercy to one among your ranks. You have been generous and considerate. You have shown kindness to one of your fellow Novices. You have chosen this person for beneficence, and thanks to you they will be spared from the trials and tribulations ahead.'

There is small pause, filled by stifled mutterings of confusion. This is not what any of them were expecting. 'Spared' – what does that mean? They don't have to wait long for the answer.

'Kez, you are their chosen one. You are to leave the island, returning now to the comfort of the mainland and to the embrace your family. Pick up your bag and proceed immediately to the doors ahead of you. You must pass through them before they close again. There is no time for farewells.'

Silence.

It is Kez herself who breaks the shocked hush that descends. 'No way,' she says, outraged. 'No way. What the hell? You can't throw me out now. I never asked for special treatment. I never do. Why would I? Why did you choose me?'

A storm of protest breaks out, guilt mixing with disbelief as the contestants apologise to Kez and plead with the Voice to let her stay. Lauren is among them, furious with herself for falling into Production's trap.

But a pair of doors on the far side of the chapter house is slowly swinging open, the creaking noise they make cutting through the clamour of voices. And with the eyes of the nation on her, Kez is drawn towards them, moving almost as if in a trance. She reaches the doors and peers through, then turns back for a moment. Lauren is near enough to see the tears on her cheeks and the anger in her eyes as she faces them for the last time.

'I guess this is it, then. Have a great time,' she says coolly, then steps through the doorway into blackness.

There is the tiniest of pauses before they run forward, catching only a glimpse of a stone staircase spiralling downwards and the back of Kez's russet head as she descends. Then the doors bang shut, fast and hard, behind her.

'You are now off air,' says the Voice, and they are left looking at each other in the silent room.

Chapter Eight

It is as though the oxygen has been sucked out of the chapter house in Kez's wake.

'Fuck's sake, the game hasn't even started! That can't just be it for her, can it? You bastards!' Frank shouts up at the ceiling.

'Hey, man, chill,' says Nate, his words unsurprisingly having the opposite effect on Frank.

Kez's sudden exit has set in motion a ripple of dismay and confusion. Hollie and Taisie are standing, shoulders stiff, hands gripped tightly. Is it guilt that has them so tense, or relief it wasn't one of them?

'But it's not fair!' says Nico. 'She hasn't had any time! Why bring her all the way here, and then just throw her out? If they can do that to her, what about the rest of us? Are they just going to chuck us out whenever, with no warning, just like that?'

'I guess they make the rules so . . . yeah,' says Jackson.

They look at each other with wide eyes. Lauren is aghast. How could they put Kez through the trials of last night only to evict her as soon as they were inside? She thinks of the weeks of tension, the build-up, the photoshoots, the evaluations, the endless journey here. All wasted.

'Bloody unfair is what it is!' Frank says, still fuming.

'Seems to me you've had a lucky escape,' Nate says slyly. 'You were the one struggling, not Kez.'

'You what?'

'I voted for you to go. I don't know why everyone else didn't do the same. You nearly had a cardiac arrest when you finally got up that hill last night. Are you sure you're even fit enough to be here?'

The confrontation comes from nowhere, and Frank is not taking it lightly.

'Say that again, you puffed-up Hollywood pretty boy. You may think you're hot shit but from what I hear you're not all you're cracked up to be. All those stunts, you "do yourself", eh?'

Frank advances towards Nate menacingly, but Lauren grabs his arm and gives a tiny shake of her head. She's starting to like Frank – the last thing she wants is for him to get punished or kicked out for punching Nate in the face. Much as Nate may deserve it.

Thankfully they are interrupted by the Voice booming out again. Lauren tenses; already she is being conditioned to fear it. But, this time, the message is something they all have been longing to hear and it cuts through the icy atmosphere.

'Novices, you may eat. A feast is laid out for you in the great hall. As you sustain your bodies, so I hope that you will reflect on everything that has transpired so far and gain strength for what lies ahead.'

Thoughts of Kez are driven out of their heads as the remaining nine of them rush through the door, falling on to the feast laid out on the table. Rough metal goblets and wooden bowls are stacked to one side, and there are boards piled with bread, and ham and cheese on huge platters. Judging by the sweaty state of the cheese it must have been left out for them to eat last night, but the accident with the portcullis means they are eating it hours later than they should have. The staleness of the bread is irrelevant, though. They are all ravenous and just about to pile as much as they can into their bowls when the Voice interjects again.

'Pay attention. Saints, you may eat whatever you wish. Sinners, as you have transgressed, you will be punished. You must only help yourselves to bread and water. Do not be tempted to share provisions, or touch anything else. If you do, you will lose another of your number.'

Nate lays a hand over Jackson's bowl, which is piled high with food, and looks him in the eye.

'Don't even think about eating that, unless you want to be the one to go home next!'

For a millisecond, it looks like Jackson might protest but chastened, he takes everything except the crusty bread out of his bowl and slopes over to Taisie, Hollie, Mac and Nico, who have sat down at the far end of the table away from all the food. The two sportsmen are furious.

'Jesus. We haven't eaten for – what is it now? – twenty-four hours. Bread and water are not going to cut it!' Mac seethes.

'They know I need to keep training while I'm in here, and they swore a hundred per cent I would have at least two thousand calories a day. This is not even close,' Jackson adds.

'Don't worry, guys,' Nate says across the table. 'It's just a game. Go along with it and I'm sure they'll give you more food.'

'And how would you know?' says Jackson, uncharacteristically combative. 'You said yourself you never watch these shows.'

'I don't need to. I have people who watch things for me, go through my contracts. You should have a better manager, Jackson. If I were you, I would have made sure the calories were written into my T and Cs, so they couldn't screw me over. When we get out, I'll give you a hand finding a new agent. Sounds like you need one.'

Mac snorts in what seems like derision and tries to cover it up with a cough.

'Thanks, but that's not exactly helping me right now, is it?' Jackson mutters darkly.

The only person visibly impressed by Nate's offer seems to be Nico, who is gazing at him adoringly.

'I could do with a new manager too,' he says wistfully. Nate doesn't reply, leaving Nico's plea hanging.

After that awkward moment they eat without speaking. Lauren can feel resentment rising off the hungry Sinners in waves. She is tempted to slip them some extra food under cover of the table, but dare not risk it, knowing the cameras are following her every move. She eats guiltily and as much as she can, not knowing when the next meal will be, watching the rest of the Saints do the same.

The Sinners, on their diet of bread and water, lick their fingers and press them into the sides of their bowls so as not to waste even a crumb. She sees Hollie whisper something conspiratorially in Taisie's ear, but from where she is sitting, she can't work out who or what they're talking about, and she only sees Taisie nod vigorously in response.

Once the agonising meal is over, the more curious among them start to look around the hall. It is only now that they notice how cold it is. Nate has automatically taken the only chair in the room at the head of the long trestle table. It has arms, and a comfortable velvet padded seat, while the rest of them are sitting on two benches that are just a narrow bare strip of wood. He is tipping his chair backwards, hands clasped behind his head, knees wide. Lauren can't work out if this mix of manspreading and bad manners is a conscious or unconscious attempt to command the room. Either way, he's certainly been quick to assume his role as leader.

'Does anyone know how to get that going? I don't expect they left us any matches, did they?' he says, nonchalantly waving a hand towards the fireplace.

Hollie and Taisie get up to have a look. Next to the fire are two old-fashioned oil lanterns, and a couple of tapers for lighting them. There is also a small box. 'There's some flint here. And some straw and wool,' says Hollie, opening it. 'It'll take a while, but we can get it lit.'

The others crowd round to watch them work, oohing and aahing as they get the sparks to catch first on the strands of wool and then the kindling. Lauren catches herself thinking that she would never have expected Hollie and Taisie to be the ones to get the fire going with just flint and material. Their practical talents don't end there, either. Taisie is inspecting the pots and pans lined up beside the chimney breast.

'Look! There's a sort of shelf for cooking things on,' she says. 'That's cool. And look at this cauldron thing. And this, what do you reckon, an ancient griddle? We can do stuff with that.'

Lauren is taken aback. In her mind, the girls are all about eye-lashes and eyeliner, not about cooking and cauldrons.

'Don't worry,' says Hollie, laughing as she sees Lauren's face 'Tai-sie's an insane cook. Literally, she does all sorts at home. She even taught me!'

Taisie rolls her eyes in Hollie's direction. 'My mum had to work a lot in the evenings when I was little. It was just her and me. I used to have childminders and that, but when I got old enough, I didn't like that she'd have to start cooking when she got home all tired. So, I kind of took it over. I like it. It's a good distraction from all the online stuff, you know what I mean?'

'Well, it'll be good to have some decent chefs in here if we ever get any ingredients,' says Lauren. 'I can't cook at all.' She gazes back at the table, unable to believe quite how much they have managed to consume in such a short space of time. All the bread has gone and the Saints, even though there were only four of them, have reduced the glorious ham to scraps. Rinds of cheese and apple cores lie scattered everywhere.

She is just about to start tidying up when the Voice starts speaking again.

'Novices, find your quarters. You may rest for one hour. Nate, you are to take the Abbot's room. Saints – that is Lauren, Jude and Frank – your dorm is reached through the cloisters. Sinners, you know who you are. Mac, Nico, Taisie, Hollie and Jackson, you will find your dormitory above theirs. You may rest until you are called.'

Nate makes the first move back into the courtyard, and the others obediently follow him in a line through the cloisters, although Frank somewhat reluctantly so.

Nate's is the first bedroom they find, clearly marked with a brass plate. The wooden slatted door is heavy and creaks as Nate pushes it. It can't be described as much more than a cell, but it is surprisingly cosy and welcoming. A fire is set in the corner at the foot of the bed, which is covered with a deep burgundy velvet quilt. As they watch, it bursts into flames.

'Wow!' says Hollie. 'I love how they do that!'

Jude, however, isn't impressed. 'If they can light fires remotely in here, they could at least have made the hall warm for us.'

There is a rickety chair beside a small octagonal desk. On the table are three objects laid out next to each other, a candlestick, a small square black leather case and a weathered-looking book entitled *Abbot's Rules*. The rest of them watch as Nate picks up the tiny case and opens it, revealing a gold ring set with a huge glittering purple stone. He takes it out with a mock imperious look on his face and slips it on to the ring finger of his right hand. It fits perfectly.

'I guess this proves I'm in charge. Better make sure you obey me, or who knows what I'll make you do!' His laugh is not entirely benevolent, and neither are the answering chuckles entirely sincere.

Looking at the perfect fit of the ring, Lauren realises Production made a pretty good guess as to who was going to be voted Abbot.

There's no way she can picture that ring adorning Hollie or Taisie's slim fingers, or even her own. How predictable, she thinks. What a cliché we are. They guessed we would vote for the big Hollywood star, and we did.

It is Frank who now makes the first move. 'All right, I'm out of here. I want to have a kip!'

The Saints' room is next door to Nate's, a small dormitory set with four beds. There are no rich bedspreads or warming fireplaces here, but it's neat and the mattresses look comfortable, already made up with pillows and thick tartan blankets.

Lauren looks longingly at the bed. A place to retreat to, she thinks, before laughing at herself as she clocks the two cameras and their glassy eyes swivelling back and forth from the corners of the ceiling. Refuge, perhaps, but no privacy.

Curious, she follows the others, who have gone up the staircase to the floor above. Judging by the comments she can hear as she approaches, the Sinners are not too happy with their lot. And when she gets to the top of the stairs, she can see why.

The Sinners' dormitory is a very different matter. There are five beds, or pallets might be a better description: wooden boards with thin mattresses on top, which seem to be made of straw, given the pieces strewn over them. There is a rough blanket folded up at the end of each and no sheets or pillows to speak of. The walls are stone, and the slit windows placed at intervals down the length of the room have no glass in them, and no curtains either.

'For Christ's sake. They know I have a bad back.' Lauren can tell Mac is losing his temper by the second. 'I can't sleep on this. And it's freezing in here.' He seems genuinely angry, fighting to hold himself in check.

'Don't worry, by the time you're all in here it'll warm up a bit,' says Nate soothingly, and Lauren notices Mac shooting him a furious look, no doubt remembering the fire and cosy coverlet below. 'You could board up the windows with something? That would warm things up.'

'And make it pitch black in here?' Mac asks sarcastically.

In response the Voice rings out at them. 'Novices, you will not alter your surroundings.'

'Jesus!' says Mac. 'Keep forgetting they're always listening, the bastards. So, no cosy room for us, I guess. If I get pneumonia, I swear I'll bloody sue you!' he yells into his microphone, then grins sarcastically at the rest of them. 'Bet they're not going to broadcast that!' he says. 'Anyway, would the rest of you mind sodding off for a bit? Going to try my best to get a bit of shut-eye.'

Lauren agrees. She wants nothing more than an hour to herself, a chance to lie down and rest and to process the events of the last day.

Five minutes later, she is on the bed she has bagged in the Saints' dorm, Jude and Frank silent beside her. They both seem to fall asleep in seconds, but Lauren's mind is racing. Kez's sudden disappearance has rocked her. It isn't just the disappearance of someone who seemed as if they might become a friend, but what it means for the rest of them.

If Kez could be banished so suddenly, what's to say that Lauren won't be next? She too could be evicted at any moment. It would ruin her chance to expose Nate for what he really is.

She kicks herself when she realises that, for the first time in years, she doesn't have a clear plan. She knows what she wants to prove and has studied her subject meticulously, for months, delving deep into his background and triple-checking her sources. She has the facts at her fingerprints, etched on to her brain, but how is she going to use them? How is she going to make Nate confess, and when?

Should she try to catch him out live on air, in front of everyone? The more witnesses the better, but it's unlikely to work and probably not worth the risk of Nate guessing what she's up to. No, she needs to be cleverer than that. She needs to build his trust, try to get to him when they're alone, or as alone as they can be under the watchful eye of the cameras. Because no matter how isolated they might feel, Lauren is only too aware that their every move is being filmed, which means if Nate does slip up, she'll have the evidence she needs.

But if something goes wrong, if things turn nasty? Well, that's just a risk she'll have to take. She's been in far more dangerous situations, after all, although this is the only one that feels personal.

Lying back on her bed, staring at the ceiling, she realises she is exhausted. She would love to take the opportunity to doze, like her roommates beside her, but her mind is too busy for sleep.

Chapter Nine

Lauren's anxious thoughts are interrupted by the clanging of a bell. As it fades away, the Voice rings out: 'Novices, please gather in the great hall where you will be assigned your roles by the Abbot.'

Lauren is intrigued to see how Nate will handle this. Who will he favour? He's clearly got it in for Frank, who never seemed to like him. Mac, too, appears less taken in by Nate's fame than the others. Will Nate want to keep him onside, or test him?

She follows Jude and Frank to the Hall, the last to join the others, who are gathered round the table. Nate is back in his seat at its head, clearly planning to commandeer the best position for the duration. *Abbot's Rules* is in his hands, the purple ring glinting against the worn leather. He opens the book, turning the pages with his forefinger and then holds it aloft.

'Hmm. A lot of stuff about respecting the Order, following the rules, et cetera. Look. Here it is:

The Abbot's first task shall be to appoint Novices to the tasks essential for the running of the Abbey. From the ranks of the Saints, he must

ISOLATION ISLAND

appoint two people to gather wood and kindling, one to tend the fire, and one to cook. From the ranks of the Sinners, two to draw water from the well, two to clean the lavatorium and the great hall, and one to maintain the reredorter. You must all complete the task assigned to you, and no one else.

God, he's loving this, thinks Lauren, just as his speech is interrupted by an avalanche of questions.

'What on earth is a rere-water?' asks Jude.

'I think he said—' Taisie starts to say quietly, but Nico shushes her.

'Does lavatorium mean the lavatory? No way am I doing that!' Hollie wrinkles her nose in agreement.

Nate puts his finger up to silence them.

'It says here the lavatorium is not the lavatory. It's a sink with running water that we'll find in the cloisters, where all the washing up and cleaning is done. But the reredorter is going to be a tough job – that's the restroom. I think you'd say toilet. And doesn't sound like there's any flushing water.'

'Are they serious? Someone has to clean it? That is absolutely disgusting'. Like Nico, Jude is clearly appalled at the idea. 'I'm sorry, but if you give it to me, I am just not doing it.'

'Don't worry,' says Mac wryly. 'You're not in line for it. You're a Saint, remember?'

Nate cuts through the babble of outrage. He is trying not to show it but is clearly enjoying being centre of attention as he doles out the worst of the roles. He tells Nico and Jackson that they are in charge of getting water from the well, trying to soften them up with comments about their combined muscle power. Nico pretends to swoon, and even Jackson looks pleased.

Next is the cleaning, an even less desirable job that will involve washing up endless plates in freezing cold water, not to mention sweeping and scrubbing. But he hands this role to Hollie and Taisie in such a deft way that, somehow, despite been relegated to being mere pot-washers, they don't seem too disgruntled.

That leaves just Mac as the last of the Sinners to be appointed. By process of elimination, he realises that his domain is going to be the toilet.

'Aye, right, I know,' he says. 'I'm on shite scrubbing detail. Thanks a bunch.'

Nate gives him a charming smile that is clearly meant to be placatory. It doesn't look as if it works.

The Saints' jobs are easier. Jude gets the vital but low-effort job of keeping the fire going, which she accepts with a tut and a nod of her head, and Nate appoints Lauren and Frank to gather wood for it. Lauren tries not to show how delighted she is by the prospect. The thought of being able to escape into the fresh air with good company is just what she would have chosen.

As for cooking, Nate promises to do that himself. He says he once played a hard-bitten restaurant cook in a gritty New York drama and did some training in a kitchen. Lauren can't help thinking that playing a chef and being a chef are quite different things, especially when all you have to work with is an open fire and some medieval cooking pots. As he jokes to Hollie and Taisie about needing some sous-chefs, Lauren can't help noticing that by dividing the jobs up the way he has, he has guaranteed that he will get to spend most of his time with the two beautiful young women. How utterly typical of him, she thinks.

Despite low grumbles, everyone sets to work. Within a short space of time Jackson and Nico have found buckets and rope and are busily working out how to operate the pulley system inside the well, while Taisie and Hollie gather the debris from everyone's breakfast and carry it out to the cloisters with surprising enthusiasm.

Together they make an entertaining picture, their tiny frames swamped by their billowing robes. Jude, meanwhile, is loudly organising the area around the fire, directing the girls where to stack plates and pots, though Lauren notices she is doing very little grunt work herself. Mac seems to have disappeared, although Lauren suspects he's not cleaning the toilet so much as trying to get some space.

She too is looking forward to getting some respite from the group. The feeling of having to be constantly 'on camera' – warm, smiling, always upbeat – is grating on her. Some of them are clearly enjoying it, doing their best, like Nate, to hog the limelight and carve out a position for themselves, but it's taking its toll on Lauren already.

She thinks of what Kez said the night before, how uncomfortable she felt about the cameras. God, was it really only hours ago she was evicted? It's unsettling how quickly her departure has been accepted. One minute it was all tears and 'We love you!', the next they're arguing about who cleans the loos. There is no trace left of her on the island, just the empty bed that she never even slept in. It's as if she has been erased. Lauren wonders if that's what being a celebrity is like: all smiles and friends while you're on a show together, then nothing.

She and Frank find some hefty baskets in an anteroom off the great hall and heave them outside. Time to explore, thinks Lauren, pushing open a small kissing gate at one end of the cloisters to find herself at the edge of a graveyard. It clangs behind them. To their right there is the square tower of the belfry, and behind that the ruined arches of the chapel lie open to the sky. The vast graveyard is quiet, its size a sobering reminder of how many lives have been spent and lost here across the generations.

The wood she gathers is rough against Lauren's hands, but it feels good to be working this way. It's peaceful outside, although the buzz of a small drone follows them, reminding them that they are not entirely alone.

'Never thought I'd find myself gathering logs with the famous Jimmy Black,' says Lauren. Frank's soap *alter ego* is a die-hard townie, who hasn't, to Lauren's knowledge, ever set foot in the countryside.

Frank gives a wry chuckle. 'I've played Jimmy so long that everyone assumes we're the same person. But I'm a country lad at heart, born and bred in the Yorkshire Dales. And we had nowt when I was a boy, no central heating. Gathered more logs than you can shake a stick at, so to speak. Never have minded a bit of hard graft. Not like Mr Hollywood Hero back there.' He makes a gesture, waving his hand grandly in an uncanny imitation of Nate handing out the tasks. Lauren laughs. 'Reckon he's never done a day's real work in his life. Thinks he was born to wear that ring. This might end up being a bit of a wake-up call, don't you think?'

'You could say that,' Lauren agrees, although she doesn't elaborate.

Frank goes on, 'I get the sense you're not his biggest fan either.'

Lauren would like nothing more than to confide in Frank, share the burden, but she can't with the cameras watching. She puts her hand over her mic and raises a finger to her lips, gesturing towards the drone. Frank grins knowingly and winks.

On their return to the monastery, they find themselves back in the graveyard, wandering among the ancient stones, trying to decipher the inscriptions despite their combined lack of Latin skills. As they reach the end, they see that the overgrown path they are walking divides. One way leads back to the cloisters. The other goes down some steps towards the octagonal structure of the chapter house, where they last saw Kez. A rope is slung across their path, 'Do not pass' written in clear black letters on a wooden sign.

'Look,' Lauren says, her inquisitiveness getting the better of her, 'that looks like it goes down near where Kez disappeared. Do you think there's any chance she's still on the island somewhere? I'd love to know where she went.'

'Only one way to find out,' Frank answers. 'Could be anything down there . . . and besides . . .' he looks around him, nods upwards and whispers, shielding his mic with his hand, 'have you noticed the drone has stopped following us? And I can't see any cameras here. Shall we risk it?'

Lauren looks at him for a second, then nods decisively, setting down her basket and stepping neatly over the rope.

Chapter Ten

Acutely aware she is breaking the rules, but not caring about the consequences, Lauren leads the way along the path, which hugs the outside of the chapter house, then feeds them into a narrow doorway on the lower level of the building.

They step through and find themselves in a tight dark tunnel, which is dank with the smell of wet stone. As it spirals downwards, the ceiling gets lower and they have to stoop to keep going. With every step, the odour becomes stronger and ranker: the smell of rotting fish. They pass a door bearing an ominous cross.

'D'you think that's some kind of crypt?' asks Lauren.

'Probably,' says Frank. 'This place gives me the heebie-jeebies. Shall we turn back?'

Lauren is just nodding her assent when she notices a sound; a rhythmic whooshing and crashing just at the edge of her senses.

'Hang on,' she says. 'What's that?'

Frank holds still, listening. 'Sounds like the sea,' he says. 'But how on earth . . .? Come on, let's keep going. Now we're here we might as well have a quick peek.'

Tighter and tighter the secret tunnel descends, winding down deeper than she thought possible, into the heart of the island. By now, they are in almost total darkness, navigating only by the touch of their fingers against the rough stone. Each footstep is an act of faith, and she can hear nothing but their breathing and their footfalls, underpinned by the sound of the sea getting closer. Her hand automatically searches for her phone to light their way, forgetting momentarily that she handed it over to an unspeaking security guard when she left her flat, what must be days ago now.

She is just about to admit defeat and turn round, when she sees the darkness is thinning ahead. Tackling the final few feet gingerly, she steps into daylight and laughs aloud.

They have descended right down to sea level. The passage opens out into a wide, low cave and water is washing on to the bottom of the steps they are standing on, threatening to splash over their feet as the waves rise and fall. It is as though they have moved from the thirteenth to the twenty-first century in one stride, because the cave is fitted out with a modern metal jetty, complete with life ring, first-aid kit and safety buoys bobbing by its side. It is far more sophisticated than the pier where they had disembarked.

So, this is where Kez disappeared to, into the cave under their feet, presumably to be picked up by a boat and whisked back to the mainland. One mystery solved, thinks Lauren, more determined, having seen the exit, that whoever is next to make that journey, it will not be her.

They must be nearly halfway back up when Frank stops her.

'Sorry, Lauren, I need to slow down, take a breather.'

She pauses and waits beside him, concerned by the way he is straining for air.

'Of course, take a minute.' Lauren doesn't want to rush him, but she's getting worried about their detour. The others will surely be wondering where they are. Frank studies her a moment, his expression uncharacteristically serious.

'Look, pet. They can't hear us here,' he says once his breathing is even. 'It's not rigged up; no wires. No cameras, no drones. And there's no way the microphones work this far underground. So go on, tell me. What is it you know about Nate?'

'I . . . I can't say. I don't want to get thrown off the show.'

'Oh, so you do know something, then?'

Lauren could kick herself for her carelessness, and just shakes her head in response.

'Don't fret yourself. Your secrets are safe with me. Anyway, I reckon I know what it is. From what I hear from some of my female friends, he has a bad reputation when it comes to women. Word is they won't work with him. Nothing illegal, from what I understand, more like . . . how would I put it?' He pauses. 'Inappropriate? No, worse. They say he's cruel. Manipulative. I feel sorry for his wife.'

Lauren takes a beat before answering. She has two questions: first, can she trust him? And secondly, equally important, can Production hear her? She fiddles with the waist-belt under her habit, pulls out her mic pack, and gestures to him to do the same. They twiddle the switches, and their red lights go out simultaneously. It's a risk, she knows, but she might need an ally and Frank seems as if he'd make a good one. In her years of reporting, her instincts about people have rarely let her down, and she likes Frank.

Before she speaks, she takes a deep breath.

'I can't say too much. We haven't got time. But, yes, essentially what you've heard is right. I've been investigating him for a while, ever since he was in a relationship with someone I know. A friend of mine, actually.' Her voice catches as Allegra's tear-streaked face flashes into her mind.

She pauses for a moment, trying to collect herself, uncertain about how much to say.

'It is horrific how he treats women. I've spoken to dozens of them.

He uses his charm and his influence to sleep with them, then when he's bored or has had enough, he turns on them, destroying their careers, turning their lives upside down. It's like a game to him.'

'I knew it. No smoke without fire. Knew he was a nasty piece of work. Won't any of your women speak up?'

'They're scared to. Like you say, it's not exactly criminal what he does. More like, malicious, controlling. It's their word against his, and if anyone is brave enough to say something he uses his army of lawyers to cover it up, threaten them. Anyone who complains is paid off or made to sign an NDA. He's completely untouchable. I've been trying to get to him for months and it's almost ruined me, so please, for God's sake, don't tell anyone.'

'Course I won't,' Frank says sincerely, and Lauren believes him. 'So, what's the plan?'

She almost laughs at this, at the absurdity of what she is trying to do.

'Good question. Now that we're both here, I want to get close to him, make him trust me. Get under his skin, make him slip up in front of the cameras.'

'You need to be careful, love. He has some powerful connections, and it sounds like he's not afraid to use them.'

'That's exactly the problem I've come up against, time and time again. But he has no one on the island to protect him.'

'Still, you should mind yourself. I've got your back if you need me. Scout's honour. No one likes a man like that, least of all me.'

His tone is genuine, and Lauren feels relief flood through her. For the first time since arriving on the island, she doesn't feel quite so alone.

Chapter Eleven

Lauren and Frank have climbed back up the twisting tunnel and retrieved their loaded baskets when they hear the bell ringing, summoning them, they presume, to the courtyard. Struggling under the weight of the wood, they pick up the pace.

Frank is joking about what other parts of a Bond villain's lair they might discover as they come through the gate, but his voice trails off as they enter the courtyard. She follows his gaze. The seven other novices are lined up next to each other with military precision in front of the great hall, stony faced.

Nate is the first to break the silence.

'Where the *hell* have you been? Are you trying to screw us all over? We've been waiting for you for over ten minutes!'

'Oh God, I'm so sorry. We were just getting wood for the fire,' Lauren stammers, embarrassed.

Frank is more nonchalant, lowering his basket in front of the well and taking his time as he does so.

'Calm down, everyone. No one's died. It's not that serious.'

'Yes, it bloody is.' Mac speaks next, picking up where Nate left off. 'We've just been given an almighty telling-off.' He waves at the loudspeaker. 'Apparently the first challenge is starting. It's timed. But it didn't let us start until you two numpties got back. Because of you they are taking minutes off the clock.'

The Voice cuts through his diatribe: 'Frank and Lauren, you have broken the rules. You have trespassed beyond the confines of your quarters, and you have turned off your microphones. For this you will ALL be punished. Ten minutes has been taken off the time you had to complete this first challenge, the Leap of Faith. Proceed immediately to the highest point. Your time . . . starts . . . now!'

'You've got to be kidding me,' Nico mutters, shooting the pair a dark look, and he's not the only one.

'The highest point? What's that mean?' says Taisie.

'It must be the top of the tall tower, over there,' says Hollie. 'Come on.'

The Novices rush headlong into the graveyard. Chastened, and still struggling to turn their mics back on, Frank and Lauren have fallen into step behind Hollie and Taisie. The two girls are jogging next to each other, their feet perfectly in tandem. Their heads are close, locked in secret conversation, and they speak so quickly that Lauren can only make out a few words.

'Just remember, every shot counts. We need to stick together; everyone will be watching. We need this. Together we're stronger than the rest of them.'

Lauren kicks herself. It has taken the social media queens to remind her this is a TV show, a competition, not some sort of bizarre holiday camp for celebrities. She needs to focus if she is to stay in the game. How could she forget to turn on her mic again? What an idiot.

They skid round the corner of the belfry, finding themselves at the bottom of the circular watchtower. Its colossal height seems overwhelming, an imposing needle of stone. Curved walls reach towards the heavens, capped by a parapet that is almost out of sight from their low angle.

'How do we even get in?' Nico asks the obvious.

'Over here!' yells Jackson. 'Follow me!' He races round the back, graceful in his voluminous robes and slippers, even at speed. They round the tower in his wake, and Nate, swinging into Action Hero mode, leads the way, making sure he is first to duck under the lintel of the low door.

By the time Lauren gets inside, five of them are already part-way up a terrifyingly delicate wrought-iron spiral staircase, which curls towards the ceiling at least fifty or sixty feet above them. It looks like it is suspended in the space, its only anchor the dusty floor. Lauren has never seen anything quite so precarious, and she is not alone. Jude has stalled.

'It's never going to take the weight of us all! Look! It's shaking.'

Jackson must have heard her. Her words are amplified in the vacuum.

'Hurry up down there, we don't have much time,' he calls. 'It's fine, just look at the wall!'

Jude tentatively puts her foot on the bottom rung, and her knuckles turn white as she grips tightly, left hand on the railing, right on the centre pole. By the time it gets to her turn, Lauren's neck is cricked from straining to see what's going on above her. With the metal structure vibrating unnervingly through her body, she is relieved that Jude is making such slow progress.

'It's OK, Jude, no need to rush,' she says, mostly for her own benefit.

'I'm fine!' Jude replies brusquely.

Lauren can only just hear her, there is so much noise. Shouts of alarm echo and repeat in the void, mixing together in a hellish cacophony.

Their ascent begins to take on the quality of an ever-recurring nightmare, as they continue round, round and round again. There is barely any illumination: slit windows punctuate the thick stone walls, letting in small rectangles of light that filter through cobwebs and dead flies, dust dancing in their beams. Lauren has to concentrate hard to place her feet on steps, her knees getting shakier as the climb continues.

Even though she can only see the back of Jude's heels above her, she senses from the decrease in the volume of the echoes that they are getting strung out, further apart.

'How far to go now?' she shouts up, hoping someone can hear her.

'Not too far, hen.' It's Mac, his earlier anger apparently forgotten. 'I'm at the top. Keep moving – you've done the worst of it!'

Lauren's lungs are heaving from the effort when she finally pushes herself through a trapdoor, on her knees with gratitude. It opens into a panelled room, the space designed for the night watchmen of old. They may not have been there for decades but there is still a low bed next to a diminutive fireplace. Nico is sitting down on the bare springs, shivering, and Jude joins him, taking his trembling hands in hers. He is whimpering.

'Omigod, this is going to kill me. I told them I hate heights. I shouldn't be up here. I'm never gonna get down again.'

Jude tries her best to placate him with gentle reassurance and encouragement.

'Come outside, guys, it's incredible!' Nothing will diminish Jackson's enthusiasm. He is by the door to the balcony, gesturing manically for them to have a look.

The girls peer over the edge, their voices blended together in shrill gasps at what lies beneath them. 'It's amazing! We can literally see for miles!'

'Man, would you look at that. Never seen anything like it.'

Nate is right. They are all right. The view from the top is utterly stunning.

It is like entering another world, a space filled with nothing but light and air. It is so overwhelming that it takes Lauren a moment to get her bearings. They are standing right at the top of the circular tower, with a bird's-eye view of the island.

She can see in all directions, out to the charcoal line of the horizon of the North Atlantic, and back towards the majestic mountains of the mainland. From this vantage point she can see the whole circumference of the island. How small it seems, how tiny and insignificant. And how far away from anyone else, unreachable without a boat.

At the other side of the monastery, she can see the huge satellite Mac mentioned, balanced precariously on top of a metal pyramid, smaller ones clustered underneath it. That must be where the TV pictures are streamed from, she thinks, and how Production control the cameras, the doors, the pyrotechnics. It is the contestants' only tenuous connection with the outside world.

Lauren thinks back to the stark emptiness she travelled through to get to the coast – no villages or even houses for miles and miles. She feels overwhelmed by the sight in front of her: it is beautiful, but it is also terrifying to get a sense of how isolated they really are.

Nate's voice snaps her back to reality. 'Come on, guys,' he says. 'We don't have time to stand here staring. Have you seen this?'

He is standing by a gap in the parapet in front of him, a couple of feet wide. Distracted by the view and the vertiginous drop, none of them has noticed that there is a thick steel cable bolted into the spire above them, which stretches taut between where they are and the belfry.

'Jesus!' Mac looks horrified.

'Sweet! I think we have to zip-line from this tower over to the next one,' says Jackson.

'OMG, this is so fun! We loved that forest high-wire we did, didn't we, Taisie? Do you remember?'

'Course I do! It was insane. *This* is insane! I can't wait.'

It's the first time since she saw Hollie on the beach that Taisie has been so animated.

'Hold up, guys. There's a sign here, tells us what's going on. Let's see.' And almost perfectly imitating the deep baritone of the Voice, Nate reads, 'Novices, this is the Leap of Faith. Prepare yourselves. This penance tests your faith, and your courage. Safety is paramount. Put on your harnesses, make sure they are buckled up tight. When your turn comes, attach both safety clips and jump. It is imperative that all of you reach the destination before the allotted time is up. Do not delay. If you fail, you will be punished accordingly.'

Nate hasn't finished the instructions before Jackson appears laden with harnesses and starts handing them out. Hearing the commotion, Nico emerges on to the balcony for the first time, crawling on hands and knees. Jude is just behind him. She is upright but hugging the walls, backing away from the edge.

'Wh-what is going on?' She sounds unlike herself, timid.

'No way,' says Nico loudly. 'I am not doing that. They know I'm afraid of heights.'

'What did he say? Leap of Faith? It looks more like a Leap of Death to me,' says Jude, faintly. 'Shouldn't someone from Production, from Health and Safety be here to oversee this?'

Nico cuts across her, his voice high and thin. 'They can't expect us to just *jump*, off that thing – oh God. No way! No way! I swear . . . I can't even stand!'

Nate attempts to take control. 'Relax, everyone. I've done this kind of thing loadsa times. It'll be fun. I think we should decide on which order we go in . . .' he begins, but Jackson is ahead of him again.

'Come on, guys, we can do this!' he says. 'We're against the clock, so we don't have time to lose. We need people who think they're OK with it to step up, to show that it's not as bad as it looks. I'll go first. Nate, you do your own stunts, don't you? You go next. Then, let's see . . . Nico, then you two girls. I'll let you figure out the order. Jude, you go after them; they can show you how it's done. Then Mac, then Frank and finally Lauren – are you OK to bring up the rear?'

Nate looks a little put out that he is no longer directing proceedings, and Hollie and Taisie, who had been standing closest to the launch platform, eager to go first, share a disgruntled glance when they hear their designated positions. Lauren catches it but notices they say nothing as they stand aside to make way for Nate and Nico.

On a mission, Jackson hauls his safety harness between his legs and over his robes and walks confidently on to the wooden boards, not in the least bit concerned by the drop below.

'Just follow my lead when it comes to your turn. It's not too far. You won't be in the air for long. It will go in a flash – just smile and enjoy it!'

The rest of them crowd together to watch, apart from Jude and Nico, who hang back, hiding their faces. Jackson reaches up above his head, yanks the pulley towards him and clips the two carabiners attached to the rope on his harness on to the giant clasp. Without a backwards glance, he runs down the ramp into thin air.

'Wooo hoooo!' he shouts, laughing, and Lauren can't help grinning in return as his flowing robes and slipper-shod feet sail away from them.

The wire buzzes with friction as he zooms away from them, and the others murmur anxiously.

'Where does it stop?' says Jude, as Jackson slides at break-neck speed straight towards the belfry. It looks as if he is going to smash face-first into its solid wall. Every muscle in Lauren's body tenses for the inevitable impact.

'Oh, my days! He's going to hit it!' gasps Nico.

And then, Jackson disappears. It's like a conjuring trick. One moment he is there and the next moment he is gone.

'Oh my God! Where is he?' It is Nico again.

Craning their heads to see more clearly, they realise that it is an optical illusion. They can just make out a window in the opposite tower. Jackson has flown straight through.

'What, is he, like, inside that other tower now?' asks Taisie.

In unison they yell as loud as they can towards where he has vanished.

'Jackson! Where are you? Are you safe?'

There is no response at all. Just the whistle of the wind over the cable.

'I'll go find him,' says Nate, who Lauren has to admit manages to make being dressed in a habit and harness look dignified. Just before he jumps, he pauses theatrically, like an actor taking a final curtain.

'Wish me luck!' he says, and leaps. 'Yeeeehaaaaa!' he shouts, and within seconds he too has disappeared into the belfry.

Nico's nerves are getting the better of him and he gives up his place in the queue to the girls, insisting that he can't go next. There is no sign of histrionics from them. They make very little fuss apart from a short discussion about who should go first. It ends up being Taisie, shortly followed by Hollie, who gives a cheery wave as she steps off, dark hair streaming in the breeze behind her, shouting, 'This is wild, but I LOVE it!'

Her elation does nothing to change Nico's mind. If anything, it appears to make him more scared, and he ushers Jude and Mac to go ahead of him. Mac has his own problems.

'I shouldn't be doing this at all really. They know the situation with my back,' he says, 'but I'll go ahead of you if you like.'

'Please, Mac, please do. I need more time,' Nico pleads.

By the time there are only three of them left at the top of the tall tower, Lauren is starting to wonder if Nico is ever going to do it, but Frank finally breaks the impasse.

'Come on, lad. Imagine what your mum will think when she sees you do this. She'll be so proud of you! You know she will.'

Nico's face softens, and that thought of home is enough to persuade him to move forward. Despite a couple more vociferous protestations, he steps on to the gangplank and clips himself on to the line. Just before he jumps, he turns round to give them a triumphant smile. As he does so, something trips an alarm switch in Lauren's brain.

'STOP! STOP! Don't jump!'

Nico freezes.

For a moment, time stands still. No one moves, not even Nico. Lauren holds her breath, praying for him to do what she says. He hesitates for another terrifying second, then takes heed of her instructions. He lets go of the rope and, instead of jumping, grabs the rails on the side of the platform, his face ashen.

'What? Why did you stop me?'

'I think there's something wrong with your harness. Get back, over here. Let me have a look.'

He unclips himself and steps back on to the relative safety of the parapet. When she is sure he is safe, Lauren takes hold of the webbing round his waist and pulls hard on the rope attached to the front of his harness. Just as her instinct told her it would, the knot slips and comes undone in her hands. Nico goes even paler.

'Oh my God, oh my *God*! Shit! I could have died if you hadn't stopped me!' he says, voice shrill with panic.

'It's OK, you'll be OK. Let me sort it out for you.' Lauren tries to reassure him, although she too is shaken by what could have happened.

Intuitively, drawing on her years of sailing experience, Lauren makes a counterclockwise loop in the rope, passes the end through it, and then back again before she pulls it tight. It is the strongest and safest knot she knows.

She can feel Nico shaking as she does it. 'Shit, shit, shit . . .' he keeps saying, looking at her pleadingly. 'I don't know if I can do this . . .' He tails off, looking terrified.

'It's safe now, I promise you. That knot isn't coming undone.' She yanks on the rope to reassure him, and before Nico has more time to process the danger he was in, or to change his mind, she leads him forward and swiftly clips both carabiners on to the pulley.

Frank, who has been watching on wordlessly, looking astonished, nods at them both and says, 'Go on, lad, show them what you're made of.'

It is with some relief that Lauren watches Nico float safely down the line and vanish through the window of the belfry.

'That was a hell of a save, Lauren. How did you know?'

'I've seen it before. It's easy to do, to tie a bowline wrong. I've done it myself, but someone should have checked it.'

'Too bloody right they should have. Second time you have saved someone's skin. We're lucky to have you here. Someone needs to have a word with Production. They can't be messing around with stuff like that. Anyone could have picked that harness and been seriously hurt.'

'They might still be,' says Lauren ominously, a sense of disquiet settling over her. The portcullis was bad enough, and now Nico's harness? For such a high-profile show, they sure seem to have been lax about health and safety. She shakes the thought away.

'Right, let's get a move on. We don't want them blaming us for dawdling, on top of everything else. Your harness is fine, mine too.'

'Agreed. Enough faffing for one day,' Frank says as he takes up his position, and just before he jumps, he turns to gives her a cheeky wink, blows her a kiss, and as he speeds away from her, he shouts, 'See you on the other side!' For the first time on the island Lauren laughs out loud.

Left on her own, Lauren feels horribly conscious of the camera drone trained in close up on her face, waiting for her to crack, but even after the drama of the last few minutes there is no way she is going to do so.

She braces herself, takes a deep breath, and runs down the ramp, whipping down the line faster than she would have believed possible. No wonder the others had screamed. She's twisting in mid-air, disorientated, seeing nothing but the gleam of light on the sea and the clouds soaring past. The wall of the bell tower is rushing up to meet her, and then she is through the window, plunged into darkness just as the handle reaches the end of its line and jerks to a halt, depositing her unceremoniously on to a crash mat below.

Thrown by the sudden shift into darkness, she looks around to see where the others are before becoming aware that the Voice is speaking to her from the walls of the belfry itself.

'Be quick!' it says. 'You have thirty seconds to get on to the next zip-wire. Unclip your safety rope and reattach it to the next line. Your fellow Novices are waiting. You must proceed with haste.'

Without pausing to take in her surroundings, Lauren follows the instructions. Another zip-line stretches out from the empty window on the opposite side, and, with shaking hands, she clanks both clips into place.

'I'm coming, I'm coming,' she mutters before she is airborne again. Picking up speed, she leaves the buildings behind, zipping over the stones and paths that flank the graveyard below, getting lower and lower. She realises she is heading for a small cove on the other side of the island from where they first landed. Through the buffeting wind she hears the cries of the others, can see them jumping about and shouting her name. She zooms down the final stretch, where she hits another crash mat and rolls on to her side in a crumpled heap just as the bell strikes in the monastery far above them. The challenge is finished, and she is over the line. They've done it.

Lying on her back, exhaustion and elation seeping from her, Lauren gazes at the sky for a second before sitting up. The others are crowding round, but the spirit of celebration she expected is absent. Instead of congratulating her, they are looking back behind her, up towards the belfry. Jude speaks first.

'Where's Frank? Is he still up there?'

For a second Lauren doesn't understand what she means. 'Frank? He's here, of course. He came down before me.'

But then she looks at the figures fanned out in front of her and counts them. There are just seven of them. Nate. Nico. Jude. Taisie. Hollie. Jackson. Mac. There is no sign of Frank at all.

'He never came down,' says Hollie. 'There was Nico. And then there was, like, a long gap. And then we saw you.'

'So, wait, Frank went ahead of you? You were last?' asks Jackson.

Lauren nods, still in shock.

'Ohmigod, you don't think something happened to his harness like mine, do you?' Nico exclaims. 'You don't think he fell?'

'No, I checked, the knot was fine. Besides, I would have seen if he'd fallen from the first zip-wire and you would have seen from the second one,' Lauren says, sounding more certain than she feels.

The others look around them, as if Frank will suddenly pop up, laughing at their confusion. But he doesn't. It's as though he sailed in through one window of the ruined bell tower and simply vanished into thin air. Mac puts into words what they are all thinking.

'What the hell?' he says. 'Frank's disappeared.'

Chapter Twelve

Lauren keeps replaying the moment Frank jumped, trying to see it from different angles. Frank careering down the line away from her, his cheerful face turning back to her in mock surprise as he sailed through the window. The flare of his hood in the wind at the last moment as he passed through it and disappeared out of sight. And then . . . what?

Where on earth has Frank gone?

As soon as they realise he's missing, the group run back to where they last saw him, hurtling towards the belfry to see if he's still there. Jackson, who is fastest, ignores the sign that says 'STRICTLY OUT OF BOUNDS' on the thick oak door, and rushes inside.

Breathing hard, hands on their knees to catch their breath, the others can hear him shouting, 'Frank, Frank! Are you there, bro?'

Seconds later he reappears. 'No sign of him. Maybe he was sent a different way and just went back? Let's see if we can catch him in the dorms!' When they reach the hall and the bedrooms, exhausted, their shouts are met by silence. Frank isn't anywhere to be seen or heard. His rough cotton bag is not on his bed. He isn't in the chapter house. As far as they can work out, he has gone.

They yell into their mics, demanding the Voice tell them where he is. But the Voice stays stubbornly silent. Eventually, they run out of steam. It's Nate who finally calls it.

'He's not here, guys. They must have got rid of him. Looks like it's game over for Frank.' Nate sounds sorrowful, but Lauren catches the briefest flash of triumph in his eyes.

As they traipse back to the great hall, defeated, Lauren imagines Frank coming down the narrow belfry staircase, disorientated and confused. He must have been running down the steps as she landed at the top. Had he tried to call up to her? Was there any sound from below? She scours her memory to see if she heard anything, but all she can recall is the insistent call of the Voice, repeating its instructions, and her mad scramble to get down the second zip-line so she wouldn't be the reason they ran out of time.

There's something so poignant about this lonely end for the fun-loving Frank that Lauren can't stop picturing it – the cameras no doubt trained on his face, producers in the edit suite trying to choose the best angle to depict his defeated trudge out of the game.

A tide of panic rises in her. If part of the game is being got rid of at the drop of a hat, she needs to hurry up and get close to Nate. But right now, there is no sign of him; everyone has come back to the great hall except for him. Jude is fussing by the fire. Mac and Jackson are slumped on the benches at the long trestle table, Mac seemingly lost in his own world, Jackson's usual high energy gone. Hollie and Taisie are sitting opposite them, side by side, heads propped on their hands in identical poses.

Nico is restless, too nervy to relax, too tired to accomplish anything useful. He keeps sitting down and then standing up to go over to the fire, kicking the logs with his foot. It's clear that the day's events have been playing on his mind, and they have on Lauren's too.

'Are you OK, Nico?'

'Yeah, I guess so. Still a bit shaky from the challenge. I don't think I've ever been that scared! But, then, everything's a bit scary here, isn't it? I mean, what with Nate nearly getting hit by that gate, and my dodgy harness. And now Frank's disappeared! It's a lot, isn't it?' He looks around furtively, as if Production are lurking in the shadows, and he lowers his voice. 'Do you think they're doing it on purpose?'

Lauren pauses for a moment. The same thing had crossed her mind, but she doesn't want to add to Nico's anxiety.

'I don't think it's on purpose. I mean, it is a reality TV show, and sure, they want drama, but they wouldn't want any of us to actually get hurt. How would that look?'

'I wasn't expecting it to be like this. Not sure what I *was* expecting, to be honest, but still, I feel lucky to be here. I only heard I was coming a few days ago.'

Given the hoops Lauren has been jumping through for what seems like months, she is intrigued.

'Really? That last-minute?'

'I was on a stand-by list. Someone dropped out. I'm not sure exactly who it was, a guy who was in a boyband a few years ago, I heard. He must have had second thoughts. And you know what it's like on these shows. They always have a specific cast list, don't they? Needed: fit young talent, quick!' he laughs, perking up and speaking more loudly now. Overhearing him, Hollie and Taisie giggle softly by the fireside.

'My agent has been trying to get me doing something like this for ages. We've been working on a rebrand of my image, to . . . well, you know how it is, to get past what happened on that talent show. So, this was perfect. It was all a bit of a rush; I only had a day to think about it, no time to get ready. But it was a no-brainer, especially when I heard what they were offering me . . .'

'Nico! You can't talk about your prize. It's, like, literally the first thing in the contract,' says Taisie.

'Oops, sorry,' Nico says, mock bashfully. 'Mouth like a runaway train, my mum always says. Besides, surely you girls tell each other everything?'

Nico is smiling, but there's a slyness to his tone that makes Lauren wonder if he's trying to catch them out. Taisie looks worried, but Hollie leaps in.

'Actually, our prize is shared. We're allowed to tell you that, just nothing else.'

'So, what, you get two chances to win it?' asks Nico.

'I guess,' says Taisie, glancing at Hollie for backup, 'but also double the chance of losing.'

'Yeah, so it's not unfair,' says Hollie, picking up her train of thought.

Nico looks like he wants to say more but Hollie carries on talking, clearly keen to change the subject.

'What *is* unfair, though, is how they randomly get rid of people with, like, no warning at all. I mean, sure, I guess we voted for Kez – not that we knew that's what we were doing – but Frank?'

'And why haven't we been told anything?' continues Taisie. 'It's weird.'

At the reminder of Frank's departure, Lauren's shoulders slump. The truth is, she's gutted he's gone. He was her closest friend in there. More than that, he was an ally. He'd believed her about Nate; he'd had her back. At least, she hopes he did. As well as feeling sad he's gone, there is a niggle of worry in her mind too. Did she say too much? Was she right to trust him? She doesn't say out loud what she is thinking, but what she is hoping.

'Maybe he hasn't left. Maybe it's just part of the show and they'll bring him back later, when we least expect it.'

Jude, having evidently finished with the fire, pipes up, 'Lauren's right. I think they just want to unsettle us, make us all feel vulnerable. And Frank was the obvious target. He liked to bend the rules – we all saw him nick that bread this morning. And they clearly don't like it if you don't do what they say to the letter.'

'Yeah. *And* he and Lauren went out of bounds just before the challenge,' says Nico.

'Good point,' says Jude.

'But why wasn't *she* punished then?' says Nico again, and everyone turns to look in Lauren's direction. She raises her eyebrows, surprised by the note of accusation in his voice.

'Did the Voice say anything to you after he jumped? About what they were going to do?' asks Jude.

'No!' Lauren answers. 'Look, I'm as confused as you are. I'm really sorry about breaking the rules with Frank, but I had no idea they were going to whisk him away like that.'

The looks she's getting still aren't friendly, but the questions subside. Lauren feels claustrophobic, longing to get out of the room into the open air, but it is dusk already, and she is too uneasy to venture out on her own.

Of Nate, there is still no sign. Probably snoozing next to the fire in the Abbot's quarters, thinks Lauren, with a touch of resentment. She tries to estimate how long they have until the next live segment – maybe she can get him on his own before then? It must surely be soon, though; they seem to have been sitting here for ever. She thinks about gearing herself up, to in some way prepare for it. The reckless thought of trying to say something about Nate live on air briefly crosses her mind again, but she knows she needs to tread more carefully than that.

'Guys, what do we do about food?' says Taisie suddenly. 'I'm hungry. Do we know what's happening about dinner and stuff?'

'Yeah, maybe you lot shouldn't have eaten every last crumb this morning,' says Jackson.

'Oh, really?' snaps Jude. 'Well, perhaps you shouldn't have broken the rules and climbed that wall. Then you could have eaten with us.'

The bickering is interrupted by Nate, who sweeps into the Hall looking refreshed. Lauren is annoyed to find that she, like the others, sits up a little straighter on his grand entrance.

'A gathering!' he says. 'How lovely. Jude, sweetheart, you've done a great job with the fire. So homely.' Jude ruffles herself, flattered by his attention. 'So, what's going on then?' Nate adds. 'The Voice woke me up. Told me to come in here.'

As he says this, the Voice itself intrudes.

'Novices, we will be live on air in five minutes. Please gather round the fire and remember, do not swear.'

As they jostle into position, the Voice goes through the familiar countdown, and then goes into full proclamation mode.

'Novices, Frank has failed to complete the Leap of Faith. As a consequence, not only is he eliminated from Isolation Island but, as punishment tonight, you will fast rather than feast. *Unless*' – the Voice seems to speak a bit louder to be heard over the predictable hubbub of protest – 'one of you can complete a penance in the allotted time. Mac, you have been chosen to represent your fellow novices. Lauren and Nico, please go downstairs to the cellars, where your provisions are housed and await the outcome. Mac, prepare yourself.'

This is all said so seamlessly that Lauren barely has time to take it in. Frank had failed the Leap of Faith? How? He'd seemed fine when he'd jumped the first time but, of course, she hadn't seen him land. What if he'd been hurt? Or maybe this was just Production's way of showing them what happens when you break one too many rules.

The Voice rolls on as a small door disguised in the stonework at the other end of the great hall swings open.

99

'Lauren and Nico, the storerooms are below. Take an oil lamp with you.'

Nico starts off immediately, taking a light from the table as he goes. Lauren is frozen. She wants to stay and watch what happens. Every face is turned towards Mac, willing him to do well, crowding round to offer encouragement. In their hunger, they are fixated on nothing else but him winning.

Nico grabs the sleeve of her habit and pulls her along with him.

'Let's go, Lauren,' he whispers. 'You don't want to be the reason we lose *again,* do you?'

Descending a tiny flight of stairs, they find themselves in a stone corridor, which is flanked left and right by vaults. Each one is closed off by a sturdy modern metal door, recently installed. Signs above them mark out numbers for the days of the week.

They stop outside the vault marked 'Day 1'. On closer inspection, they see that there are two separate doorways in each section. On the left, a sign declares 'Feast'. On the right, 'Fast'.

'Ohmigod, come on, Mac,' says Nico. 'We *need* this Feast. I'm starving.'

Both of them have turned their faces upwards, straining towards the ceiling as if they might be able to hear what's going on.

'What do you think they're making him do?' asks Nico.

'No idea,' says Lauren. 'Can't hear a thing. Just glad it's not me.'

'Me neither,' says Nico fretfully, and then, after a long pause: 'Feels like we've been down here hours.' His face is yellow and elongated in the strange light.

They both jump as the Voice booms out from a grille in the wall right next to Lauren's head.

'Lauren and Nico, take what you can from the storeroom that opens first.'

They stand up straight, transfixed by the lockers in front of them.

In the pause that follows, the red light of a camera winks at them from the walls. Then a click, and a door swings open. The right-hand door. The 'Fast' door.

Mac has failed the penance.

'Today, you will be fasting,' confirms the Voice.

'Oh God, no,' says Nico.

Trying to hide her own disappointment, aware the cameras will be waiting for a reaction, Lauren follows Nico in without much hope. They find themselves in a sort of pantry, shelved on the back and sides. There's certainly not much food to be had. Some small sacks of what looks like oats, two loaves of dense rye bread, some misshapen vegetables, not all of which Lauren can identify, but among them might be potatoes, a cabbage, leeks. Some pale green bulbs that might be fennel. A large chunk of pale-yellow cheese. It is unbelievably basic.

'Seriously, is that all there is?' Nico is incredulous as Lauren kneels down to search the bottom shelf, but it is in vain. After a few seconds she stands and raises her empty hands. 'Yeah. That's it, apparently.'

She tries not to think about what might lie behind the other locked door as they carry all they have upstairs.

The scene they walk into is one of strained camaraderie. Mac is sitting on the end of one of the benches, head in hands. Taisie and Hollie stand either side of him, patting his shoulders.

Jackson is crouched in front of him. 'Seriously, bro, don't worry about it. It'll be fine,' he is saying.

Jude and Nate stand back slightly from the others.

'It was a memory test. He nearly made it,' says Jude briefly. 'They asked him a question about each of us. He didn't know exactly what time Jackson ran the 1,500 metres in. He was only two seconds out! Ridiculous, he was so close!'

They crowd round Nico and Lauren, examining the contents of the trays. Mac stays where he is, gazing at the floor.

'Goodness, not much there, is there?' says Jude.

'It's not that bad,' says Nate. 'We've got oats – that'll make some hearty porridge, right?'

'Yeah, watery porridge,' mutters Nico, but Nate continues as though he hasn't heard.

'We've got bread. We've got vegetables. It's not so bad, trust me. I had to do a bit of fasting for a role once. Did me no harm. Might even be good for us!'

There's a muttered sort of acceptance as Nico and Lauren set the trays down on the table, although Lauren notes that Nate isn't actually offering to make the porridge or suggesting anything else.

'We need a little ceremony! Come on, let's make this fit for a king. Or an Abbot,' says Nate, setting out the bread and cheese as though they are the centrepieces of a grand feast.

Hollie and Taisie have grabbed the oats and are conferring, their heads bent towards the fireplace where they have rigged a cauldron up to one of the hooks inside the mantel. Hollie starts expertly chopping the vegetables, as Taisie lifts the cauldron lid, and an undeniably delicious smell comes wafting towards Lauren.

'How on earth have you managed that?' she says.

Hollie giggles. 'It's a kind of a stock. We boiled up the hambone that was left over from earlier. And we did some foraging outside. There's a patch that must have been, like, an old herb garden or something. It's mostly overgrown. But we found some of these!' She holds up what Lauren dimly recognises as bay leaves.

'So, we reckon' – Taisie picks up her thought seamlessly – 'if we add in some of the oats and bits, it'll make a kind of pottage.'

Lauren raises her eyebrows in amazement, simultaneously chastising herself for being surprised that Taisie knows what pottage is.

'Ham porridge! Gross!' says Nico.

'No, *pottage*. Think of it as, like, an organic soup you'd get in a posh restaurant. It'll be delicious, just wait,' says Hollie.

Lauren is impressed. The girls had said they could cook, but she was imagining mostly TikTok-friendly dishes garnished with trendy ingredients. Buddha bowls and colourful tacos; food with more style than substance. Not boiling up bones for stock and foraging in weed patches. She becomes uncomfortably aware that the girls are watching her carefully.

'We're not, like, total idiots, you know,' says Hollie.

'Yeah, and we know about cooking on a budget. I kind of had to, when I was young. My mum and me, well, we didn't have much money back then.'

Hollie nods and squeezes her friend's arm. 'Yeah, Taise,' she says, 'You and your mum could make anything taste amazing. So, let's go for it.' She tips the bag of oats into the steaming pot. 'Just wait, you guys!'

Fifteen minutes later, the great hall has been transformed. Jude has lit every oil lamp she can find, and at least half a dozen candles. Nico has laid out the dishes and cups as though they are actually having a feast and set jugs of water down the table as if it were wine. The flames from the fire are dancing, casting a flattering light and dancing shadows, and the girls are ladling their pottage into bowls.

Nate stands at the head of the table, brandishing a huge carving knife and fork.

'Attention, ladies and gentlemen,' he says, plunging the fork into the bread and attacking with a flourish, as though it's a Thanksgiving turkey. 'Dinner is served!'

His ability to transform the atmosphere is admirable, but it can't disguise the reality that when they tuck into their food there isn't quite enough to eat. The girls have done their best, and the stew is delicious – tasty chunks of vegetables in a thickened broth. But there is only enough for one tiny bowl each, and they have demolished the bread and cheese almost before it has been handed out. Lauren can see Mac sweeping up crumbs again with his forefinger to get the most out of the meagre rations.

Most of them try to rise above the fact that their stomachs are still complaining. But Jude cannot let it rest, venting to anybody who is in earshot about the conditions.

'It's just not good enough. They told me we'd have to rely on ourselves. But they also told me that food would be provided. This isn't food – sorry, girls, you've done a great job, but there's not enough for eight of us. And sleeping outside, being made to jump off towers. I mean, something might go really wrong here. It nearly has, twice. Look at what happened to Nate! And then Nico. They could both have been killed. Do we think there's even a medic on site?'

Mac tries his best to soothe her, reminding her that he is a paramedic, that he has been given instructions on how to get to the medical stores, as well as a key to unlock them. And they all did first-aid training. But she's on a roll now, and it is only Nate who can still her long list of complaints.

'Jude, we're doing great. *You*'re doing great. Imagine how this is playing back home. They need it to look like we are having a hard time, so they can justify paying one of us the big bucks when it's all over. Think about what they have offered you. I know, for sure, if I win, whatever they make us do, it'll feel like it's worth it.'

A hush falls around the table. Lauren wonders what they could possibly have offered Nate, the man who has everything. And gets away with murder.

When he puts out his hand to hold hers, Jude softens.

'It's only for a couple of days. You've got this.'

'I suppose you're right,' she says stiffly. 'Thank you.'

With that, the girls stand up to clear the plates, Mac automatically rising to help them.

'No, don't do that,' says Jude. 'Remember what the Voice said. We need to stick to our own tasks. We don't want to be punished again.'

'Oh, yeah? How come Nate let the girls cook, then?' mutters Mac, but he lets the moment go. The girls work quickly and efficiently, Hollie singing quietly to herself while she bustles about, and soon the Hall is clear and they are all trooping to their respective beds, tired but still hungry.

Chapter Thirteen

Lauren wakes with a start and stifles a scream. In front of her looms a large white face, lit eerily from below, peering out of the darkness into her dreams. In the background, an insistent bell. She is terrified.

'Lauren! Wake up! We need to get to the chapter house. *Now.*'

It takes Lauren a moment to work out where she is, eyes straining to focus in the gloom. She sees bare stone walls and a narrow bed – oh, yes, the Saints' dorm, Eilean Manach, the monastery. Jude standing over her in what must be the middle of the night.

'What's happening? What time is it?'

'Just get up!' Jude's command galvanises Lauren. She can just imagine her using this tone to order people around on her rise to multi-million-pound success. It's not the best way to start the day, but it is effective. Even though everything in her aching body is screaming at her to lie back down, she swings her legs off the bed and sits upright, her feet recoiling as they brush the stone-cold floor.

She squints at Jude, realising that the light is coming from an oil lantern she is holding in front of her.

'Didn't you hear the Voice? Lucky you! It's Matins, apparently – I think that means it's about three a.m. Time for the next task, anyway.'

'You've got to be kidding. Can't they give us a break for just one night? Everyone is exhausted!'

'Apparently not,' says Jude curtly. 'I think everyone else is getting up, so get a move on.'

Lauren shuffles her feet into her fluffy slippers and follows Jude and her lantern out of the dormitory. The cloisters feel cavernous and ghostly in the dark, the circle of glowing light from Jude's lamp casting an inky shade on the old stone. Their footsteps are unsteady on the sloping flagstones, and both of them are shivering in the morning air. The faces of the cherubs, innocuous and comedic in daylight, now look like gargoyles glaring down at them.

By the time they make it to the chapter house, Nate, Mac and Jackson are already there, their hulking shadows filling the space. Mac is clearly in discomfort. He has his hands high above his head, holding one in the other fist, and is stretching out his back with a pained look crumpling his forehead. Nate is hunched in his robes, hood pulled up over his face, hugging himself against the cold. He seems somehow diminished, smaller than the cheerful host who presided over last night's meal. It is only Jackson who looks fresh-faced and ready for anything, as if he doesn't need sleep, doesn't need food, and doesn't need a comfortable bed.

Gruff 'Good mornings', and 'Hey, how are yous?' are exchanged before Nico, Taisie and Hollie stumble in. Even the girls look dishevelled now, bleary-eyed and bewildered.

'Oh my God, I haven't slept at all. That dormitory is so *cold*. Taisie and I had to share a bed and even then, we were frozen.'

Taisie is apparently too discombobulated even to agree with Hollie. She drags herself over to one of the scriptorium desks and lays her head on it.

Nico is surprisingly more upbeat. 'Better than last night, in the cloisters. Least we got to lie down, get a bit of beauty sleep. Think it worked?'

Nobody can think of any answer to this, so they lapse into silence, broken after a moment or two by the Voice resonating from the rafters.

'Good morning, Novices. The hour is Matins, and we have chosen this time for your next task, the Crossing. Make your way to the cove beyond the graveyard.'

'Do you reckon it's the one we landed on after the Leap of Faith yesterday?' says Jackson, taking off towards the door. 'Come on, let's get it over with, and we might get something decent to eat!'

The night is crisp and clear, and, with their cowls pulled over their heads to stave off the chill, they make their way gingerly along the narrow path to the shoreline where they had landed from the zip-wire. It's still dark, but as they progress a set of torches bursts into flame in front of them, a reminder that someone is watching their every move and pressing buttons accordingly.

At each switchback on the winding track Lauren glimpses the giveaway red beam of an infrared camera and hears the familiar hum as it focuses. Dressed as they are in identical robes, it is difficult to tell who is who in the dark. Only Mac, at the head, is clearly distinguishable by his six-foot-six frame. The others trail behind him like a group of penitents taking part in an ancient pilgrimage.

The stone path takes them over the springy heather, which then gives way to shingle. Lauren can feel how bumpy and sharp it is through the flimsy soles of her slippers. A cluster of burning torches leads the group to an unexpected sight hidden behind a line of rocks: a collection of what appear to be tarred domes looming out of the ground, like the carapaces of turtles washed up on the shore.

They hadn't seen them when they landed yesterday, so either they hadn't noticed in their confusion after losing Frank, or Production must have sneaked over under the cover of darkness, to covertly place them on the beach. The thought of anyone creeping about unseen sends a shiver down Lauren's spine. They count six of them in total, four so small they can pick them up with outstretched arms, two of them bigger, more than six feet across.

'What on earth are those?' Nico articulates what most of them are thinking. 'And how did they get there?'

As it happens, Lauren knows what they are.

'They're boats,' she says, as Jackson turns one over. The shell tips and rolls on to its back, revealing a hollow basket-work frame of interwoven wooden slats bent to form an exoskeleton, a makeshift bench running across the centre. 'Or a kind of boat, anyway. It's a coracle. Monks used them for fishing and transport. They're meant to be light enough that they could carry them down to the shore, but buoyant enough that they could take them out to fish.'

The others are beginning to look at her as though she is responsible for planting the coracles in the sand herself. She talks a bit faster. 'Well, that's what I think they are, anyway. But these two' – she points to the larger ones – 'are a bit odd. They're usually just for one person, but it looks like those might be for two.'

'You mean we've got to get in those?' says Jude, horrified. 'Surely not,' she whispers. Fear seems to have overtaken her. In spite of the light from the circle of torches, she is still clinging tightly to her lantern and her hands are shaking a little.

Jackson is as enthusiastic as ever. 'Where do you think we have to get to?' he says, as he goes over to a pile of what look like sticks lying on the ground. 'Paddles!' he exclaims.

He holds them up triumphantly, and then whirls round as a dazzling flash and a whoosh detonates from the water behind him. The night is shattered by brightly coloured fireworks. Arches of light fizz high into the sky. Explosions echo across the water, splitting the silence. The Novices watch mesmerised as the tumbling sparks illuminate the shape of the tiny islet in the middle of the cove and reveal the outline of a Celtic cross standing at its centre. At the base, a bonfire springs into life, and its orange glow spreads towards them across the water like a path.

The Voice rings out at them, this time from a speaker, which must be hidden in a rock near where they found the coracles.

'Your task is before you. You must take these vessels and use them to reach the Cross of Fire. Once there, you will find the object of your quest. Bring it back to this shore. You have one hour to complete your next penance.'

As the Voice subsides, Lauren catches Jude's expression. She looks appalled.

'I don't think it's actually that far, ' says Lauren, looking out at the island. 'As long as there are no strong currents I reckon it won't be too bad.' Her reassuring words seem to make no difference.

The first dilemma to solve is who should go in the single coracles and who should take the pairs. Without anyone saying it out loud it's clear to all of them that the least capable is going to be Jude, and if she is to get across, she needs to be paired with someone strong.

'Hey, Mac, buddy, how about you go with Jude?' says Nate, heading to one of the smaller coracles for himself.

'Don't think that's going to work, chief,' says Mac, gesturing to the size of the coracle and his own enormous bulk. 'I'd just flip her straight out of that thing. Why don't you take Jude, then, Taisie and Hollie, you can share, and the rest of us will make do on our own.'

Nate's mouth tightens in what looks like irritation. Whether he doesn't like being ordered around by Mac, or he just wants his own boat isn't clear, but within seconds he is genial again, concurring with Mac and chivalrously putting out his hand to steer Jude towards the waterline. She nods almost imperceptibly at first, clearly relieved not to be on her own. And then, realising it is Nate she is going to be with, she flashes a more genuine smile.

'You'll keep me safe, won't you?' she says coyly, a little of her spirit returning.

Getting into the coracles turns out to be a nightmare. The round-bottomed boats sit shallow in the water, and the slightest movement in the wrong direction threatens to tip them over. By the time she's got the hang of steering, Lauren realises that a mini argument has broken out between Jude and Nate. Jude is intent on carrying her oil lantern on to the boat. He is trying to persuade her to put it down, and by the sound of it trying his best to keep his tone firm but jokey. But she is adamant.

'You don't know whether we're going to need it. You of all people know we can't trust them to keep us safe. Anyway, you're strong enough – surely you don't need me to help paddle, do you?'

The slight needle in Jude's tone, and the ever so subtle questioning of his masculinity are enough to change Nate's mind. 'Of course, I don't!' he snorts, and with admirable skill he pushes them off the shore and starts to navigate a straight line towards the burning cross.

Lauren chuckles to herself. Well played, Jude, she thinks as she sets off in their wake just as the Voice calls out from the beach, 'Forty minutes remaining.' Hearing how little time they have left, their efforts become a mad dash towards the islet and Lauren's arms ache with the effort of keeping up.

Unsurprisingly, it is Mac who reaches their destination first, planting his paddle firmly on the seabed in the shallows and leaping into the water to shout back to them.

'Careful you lot, it's bloody Baltic in here. You don't want to fall in. I'll lift some of you out. Jackson, Nate, Nico, can you sort your-selves out?'

He starts with Taisie, who screeches as her and Hollie's boat rocks alarmingly at the shift in weight.

'It's OK, Taisie, I've got you. Hang on to my back . . . gently does it.'

He carries her over his shoulder like a firefighter and deposits her safe and dry above the waterline. He repeats the manoeuvre on Hollie and Lauren effortlessly, then turns back to Jude, who is sitting in Nate's boat, still clutching the lamp.

'Don't worry, I'll take her,' says Nate. It occurs to Lauren that Mac is well on his way to becoming the *de facto* leader, a further threat to Nate's fragile male ego.

'You sure, pal?' says Mac, and steps back. He doesn't move far, waiting instead just a step away from them to see if his help is needed. Lauren wonders if Nate has clocked this too.

She can see Nate gesticulating, asking Jude to put down or put out the lantern. Jude is shaking her head vehemently. She is fixated with carrying it to the shore.

'I can't carry you if you have that thing,' he says, but she shakes her head, until Mac reaches out a long arm and takes it from her gently.

'I'll take it to the beach for you.'

With that resolved, Nate copies Mac's action and slips out of the boat into the knee-deep water. He smiles at Jude, lifting her in his arms before swinging round and carrying her to dry land, where he sets her down with a flourish.

'There you are, ma'am.'

'Thank you,' she says, recovering some of her poise. Lauren notices she glows visibly in the presence of Nate, though not enough to let go entirely of the reassurance of her lantern, which she takes back from Mac as quickly as she can.

Now they are all on the sand, their focus becomes working out what they are meant to find on the island.

'C'mon, guys, quick. We need a win this time round,' says Jackson, making for the cross with Nate hard on his heels.

Jude sets off after them, trying to say something to Nate. But he is just too far ahead, and she is rushing to catch up. She looks clumsy and uncoordinated, hindered by her over-size slippers on the damp and heavy sand.

Nate doesn't see her trip. Doesn't see her fall towards him. Doesn't see her put out hands to save herself. He doesn't see the burning lamp hurtle through the air, or the arc of oil being released skywards and splashing over his back.

A tongue of bright yellow flame catches the bottom of Nate's habit and, in a flash, licks up past his waist, igniting his clothes.

Taisie and Hollie are the first to react, but their terrified screams are drowned out by Mac roaring, 'Nate! STOP! COVER YOUR FACE.' With no more warning than that, he slams into Nate from behind, wraps his powerful arms around his thighs and dumps him on the ground with the full force of a mighty tackle honed on the rugby pitches of Glasgow, rolling him over on the wet sand.

The others stare on, aghast, the silence only broken by the familiar whine of a drone above them.

Nate is the first to move. His feet twitch, followed by his fingers. Then, very slowly he pushes himself up on to his fists, shakes his head, pauses for a moment and still on all fours he roars, 'What the HELL? What are you DOING? You ASSHOLE!'

His outrage bounces across the water.

Mac hoists himself upright on to his knees, holding his hands up in front of him in surrender.

'You were on fire! If I didn't put it out, you'd have burned alive!'

But Nate's blood is up so high it's as if he doesn't hear him. 'You don't touch me, do you understand? Don't. Lay. Your. Hands. On. Me.' From where Lauren is standing, just behind the two of them, she sees his hand tighten into a fist. He is straining upward, Mac's bulk towering over him. His eyes have narrowed, his breath is coming quickly. 'You should get back down on your knees and apologise to me. *Nobody* lays a hand on me without my permission, do you understand? Do you UNDERSTAND?'

'Yeah, right,' says Mac sarcastically. 'I understand. You bet I do. Next time I'll just let you burn.' Ostentatiously, he turns his back on Nate, and bends down to where Jude is half-raised from where she has fallen, snivelling with tears in her eyes. 'Jude, hen, are you OK?' he says.

Nate looks at her, as though only now seeing where she has fallen, and then his gaze travels slowly down to his own feet, the trickle of smoke rising from a charred spot on the side of his habit, the lamp lying where it came to rest on the sand. He blinks, as if he is trying to make sense of what just happened.

Jude is gazing in horror at the bottom of Nate's habit. 'I'm sorry. I'm so sorry, Nate,' she says. 'I didn't mean to. I just tripped, and it went flying out of my hands. Christ, you could have been seriously hurt! Are you OK?'

The others crowd around her to dispense hugs and comfort, so it is only Lauren who witnesses the struggle that passes across Nate's face as he looks at her. Pure hard anger crashing up against confusion. There is a moment where the warring emotions struggle to get mastery, and then she sees Nate's hand relax, his fist uncurl. She can almost track the thoughts going through his brain and catches the sly glance of his eyes as they flick to the camera drone, which is hanging in the air, not far away.

Almost immediately, an apologetic frown crinkles his forehead, and he sinks down to his knees in front of Jude, who is trembling.

'Jude. Darling. It's fine,' says Nate. 'It wasn't your fault. Are *you* OK?'

She nods as she climbs to her feet, helped up by grasping one of Mac's strong outreached hands.

Meanwhile, Nate's apology continues. 'Mac, I'm sorry, big guy. I didn't realise what you were trying to do. I thought you were kidding around or something. You caught me by surprise there, buddy. Didn't realise I was actually on fire. But hey, I owe you, man, I really owe you. If it wasn't for you, I'd be lit up like one of those torches.'

He holds out his hand. Mac hesitates for a moment, then shrugs and takes it. Nate pulls him into an embrace, clapping his arm around Mac's shoulders, and even though Mac's brow is furrowed, he submits.

Chapter Fourteen

After that, they lose the task, all of them too shell-shocked to get their act together. Jackson is picking up the spent lantern, Jude is putting her slippers back on and Nate is inspecting the damage to his robes, when the Voice of God blares out from the night.

'Novices, you are out of time. Once again, you have failed,' it says.

It is almost a surprise to be reminded that they are in the middle of a penance. Nobody even bothers to search at the base of the cross to discover what it was they were meant to find, not even Jackson. Defeated, they make their way back to the shoreline, and as they do Lauren falls into step with Nate and whispers under her breath, so no one else can hear her.

'Gosh, that was close. Are you actually OK? Did you get hurt?'

He turns his slate-grey eyes on her and holds her gaze steadily, as if he is assessing her again.

'Yes, thanks, all good. No real harm done. But thanks for asking. Dunno about you, but I'm starting to feel kinda unsafe round here. Like, I'm trying not to get killed *and* work out who's friend or foe. But you've got my back, right, Lauren?'

'Sure,' she answers as convincingly as she can, trying not to show in her voice the chill that's run down her spine. Is there something behind his words or does he believe she's an ally? She knows she's playing a dangerous game, cosying up to him, but she needs to hold her nerve.

'Want to have a chat later? Away from . . . everyone else?' she manages to say.

'Yeah, let's find a moment. Come find me,' he says, then walks ahead of her, catching up with the others.

They climb into the coracles and straggle back across the narrow channel. Stripped of the adrenaline that had lent her strength on the outward crossing, Lauren watches as the gaunt silhouette of the monastery draws her back and tries to calm her racing thoughts, Nate's parting words echoing in her mind. It'll be her first real opportunity to speak to him alone. She'd better not blow it.

Once they are back on Eilean Manach, the Voice instructs them to return to the great hall, where they are told they should wait until the next live segment. 'You may not break your fast until after that moment,' it adds ominously.

As they make their way back up the path, the flaming torches begin to gutter and die out. It is almost dawn but not quite. On the horizon they can sense the first tendrils of light tentatively stretching skywards. In the great hall the fire has completely died down. Jude fiddles with it, trying single-handedly to get the embers to ignite, until she eventually gives in and asks Jackson to help her.

Every single one of them is drenched. Mac, having gallantly helped everyone in and out of the coracles, has the worst of it. His clothes are soaked all the way up to his chest. Nate's habit is still covered in sand. The hem is badly singed, and there are dark spots of oil splattered all over the back. He looks more bedraggled now than Lauren has ever seen him.

When the fire is alight again, Jude turns to Nate.

'Nate, you can't wear that all day, you'll catch your death of cold. It's soaking! And burnt. I can't tell you how sorry I am.'

'Don't worry, don't worry. I'm fine. And there's nothing to change into.' Nate tries to reassure her, his arm draped affectionately over her shoulders. 'Anyway, we're all in the same boat, aren't we?'

'Yes, but this is ridiculous. Everything wet. So little in the way of food and supplies. And no help whatsoever. How do they expect us to manage?'

Lauren is oddly pleased that Jude's habitual grumbling has returned. Clearly, she is feeling more herself.

'For sure,' says Nate, 'it's definitely a bit more hardcore than I thought.'

'I guess that's how the monks had it, though,' says Mac. 'They must have been tough to survive out here. If we want to stay, that's what we're going to have to prove we are, too. That we're hard enough. If you aren't up for it, then I'm sure they'll let you go home. I, for one, am here to stay.'

'Same,' says Jackson, 'but I'm not going to sit around here freezing. Come on, we need to get moving, get out of these robes and get dry.'

He strips down to his thermals and lays his wet clothes over the bench. In minutes, the great hall looks like a medieval laundry. All of them, even a still grumbling Jude, follow his example, apart from Nate. He has retired to his bedroom again, presumably to dry his things in private. Lauren makes a mental note: the fact that he is always sneaking off alone gives her ample opportunity to talk to him without anyone else overhearing, except of course, Production. For now, she decides to bide her time. The moment needs to be right.

In the meantime, she looks around at everyone, dressed incongruously in their dark thermals. They are all almost unrecognisable from the moment they arrived on the island. The lack of sleep and make-up shows most visibly in Jude. Her perfect bob has lost its distinctive volume and is hanging lankly, and her lips look thin without her red lipstick. There are dark shadows under Nico's eyes, and Mac looks like he is permanently in pain, the creases on his forehead more deeply corrugated than when he arrived. He is stretching again, clearly unable to get comfortable. Even the effervescent Jackson looks diminished, as if he is already losing weight.

As for herself, she hardly ever wears make-up so the lack of it won't be making much difference, and she has scraped her hair back in a high ponytail, though she can feel how greasy it is. Out of all of them it is only the girls who are still managing to look glamorous. She has to admire them for their fashion skills: they have tucked in their thermals artfully, so they hug their perfect figures, their hair is plaited tightly, every strand in place, and their laminated eyebrows haven't moved a millimetre. No wonder they have legions of followers. If they can pass this off as a good look, they can sell anything.

Lauren is just thinking she might help herself to breakfast if there is anything to eat, whatever the Voice's instructions, when she hears it boom out over the hidden speakers.

'Novices, put on your robes and head to the chapter house. You will be live on air in five minutes, so make sure you're dressed by then.'

There is a scurry to fling habits on, still damp and now faintly steaming, before they rush into the smaller room next door. They get there just in time for the countdown. Nate, roused from his slumber, makes it with only seconds to go.

'Novices, you have failed to complete another penance. Because of this, one of your number will be exiled from the monastery later today.'

'Already?' says Nico 'We've lost Kez and Frank, and now another one goes? No way.'

But the Voice surges on, ignoring the interruption: 'This expulsion will be at the discretion of the Abbot. He must make his choice later tonight. His decision will be final. Until then, you are dismissed.'

A beat passes before a hubbub of outrage rises from the contestants.

'What the hell? *Nate* gets to kick one of us out of here?'

'Like, no discussion or anything? Just tells us to leave?'

'How is that fair?'

Nate raises his hands to placate the others. 'Guys . . . guys . . . this is the game you all signed up for! Come on!'

'I can't listen to this,' mutters Mac, banging out of the chapter house door. 'I'm out of here.'

A camera swivels to watch him as he goes.

'You are off air.'

Chapter Fifteen

Once their protestations have died down, they gather by the fire to share out the tiny amount of oats they reserved for breakfast and make some porridge. As soon as they have eaten, Nate slopes off to his bedroom again and everyone except Mac and Lauren accept Jackson's suggestion to see if it's worth trying to take the coracles out to catch some fish to eat. Even Jude follows, saying she will be the safety monitor on the beach.

'You don't want to join them?' Lauren asks Mac as he scavenges the last of the food.

'Couldn't really face being around people for a bit,' he says. 'Sorry. Not you, obviously.'

Lauren laughs, but she knows what he means. She'd happily wile away the time just in Mac's company but wonders if now could be a good time to talk to Nate, especially with the others gone.

'Just going to pop to the dorm a sec,' she says. Mac grunts in response.

She heads towards the Abbot's quarters, heart racing, but as she approaches the door swings open and Nate strides out.

'Oh! Hi! I was just coming to find you,' says Lauren, a little breathlessly.

There's a glint in Nate's eye and again Lauren feels a chill run down her spine. Could he know what she's up to, or does he think she has something else in mind? No, she tells herself. Most likely he'll just be thinking she wants to save her skin before the eviction later.

'I need to get out, clear my head,' he says. 'What's everyone else up to?'

'It's just Mac and me here. The others have gone to try and catch fish.'

'Awesome, I'll catch up with them,' says Nate. 'See you in a bit.'

Lauren barely has a chance to respond before he dashes off, leaving her feeling slightly deflated. Contrary to his earlier invitation, is Nate evading being on his own with her? Or does he just not want to pass up the chance to show off his hunter-gatherer skills?

She returns to the great hall, determined to try again later, and fetches herself some water before heading to the long table. She and Mac sit in comfortable silence for a while, lost in their own thoughts, Mac drumming his fingers on the table from time to time.

Eventually, Mac bursts into speech, as though he can contain himself no longer. 'I just don't get it. How come nobody else sees it? He's just bloody awful. You saw what he was like with me. He was just itching to lather me. Would have, if the cameras hadn't been there. What an idiot. As if he could! I'd like to see him try. But now he – *he* – gets to kick one of us out? How the hell is that fair?'

Lauren shushes him before he can go any further; she can hear the others coming back from what looks like an unsuccessful fishing jaunt. Nate sweeps in first, Nico close behind.

'Sorry, guys, we didn't catch a thing. Couldn't even get in. Though Nate came close,' says Nico, looking at him devotedly.

Nate holds up his hands in a show of humility. 'Not close enough, sadly. But we had a good time trying, didn't we, girls?' he says to Hollie and Taisie, who are next to appear.

The girls giggle. 'Yeah, it was fun,' says Taisie. 'But the sea is too rough right now, even for Nate.'

There's something that makes Lauren queasy about the way the young women press slightly too close to Nate, laugh a bit too long at his jokes. Although maybe they're just staying on his good side, now that he carries their fate in his hands.

They drape themselves around the great hall in small groups. Nate is in 'his' throne, which no one else dares to touch, and there is nowhere else comfortable to sit. Nico makes a foray back to the dormitories and brings back the mattresses and meagre bedding from the beds meant for Kez and Frank. 'They never even got to spend a night in them,' says Hollie sadly, but Lauren is grateful as they turn them into makeshift cushions around the fireplace. Hollie and Taisie occupy themselves by giving each other more elaborate braids, and then offer to do Lauren's as well. Settling on the floor between them, Lauren asks how they're doing.

'All right, I guess. Bit of a weird way to start the day . . .' says Taisie as she pulls on Lauren's hair. From where she is sitting, Lauren sees Hollie glance at her quickly, a warning flash in her eyes.

'Yeah, we're exhausted,' says Hollie, then falls silent, closing the conversation down.

It is not the first time Lauren has seen her do that. They are not alone in being reluctant to go over the last few hours. As far as Lauren can work out, nobody wants to talk about Jude throwing the oil or about Nate and Mac squaring up to each other. It is classic game-play, thinks Lauren. No one, apart from Mac, wants to speak ill of Nate and jeopardise his or her future on the island.

There is speculation about who he is going to banish tonight. Feverish bouts of conversation break out in hushed tones. Lauren catches Mac's name over and over, and even her own once or twice before the whispers fall silent at her approach. Nico keeps declaring that he is sure it's him. He's been so hopeless in the challenges, he says. The girls keep their own counsel, saying only that it must be really hard for Nate to have to choose.

Only Mac holds himself entirely apart from it all, sitting at the other end of the Hall and chatting briefly to the few people – Jackson, Hollie and Taisie, Lauren herself – who occasionally stray over to him and exchange a few words.

The rest of the day passes painfully slowly. The Voice of God is quiet. Lauren imagines the programme editors must have a mountain of material to work with. They wouldn't have been expecting that confrontation on the beach and Lauren knows they'll be hyping it up. What is the story they are telling the audience? Did they catch Nate's clenched first, that flash of fury on his face? There were cameras everywhere. They couldn't have missed it. But would they put it in the edit? Or are they choosing the pictures to exaggerate the danger Jude had put him in, to make him look gracious, magnanimous even?

She knows the answer; she could write the script herself. Of course, they aren't going to portray their biggest signing negatively. They can't afford to. Production will be working hard to reinforce his carefully nurtured reputation as a Hollywood hero.

Soon, like everyone else, Lauren's thoughts turn to food. It feels like days since they had a proper meal, and the nagging gnaw of hunger means that food is becoming their main topic of conversation. Jackson is obsessing about calories again, furious that the promises he was given have been broken. The others keep returning to their favourite snacks, what they would die for, and what they would have as their last meal. As the roll call of food – 'Sunday roast!' 'A juicy burger!' 'Perfect fries!' 'My mum's jerk chicken!' – flows over her,

Lauren's mouth waters, but what she is really dying for is a coffee. In normal life, she has a black coffee in her hand day and night and she failed to heed Production's warning that it might be a good idea to wean herself off it before she came to the island.

She bonds with Nico about this, and the dull thudding caffeine withdrawal headache they are both fighting. Lauren tells him to drink more water – the water from the well is surprisingly sweet – but Nico is nervous about it.

'No idea what's at the bottom of that thing,' he says, and he holds back, not drinking until it has been boiled up on the fire and cooled.

The boredom of having nothing to do affects them all differently, and Lauren takes the opportunity to observe her fellow contestants. Nate is holding court at the long table, waxing lyrical about some film role or other, Jude and Nico listening intently.

Hollie and Taisie are looking around for extra food, mostly in vain. The dynamic between the two young women interests Lauren. It's always Hollie who takes the lead, often speaking for both of them, chatting to the others. Taisie is more reserved. She tends to defer to Hollie even on small decisions, although Hollie almost always gives her smiling assent. Lauren wonders about their lives – do they have boyfriends, a wider circle of friends? She knows they met at school, and that their make-up channel took off before they even did their A levels. Strange to have fame at that age, she thinks. And even more impressive that they had the business sense to turn that fame into a real brand. But how claustrophobic it must be at times, to be so dependent on your best friend and business partner. Does either of them ever long to break away from the other, she wonders.

If so, there's no sign of it. In here, they tend to talk most to Nico, and they are sweet and affable to everybody without exception. But they seem most at ease when it is just the two of them. Like right now.

They have been foraging again in what had looked to Lauren like a patch of weeds outside. When they return, she can hear animation in their quiet voices as they discuss what they can make with the herbs they have found.

Jackson has found something to occupy his restlessness: making endless trips to and from the well and filling with water every vessel he can find. Looking at everyone's mystified face, he grins.

'For training,' he explains briefly, and sets about cobbling together a makeshift weights machine. It involves balancing the full water buckets on the ends of the narrow wooden benches, which he then lifts while lying on his back, laughing as he dodges the water that inevitably spills. His drive and relentless good humour are impressive, thinks Lauren, as she watches him next do a round of press-ups. Nate has by this time left his throne and moved to Jackson's side, offering him encouragement and advice. Lauren notes, however, that he never joins in, probably unwilling to compete with a real-life Olympian.

Mac, in contrast, is still sunk in gloom, clearly obsessing about tonight's eviction. He's a man of contrasts: great in a crisis, and a natural leader, but given to melancholy.

'Can't do it, not with my back,' he says when Jackson suggests he join in on the training. 'I think I might have done something to it on that bloody zip-wire, and those so-called beds haven't helped.'

The atmosphere is not improved by the fact that the weather outside has turned. Low clouds stalk the horizon, and an odd gust of wind fitfully shakes the slate roof tiles outside.

The strain grows as the sky darkens. Eventually they fall silent, until there is no sound but the crackling of the fire and the howl of the wind outside. It is almost a relief when the cloister bell rings, summoning them to the chapter house.

'The hour has come,' the Voice says, 'for the Abbot to make his choice. You are each to pack your belongings and gather by your desks as quickly as possible.'

Five minutes later, their bags in their hands, they are listening to the countdown and for confirmation of Nate's decision. Without any instruction to do so, they have arranged themselves in the same positions they took that first day when they inadvertently sealed Kez's fate. Nate is the last to come in and stands in front of them. He is holding the *Abbot's Rules* book and has pulled his cowl up over his head. Presumably to look more official, thinks Lauren, but however he dresses it up there is no disguising that his decision will be costing someone their place on the island and the chance of winning the prize.

'I have thought long and hard about this,' he begins, looking at each of them in turn with great sincerity. 'And this is what I have decided . . .' He leaves it a beat, taking a moment to hold the gaze of each of them with sorrowful eyes. His sense of timing is pitch perfect. It is almost as if he is being directed. Production must be loving his poise, but in the room the empty seconds are agonising. 'I refuse.'

He lifts his eyes up towards the ceiling, as though conversing with the Voice itself. 'I refuse to take responsibility for ending this journey for any of us. I refuse to turn anyone out of here. How could I? Every single person in here' – he sweeps his arm theatrically through the air – 'has become a dear friend to me in the last few days. They are like family to me. You cannot ask me to banish any one of them. If you demote me from being Abbot because of this, that is your decision. Here, take this ring off me. I don't care. I'll go to the Sinners' dorm and sleep there tonight. Whatever you say, I am not betraying my buddies.'

There's a long pause. Then the Voice responds, implacable: 'Your position is noted. However, be advised that at least one Novice must leave this monastery tonight. If you, as Abbot, refuse to make that choice, then you yourself must forfeit your place and descend the banishment stairs. You have three further minutes in which to make up your mind.'

'That's me done, then,' says Mac quietly beside Lauren, so only she can hear. 'There's no way he's sending himself home, is there?'

A gaggle of the others – Nico, Jackson and Jude – have gathered round Nate, pleading with him that he mustn't fall on his sword. Lauren too is desperate for Nate to stay. She hadn't even considered the possibility that he might be sent home before her. Without him, her whole purpose here is lost.

She finds she is clenching her fists with the tension – and the horrible realisation that for Nate to stay, then almost certainly Mac will go. One more ally lost, she thinks. The only one who really sees through Nate. She can't bear the thought of Mac leaving the island, but that is preferable to Nate going.

Nate, meanwhile, is sitting, head bowed, as though the responsibilities he has been charged with are too heavy to bear. He stays that way for almost the full three minutes. Then he stands up, before the Voice has a chance to summon him.

'I have made my decision,' he says, 'and I'd like to explain my reasons. This has been a terrible choice to make,' he continues. 'But all day I've been thinking about what everyone is getting out of this experience. For me, it's been an amazing chance to see this beautiful place and get to know an awesome bunch of people. And just do something different, you know? Take some time out, be in the moment. But I think there's one of us here who isn't happy on this island. I know everyone wants to win this thing. But I don't think that being here is making someone their best self. So, for that reason . . . and with a heavy heart, the person I am exiling . . . is . . .' Again, he stops for a beat before he looks up at them all. 'It's Mac.'

'No shit, Sherlock,' says Mac under his breath, as the others gasp. Some not very convincingly.

'Mac, I'm sorry. I really am. But I've been watching you today, sitting on your own. I just don't think you're happy here. I know you've given so much to the challenges. And I think you're a great, great guy. But I don't think this is the right place for you right now. It has to be you, Mac. And I think you know it too.'

'You would say that, wouldn't you?' says Mac with barely repressed fury. 'Well, I have some things I'd like to say to you right now. For a start—'

But at this point the Voice cuts him off. 'Mac, you have been chosen for banishment. Please turn round and leave the chapter house. There is no time for goodbyes. Your time as a Novice has come to an end.'

There is a click and a whine from behind them, as the doors to the stone staircase start to open.

'Fine,' says Mac, shooting one last venomous glance towards Nate. 'I'm going. Don't worry. You enjoy yourselves. And I'll see you on the other side.' And on that note he turns and walks the distance to the doorway in three quick strides, his huge frame filling the archway. Without glancing back even once, he descends the staircase and the doors close behind him.

The Voice confirms what they have already guessed.

'You are off air.'

Chapter Sixteen

The dusty air of the chapter house feels dense and suffocating, crowded with unspoken accusations. Looking around, Lauren sees on her fellow Novices' faces a mixture of relief and disbelief. They are growing accustomed to the emotional shockwaves left in the wake of every departure, the appearance of a ghostly void where one of their number once stood. But of everyone to leave so far, to her, Mac's absence is the biggest loss. Lauren feels it like a physical blow to her morale. Over the last forty-eight hours, he had become a stalwart of their team. Everyone, except Nate, liked and trusted him.

In the end it is Nate himself, in a voice that sounds on the verge of cracking, who breaks the silence. 'Oh God. That was awful. I can't believe they made me do that.'

So that's the tactic, Lauren thinks. Invite pity and point the blame elsewhere. Although it doesn't seem to be working.

'Seriously, mate? Why him?' says Jackson.

Hollie joins in, 'He was always so kind to us,' as Taisie says at the same time, 'He helped everyone.'

'Like, last night in the dorm he was trying to make sure we weren't too cold . . .'

'. . . he even tried to give us his blanket . . .'

'. . . it's going to be so strange here without him.' Their words tumble out in a rush, their sentences overlapping. Lauren has noticed before how they do this, but it seems to be intensified in times of stress.

Nico is the only one at first to speak up in Nate's defence. 'Guys, it's a game. We're all playing it. He had to choose someone. Who would you rather it was? Me? Jackson? One of you?'

No one has an answer. But nor do they continue berating Nate. Instead, shoulders dropping, they begin to shuffle towards the relative warmth of the great hall. Lauren, leading the way, is nearly out the door, when a loud bang makes her freeze. It is coming from the other doors to the chapter house, the ones that lead to the banishment stairs. Horrified, they watch as the doors shake under the force of several blows.

'What the hell?' says Jackson.

As he speaks, they see one door is being forced from the other side, emitting a squeal of protest as wood grinds over stone. Huge hands appear in the crack, then enormous forearms. And then Mac stumbles in, practically falling across the threshold. Water drips from his hair and his habit; he is soaked, and he seems to have lost one of his slippers. As for his face, it has transformed into a ruptured mask of panic mixed with fury. He is heaving for breath as he tries to explain what happened.

'Jesus, I thought I was never gonna get out of there. I went all the way down, through an underground cave to a jetty, but the bloody sea is raging. There's no way in hell any boat is getting near it. The waves are smashing against the rocks.' He stops to take a breath. 'There's water everywhere. Waves were washing all over me. I can't believe they even let me go me down there. They must have known it's blowing a hoolie and nothing could reach me. How effing stupid and dangerous.'

There's an astonished silence, and then a familiar boom.

'Novices, as you can see, Mac is unable to leave the island at this

131

moment. We are currently dealing with some weather issues, but you are safe and the game will continue. In order to maintain its integrity, please take Mac to the gatehouse, which you will find above the port-cullis. He will find a comfortable chamber there ready for him where he can wait until we can get him safely off the island. The key is in the door. Please lock it behind you and leave him in there. He is no longer part of *Isolation Island*.'

'What the actual hell?' Mac is incredulous. 'Don't be ridiculous. No one's locking me up anywhere. Not in a month of Sundays. That was never part of the deal. I'm staying right where I am, with you lot.'

For a moment, there is resounding silence. The others still haven't processed Mac's exile, let alone his unexpected reappearance. Lauren notices they are all avoiding looking directly at him. His return has thrown them into confusion and there's no pre-worn TV script for how to behave. The girls have physically withdrawn from the space in the middle of the floor, moving as far away from the drama as possible. They lean in close to each other, whispering. Taisie looks as though she is pleading and, as Lauren watches, Hollie shakes her head emphatically, just once.

Nate clears his throat, taking charge. 'You're going to have to do what the Voice says. I'm sure Production has this all worked out,' he says.

'Yeah, right,' says Mac. 'And that includes nearly killing you by mistake, and incarcerating me, does it?'

'It was fine, I am fine. And it's hardly incarceration. It's just having you sit out the game,' says Nate.

'Oh, yeah? Well, how would you like it? Suits you, though, I reckon, me being locked away. You really don't care for anyone who takes a bit of your limelight, do you? You want to be careful you don't start looking like Nasty Nate. We're not the only ones watching you.' The venom in Mac's voice is chilling as he gestures towards the ceiling with its watching cameras.

Nate throws his chin up, apparently not wanting to dignify this with a response, but naked aggression crackles in the space between them.

It is Jude who brings things to a halt, stepping in front of Nate as if to protect him. 'OK, you two, calm down. There's no need to make it personal. But I think Nate's right. Don't forget it's a game, like he said. We all signed up to it, and we need to obey the rules. If we don't, none of us will win this. What's the harm in just waiting till you can leave, somewhere a bit more comfortable?'

Mac rounds on her. 'It's inhuman, that's why. How would you like to be locked up?'

'Why don't we vote on it?' Nate says. 'Mac doesn't get a vote since he's officially out of the game. But the rest of us can decide together. Raise your hand if you think we should send Mac to the gatehouse?'

It's definitely a gamble Nate's taking, thinks Lauren, watching the others. At stake is not only Mac's freedom but Nate's authority. Slowly the hands go up. Jude's first, and then, more reluctantly, Nico's. Jackson says firmly 'No', at the same time as Lauren shakes her head, and both keep their hands down by their sides. Three versus two.

What will the girls do? She can feel the anxiety rolling off them as all eyes turn to them. She has noticed they never like the spotlight on them in these uncomfortable moments; they shun conflict. A quick glance passes between the two, unreadable to anyone else. Hollie speaks first, quickly backed up by Taisie.

'It's probably, like, way more comfortable than here . . .'

'. . . got a decent bed . . .'

'. . . definitely going to be warmer than the Sinners' dorm.'

'And we'll bring you your food – promise we'll give you the biggest portions.'

Slowly, both of their hands rise into the air, though their voices fade out in the face of Mac's fury. They quickly drop their arms, stepping back one more pace from the others and gazing determinedly at the floor.

But their vote is cast. Mac is banished. He is going to be sent to the gatehouse, whatever that means.

Jackson and Lauren meet each other's eyes with a rueful expression, and Jackson raises his eyebrows, but before either can speak, Mac's face has turned dark as thunder. 'What the feck, you bunch of spineless eejits, just look around you. Nate is playing you all for fools!'

With that he slams his way out the door and bangs it behind him. They hear his wet footsteps echo down the passageway. It is an almost comical sound as one bare foot alternates with the slap of a sodden slipper.

'I'll go with him,' says Lauren, picking up the slipper he dropped on the threshold and putting it into Mac's cotton bag, which he has left behind in his rage. 'Someone needs to check he's OK.'

'And lock him in!' she hears someone say. Was it Nate or Nico? She can't tell.

On her way she snatches up an oil lamp, then hurries to catch up, worried about what state Mac will be when she reaches him. Something is niggling at her, and it's not just the drama of the last few moments, but a small detail that has caught her attention, something about the Voice itself when it dropped its latest bombshell. There was some quality she cannot put her finger on, something subtly different about the language and the tone.

And then it comes to her. Just the one word: 'please'. Throughout all their time on the island, the Voice has never sounded anything less than commanding, never used a request where an order would do. It has never said 'please'. That small word is a giveaway: it makes the Voice sound uneasy, as if it is no longer entirely in control.

Something, she can't tell what, has changed. It is as though the Voice itself is scared.

Chapter Seventeen

Stepping through the doors into the night, Lauren gets a shock. Even in the relatively sheltered courtyard, the force of the wind is alarming, threatening to blow her off her feet. It is whipping at her robes as she struggles to match Mac's furious pace, whistling over the roofs and towers. Angry gusts are whisking leaves and dust up in flurries, stinging her eyes. There's an ominous rattle coming from the pyramid of scaffolding in the moat that holds up the communication satellites. It is dark, but she can just make out the outlines of the antennae and satellite discs, incongruous against the sky.

Ahead of her, Mac is running towards the portcullis and Lauren follows him, both instinctively pulling their cowls tight over their heads. She catches up as he reaches a small door into the side of the gatehouse, its lintel giving them some scant protection. They grab for the latch at the same time, their hands meeting as they scrabble to turn it. Then it gives, and they throw themselves into the ancient building, banging the door shut behind them. Letting their cowls fall to their shoulders, they grin at each other. In the light from the lantern, their faces gleam, eyes bright, exhilaration still filling their lungs as the sound of the storm outside drops, muffled by the hefty planks of oak.

'Bloody hell,' says Mac.

'That's quite something,' agrees Lauren, laughing. 'No wonder the boat couldn't get to you.'

She regrets her words immediately, because the smile drops off Mac's face in an instant, replaced by a scowl.

'Cannae believe they're doing this to me,' he says.

'"They" who?' replies Lauren. 'You mean Production, or the others?'

This wins a reluctant grin from Mac. 'Oh, all of them, the bastards.'

The first turn of the stairs brings them to a tiny door – half-height – that opens into a room that is dwarfed by Mac's size. Lauren remembers briefly passing it when the Saints first gained entry to the monastery but, in the excitement, hadn't thought to go to look inside. She holds up the lantern; the only furnishings are a single bed and a tiny chair. There are a couple of small windows on each wall with views over the whole monastery.

'It's like a secret hideaway. I suppose when the monks lived here, they would have had a night watchman sleeping here.'

Mac is less concerned with the history of the room than with its comforts. He's examining the mattress, piled with thick blankets. There's a fireplace and a couple of logs. All in all, thinks Lauren, it could be a lot worse. Production must have anticipated that some-body might need to be separated from the others. Was everyone who was banished actually meant to leave the island?

'Do you think Frank stayed here for a bit?'

'No idea. I s'pose he could have, he disappeared so quickly. It would have been a great place to hide him.'

'Well, either way, this will be better for your back, won't it?' she says.

Her attempt at optimism doesn't work.

'Thanks, hen. I'm not so worried about the creature comforts. It's the fact they want me locked in. I'll go mad in here. It's not decent, locking someone up. And surely some kind of a health and safety issue? What the hell do they think I'm going to do, creep back in the night to steal a bit of porridge or something? I'll sit the rest of this thing out till they can take me away. But there's no way you're locking me in here. I'm sorry, nothing against you, but no way. And if the others come over here and try anything, I won't let them. I'll fight back!'

His voice is rising as he speaks, real anxiety beginning to creep in. He's not messing about – clearly he really can't cope with the idea of being shut in. But Lauren thought about this the moment she made the decision to follow him. Glancing up at the camera, which she can see glinting in the corner, she turns her back to it and lowers her voice, tapping her foot against the base of the bed to drown out what she is saying.

'Look, you know I don't think you need to be in here at all. You saw how I voted. I'm not going to be able to change the others' minds, but I'm not going to lock you in either. I'll just leave it unlocked. I'll make sure it looks like I've turned the key, and that the camera can't see what I'm doing.'

'What about when they come to bring me food?'

'Easy. I'll work it so it's either me or Jackson who bring it. It's not like you actually want to see the others anyway, and I doubt they want to face you either. There's no way I'm locking anyone up – I'm not a bloody prison officer. The Voice can penalise me all it wants, but I reckon it won't even notice. I think it's probably more worried about the weather.'

Relief floods Mac's face as he nods. 'Thanks, Lauren,' he says softly. 'I really appreciate this.'

'Here,' she says, handing over his bag. 'Better start making yourself comfortable.'

She leaves him crouched over the fireplace, coaxing a flame out of the kindling. Even though the room is dry and getting warmer, and she knows he has all he needs, she feels complicit in something horribly wrong as she says goodbye, closes the door, makes a pretence of turning the key, and heads down the narrow stairs. She can tell how much he fears the isolation, the forced hours in his own company. His vulnerability is at odds with his tough rugby captain persona and it's shaken her. She worries about him as she fights her way against the wind across the courtyard, moving as fast as she can to reach the light and shelter of the hall. In the darkness, it feels as though she is being pursued by a thousand eyes.

She is about to open the huge double doors and go back to the others to tell them she has locked Mac in, when she changes her mind and turns left instead. She's willing to bet Nate has retreated to his room as usual, and she needs to get him alone, to build on the camaraderie that was forming between them. Especially as she voted against him about Mac. With renewed purpose and fast feet, she heads down the corridor towards the dormitories. By the time she gets to the door marked 'Abbot', her heart is racing. She takes a deep breath to focus and knocks gently, not one-hundred-per-cent sure there will be any answer.

'Yeah?' He sounds expectant. 'Who is it?'

'It's me. Lauren.'

The latch jolts open so quickly she takes a step back in fright. It's as if he had been waiting for her right by the door. Nate's voice is low and husky, and that knowing look is back on this face. 'I've been wondering when you would come back to see me.'

He ushers her in and Lauren is greeted with a cosy scene – the fire burning brightly in the hearth, a candle flickering on the mantelpiece – and it is warm, much warmer than anywhere else in the monastery. No wonder he spends so much time in here. She is aware of his proximity as he shuts the door quietly but firmly behind her and turns round to sit on his ruffled bed.

'Here, have a seat,' he says, offering her a place beside him and patting the mattress before running a hand through his hair. She knows that to play this right, she should probably sit next to him, but can't quite bear to do so. Instead she opts for the wooden cross-back chair by the octagonal desk. The small leather box that had his ring in it is still there, as is the Abbot's rulebook.

'I've locked Mac up. He was furious about it. I feel terrible, but it's done now.' Lauren hopes Nate believes her.

'Don't feel terrible. I know you guys were close, but you did the right thing. It's a game, we have to play by the rules. And besides, we all know he had a temper on him. Personally, I'll be glad to see the back of him. Sooner they get him out of here the better, far as I'm concerned.'

Lauren forces herself to agree with him.

'Yeah, I guess you're right. It's just . . . a weird situation. Doesn't feel like Production has everything under control, does it? I mean, with all that's been going on – the portcullis, the harness, and now this storm . . .'

'To be fair, they can't control the weather.'

She gives a nervous laugh. 'Of course, you're right. I'm just being silly. Guess I'm a bit scared, to be honest. And I'm not the one who was set on fire and nearly crushed by a gate! You always put on a brave face, but it's a lot. You can talk to me, you know, if you're not OK?' She hopes she's not laying it on too thick.

'Don't you worry yourself about me, Lauren. I'm fine. And I think you know that.' He raises his left eyebrow and locks his piercing eyes on to hers before he continues, 'I think we both know that's not really why you're in here.'

She takes a sharp intake of breath and her heart contracts, but she manages to keep herself stock-still as anxious questions accelerate through her brain. Does he know what she's doing? Has he known all along?

'Sorry, I don't understand,' she replies slowly, pleased that she manages to keep her voice from trembling.

'Oh, come on! Why else would you keep trying to get me alone, trying to have cosy little chats? It's obvious to me, to everyone here.'

'I don't know what you mean. I just wanted to check you're OK.'

He rises from the bed and takes a step towards her, a wolfish look in his eye. Lauren's heart is hammering uncontrollably now.

'Seriously, Lauren, stop messing around. You know *exactly* what I mean. Don't worry, you don't need to pretend you're just here to check up on me.'

'I am! I am worried. I have been ever since the portcullis nearly fell on you. Then the incident with the oil and all the pressure of having to evict someone. I can only imagine how much that must be weighing on you. I just want to help. You can trust me . . .'

He takes another step towards her, grin widening. He's right in front of her now and brushes a finger lightly down her cheek. 'I do trust you, Lauren. And you can trust me too . . .'

Lauren inadvertently jerks her head away. His expression darkens, but he doesn't back off. She suddenly realises she's put herself in a potentially dangerous situation.

'Stop playing games,' says Nate in low voice. 'I know what you're after.'

Suddenly the room feels too hot, and claustrophobic as if the walls are closing in. She feels cornered. Images from the last two years flash before her. The distraught faces of dozens of women she has spoken to about Nate, the details of the appalling experiences, their tears, their anguish, their frustration. Allegra, her best friend, crying and broken.

She pauses before she answers, struggling to think of a way to reject him without angering him even more. An infinitesimal silence stretches between them, until Nate speaks again.

'I know exactly what you want. You want what everyone else does, a bit of Nate Stirling. Well, come on, come and get what you came for.' He is laughing now, gesturing towards the bed. She doesn't move. She is frozen to her seat. 'It's no big deal for me. I'm used to it.' He bends over her and whispers in her ear, 'And, don't get me wrong, you're an attractive young woman. We can have some fun.'

Lauren feels a visceral sense of terror as his breath tickles her ear. But, underneath the fear, is a small thrill of triumph. Is it possible that Nate has forgotten about the cameras that are trained on them at all times? To anyone watching, it must be clear from her expression and body language that she feels threatened, that she doesn't want this. The real Nate Stirling is exposing himself for everyone to see. She can hardly believe her luck.

'*No*,' she says firmly, so there can be no confusion. 'That's not what I'm here for. Or have you forgotten that you're married?'

Instantly the smile is wiped from his face and he backs off, if only slightly. She sees a flash of fury, the same one she saw on the beach when he turned on Mac.

'Lauren, don't pretend to care about my wife. Stop being such a tease. Either get over here or get outta here because, believe me, there are plenty of others here on this island who would be begging to sleep with me.'

'Jesus, Nate, who do you mean? Jude? The girls? Good God, they're young enough to be your daughters.'

He is sneering at her now, leaning towards her. 'That's never stopped anyone before.'

The image of him with Hollie or Taisie is too much for Lauren. She has no doubt he wouldn't hesitate if the opportunity arose to sleep with either of them. And then he'd destroy them. She feels sick; she needs to get out. She gets to her feet unsteadily and is standing up to leave, to escape, when he grabs her left wrist.

'Come on, Lauren, you know you want to.' He breathes heavily into her face.

Using all her strength she twists out of his grasp, pulls away from him and manages to get her right hand on to the latch to open the door. Before she does, she is interrupted by a deafening two-tone wail. It is the unmistakable blast of an emergency alert. It is so loud it and so unexpected it stops them both in their tracks. They look up to the ceiling as there is a strange crackle over the loudspeakers. The Voice is trying to talk but no words come out.

A moment later, with no warning, a new voice speaks. Gone are the booming tones they are accustomed to, replaced by a woman whose voice has a definite waver to it.

Her words are coming hard and fast, but Lauren doesn't need to hear the words to know that something is very, very wrong.

'Novices! Make your way to the great hall immediately. This is not a drill. Go immediately to the great hall! THIS IS NOT A DRILL!'

Lauren sprints out of the door through the cloisters, Nate hot on her heels. The sky is dark and menacing, and an ominous rumble of thunder reverberates in the distance. They round the door into the great hall just behind Jackson, followed closely by the girls, and Nico and Jude pull up in their wake. All of them are panting as they come to a halt in the middle of the hall, gazing up at the speakers above them as they wait for the next announcement.

A kind of screech comes over the airwaves, then the new voice starts talking again, in a tone that is striving for businesslike but just missing the mark. It's clear the person is reading, awkwardly and hurriedly, from a script.

'Contestants. Um, sorry, Novices. This is important, you must listen carefully. There is a once-in-a-hundred-year storm crossing the Atlantic. Storm Logan is heading directly towards the north-west coast of Scotland. It is due to hit tonight, in the next couple of hours. We will be in the epicentre. We have been warned it will cause widespread damage and looks likely to be severe for at least forty-eight hours. We cannot get to you. Repeat. We cannot get to you. It is too dangerous.'

There is a stunned silence, before the Voice continues.

'The wind is too strong for an aircraft and the sea too rough for a boat. Rest assured, though, you are completely safe where you are. The monastery on Eilean Manach has survived for centuries. But to stay out of danger you must obey these rules. You *must* remain together here in the great hall. You have twenty minutes maximum to retrieve your belongings and anything else you need. After that, you must close the doors, and do not leave until we say you can. The great hall is the only place where we can guarantee your safety.

'We have opened all the locks to all the doors. This includes the storerooms, so take what you need. I repeat, you have twenty minutes. After that, shut the doors and stay where you are. We will come and get you when the storm has passed, when it is safe to do so. You must stay within these walls.'

Just as suddenly as it came, the Voice has gone.

Jude is the first to react. 'What are you saying?' she yells at the ceiling. 'What does "once in a hundred years" mean? How can you know we're safe?'

The others chime in: 'Can't you get us out of here?'

'How long are we stuck here?'

'Oh my God. What are we meant to do?'

A short buzz over the airwaves signals that someone is trying to answer them. It crackles again and then stops.

They all shout at once.

'Hello? Talk to us! Are we safe? Can't you get us out of here?'

There is no response. Nate gestures for them to be quiet and then shouts as loudly as he can into his microphone.

'Hey, you, Voice of God, whoever you are. This is Nate Stirling speaking. I want to talk to whoever is in charge of this mess, do you hear me? Now. Not later. *Right now!*' The rising pitch of Nate's voice indicates he's losing his cool. But even an order from him makes no difference. There is still no response, nothing at all.

After a while they stop shouting and look at each other, dread etched on their faces. Finally, Jackson takes control.

'Right. They can't hear us, but we heard what they said, so let's get organised. Let's get our things, quickly. We need our stuff. We need water, the rest of the mattresses and blankets and as much food as we can find in the storerooms. Go, go, go, everyone. Lauren, you go and get Mac. There's no time to lose.'

But before they can obey him, they hear a noise from outside: the sound of the gale growing into a howling scream. They run to the doors of the great hall, venturing out into the darkness. Already, they can barely stand against the power of the wind, it is so loud they can't hear each other's shouts, and have to gesture at each other as the breath is knocked out of their lungs. And then, to their horror, they hear a new noise, a sinister metallic rattle, which seems to be coming from just outside the courtyard.

'It's the communications platform!' yells Nico as loudly as he can, pointing across the roof of the right-hand cloister. And sure enough, the metal framework that holds up the dishes and cables is shuddering, wires vibrating in the wind, antennae whipping wildly backwards and forwards.

'It's not safe! We have to get inside!' screams Jude, but just as they turn to run, an enormous tearing sound rends the air as the platform starts to crumple. There's an infinitesimal pause, and then a thumping crash as the metal structure hits the outside wall. Satellite dishes clang to the ground, pylons scatter and shards of plastic and bent poles clatter into the moat.

Speechless, the seven of them stand open-mouthed, facing the space where the communication system – their entire connection with the outside world – used to be. The shock roots them to the ground, the trance only broken when an enormous figure flies out of the gatehouse door towards them. It's Mac, his robes streaming behind him in the wind, his cowl whipped back to reveal he is raging.

It's only when he gets within a couple of metres that they can hear the words coming out of his mouth.

'What the bloody hell is going on?' he screams.

Chapter Eighteen

No one has time to explain the details to Mac, and Jackson is the one to shout.

'Massive storm on the way. We need to get ourselves inside, like *now*!'

Panic takes over. It is utter chaos. Lauren has no time to think through her confrontation with Nate or its implications as they rush helter-skelter in different directions to grab what they can before their time is up. She sets off with Nico, Hollie and Taisie to the storerooms, the four of them tumbling over each other in their haste to raid the supplies. When they reach the corridor, every single door, Feast and Fast alike, is swinging open on its hinges.

After days on thin rations of strange soup and dry bread, the cornucopia that meets their eyes is overwhelming. The first 'Feast' store, the one that had remained locked after their failure at the Leap of Faith, turns out to be a giant larder filled to the gunnels. There are enormous loaves of bread, jars of jam and honey, huge bowls of fruit, side by side with baskets of vegetables. Giant canisters turn out to contain coffee, tea and sugar. There is even a refrigerated section with juices, milk, butter and cream, and massive precooked joints of ham, alongside bacon, sausages and eggs. With so much choice, Lauren can't decide what to grab first and she takes a moment to decide what is a priority.

The others aren't so circumspect. They rush from cellar to cellar, grabbing as much as they can carry. Nico is an apparition of avarice, dashing past with two bumper loaves of bread, one under each arm, a huge pack of cheese wrapped in brown paper under his chin, in his hands what appears to be a whole roast chicken balanced on a platter.

'Going to take these up first! Back for some more in a minute!' he mutters through his clenched teeth.

'Hollie, Holls, OMG! Look in here!' Taisie's voice, coming from the second-to-last of the storerooms, is muffled but ecstatic. Lauren sticks her head round the door to find the girls grinning from ear to ear. Behind them are shelves full of bottles. The labels are deliberately old-fashioned, clearly made specially by Production, each one declaring its contents loud and clear: whisky, wine, beer and mead, stored in big earthenware jugs.

'Must have been planning a big feast for us,' said Hollie, loading bottles first into Taisie's arms and then her own before running upstairs with her booty. Minutes later they are back for more, diving into the final storeroom this time. Lauren leaves them to it, finding an old box and loading it with more sober treasure: a side of ham, some butter, a stack of biscuits. When she returns, most of the others have gathered in the great hall already. Nate has piles and piles of bedding, Mac and Jackson are carefully laying out the food along the table, unable to believe their luck, and Jude is tending to the fire, debating what to cook.

'We need Hollie and Taisie. Where the hell have they got to?' shouts Nate.

Their return causes every jaw in the room to drop. They have found a stash of props and costumes, presumably meant for some tasks that had yet to happen.

After days of seeing everybody dressed in identical brown robes, the effect is electric: their appearance lights up the room. They are wearing matching bright orange and white harlequined jester's outfits –complete with floppy felt capes. Somehow the girls have managed to make the comedic outfits look graceful. The tops are nipped in to their tiny waists, the skirts are flaring out, and the capes draped over their shoulders look like petals, the tip of each decorated with a tiny bell. They hand Nico a floppy velvet minstrel's hat with a curling feather, which he accepts with glee.

Not only have they changed, but they are laden with musical instruments; something that looks like a lute, and a set of bagpipes and what might be a flute.

'There's a drum and some tambourines down there too,' said Hollie.

'Think somebody wanted us to have a party,' says Nico, examining one of the bottles and shaking it gleefully.

Nate holds up his hands. 'Hang on there, Nico. I like what you're thinking but we need to make sure we're safe. We must be nearly outta time.'

With that, a massive gust of wind slams against the giant oak doors. They smash open, hitting the walls with a shuddering bang, and it takes the strength of both Jackson and Mac to heave them closed again, by which time they are both soaked. When they have successfully done it, Mac turns the giant key in the latch, breathing heavily.

'They weren't messing: it's hell out there. None of us are going any-where tonight.'

Nate, apparently satisfied they are safe, has already opened a bottle of whisky and is pouring out large measures into bronze goblets.

'Only one thing for it, then. Let's have a drink.' He puts the top back on before flipping the bottle with a barman's flourish and then hands the drinks around. 'I think we deserve this. Cheers, guys. Here's to Isolation Island! Here you go, Lauren, down this!' he says, grinning at her, giving her a conspiratorial wink as he passes her a drink. 'No hard feelings, eh?'

Lauren can't believe his chutzpah. Only half an hour or so ago he was making a pass at her, turning nasty when she rejected him. And now he wants to breeze over it, pretend it never happened. If that is how he wants to play it, that's fine by her; she has what she needs. She takes the cup he is offering and smiles back.

After days of barely any food, neat whisky is a punchy way to start, but everyone except Mac downs their drinks. He refuses, muttering under his breath, 'Not for me, pal, thanks,' and starts inspecting the bagpipes.

'Don't think I've ever had whisky,' says Hollie.

Taisie nods in agreement and her eyes water as she says, 'Me neither. *Wow*, that's strong. But I think I like it.'

Fuelled by alcohol on empty stomachs they all pitch in to cook, coming up with a feast of chicken and cold ham, accompanied by baked potatoes cooked in the ashes and bubbling with melted butter and cheese, sprinkled with rosemary foraged the previous day by the girls. More bottles are set out the length of the table, together with jugs of mead and water. The water is being ignored by almost everyone, but not the mead. Taisie and Hollie even cobble together a pudding of stewed plums and apples topped with dollops of cream.

As they devour the food, the hall is filled with the sound of good-natured laughter and gentle teasing accompanied by the drumming of rain outside and the occasional rumble of thunder.

Lauren is too preoccupied with her own thoughts to join in the chatter, and she lets it wash over her. She feels shaken by what happened with Nate; how he spoke to her, how blatant he had been. She's not sure what would have happened if she hadn't slipped her wrist from his grasp, if the emergency siren hadn't sounded.

But, she reminds herself, there is the positive: by showing his true nature he has played right into her hands. Surely, with all that caught on camera, including the moment he lunged for her, it will be enough to convince others to blow the whistle. An entire production team will see it.

When it comes out, maybe the women she has spoken to will finally go on record and tell their own stories. And at last Lauren will be able to bring down the man who destroyed her best friend. Of course, she can only speculate but, for the first time since getting to the island, she lets herself relax a little and reaches for a cup of mead. It's far from a confession, but it's huge progress.

But as she watches him joking and laughing with the others, she now faces the more immediate problem of being stuck with Nate in the middle of a storm, cut off from the outside world. She'll just have to be careful not to be alone with him again, and hope she's done enough.

Once they have had their fill of food, the volume in the great hall rises. Down the end of the table, Mac is trying to teach Jackson to play the bagpipes, with predictable ear-splitting results. Hollie and Taisie, who are looking ridiculously perky in their matching jester's outfits, are indulging in some strange chemistry, mixing up soot from the fire with oil they have found to make eyeliner, and some beeswax from a candle with some red berries for lip gloss. Their plan is to give Nico a makeover.

'We did a thing on how to make your own make-up, like they did in medieval times. These are rowan berries,' explains Hollie. 'Want some?'

Lauren laughs and shakes her head, marvelling again at the resourcefulness of the two young women. 'Don't worry, they look poisonous, but we have boiled them, so they're not.'

Taisie adds with a smile, 'Mum was a make-up artist before she had me. She once worked on this period movie and the director was, like, super-method. He would only let her work with materials they'd have actually used at the time.' Taisie is still smiling, but her voice is choked with emotion.

'She sounds like a pretty inspiring woman, your mum,' says Lauren.

'Yeah, she was,' agrees Hollie, and Taisie nods through her tears.

The girls go back to their make-up alchemy, and Lauren turns her attention to Jude and Nate on her right. They are deep in conversation. Given how Lauren's last interaction with him turned out, she wonders what they're discussing. They both look engrossed. Nico has been trying to pick a tune out on the lute and when his strumming turns into a recognisable tune, one by one every conversation falls away. Nico's right hand ripples over the strings, and softly he starts humming, then raises his voice into a melody that they all recognise.

'It's "Stand by Me"!' exclaims Jude in delight. As Nico sings of dark lands and moonlight nights, there is a spellbound hush, with only the odd crackle and hiss from the blazing logs to accompany him.

Outside, the wind is fierce, its force buffeting the windows and rattling the latches. Mac and Jackson pull over one of the wooden benches and position it in front of the doors to made doubly sure they aren't blown open again.

Lauren lapses into a reverie. Part of her brain is still ringing with the surrealness of her circumstances, trapped on an island with people who amount to strangers, among them the person who has derailed her career and done so much worse to others. And yet the food and the drink, the candlelight and the music allow her to silence that voice for a short while, to let the magic of the moment flow.

As Nico reaches the chorus for the third time, they all join in singing, and Mac tucks the bagpipes under his arm and underscores the whole thing with a plaintive chant. Lauren is amused to find her eyes stinging, tears blurring her vision as they reach the final line. The rollercoaster of emotions of the last few days are getting to her.

Then Nico gives a wicked grin and changes the tempo of the chords to something fast and insistent, a beat everybody knows. 'When I wake up . . .' he sings, foot thumping on the floor.

'"500 Miles"!' cries Mac, putting down his bagpipe and grabbing Jude's hand. 'I love this one.' Joyfully he holds his other hand out to the girls, and before Lauren knows what she's doing, she too is up and dancing, arms aloft, chest pounding as Nate and Jackson join in. Every one of them is on their feet, swinging each other through the hall in a whirling frenzy.

A round of applause, foot stamping and hollers go up for Nico, who stands up and takes a bow, grabbing a glass from the table and draining it.

'Oh my days, my mum is going to love that when she sees it on the show!' and he bends over, hands on his stomach, laughing.

At the mention of 'the show', it suddenly dawns on Lauren that there is something important missing from the scene. Subconsciously she had registered it a while ago, but she can't quite pinpoint exactly when. The cameras. They aren't working, and they haven't been for some time. She glances round the room, checking. She can see five of them, and she is right: not one of them is moving. The familiar whirr of their lenses refocusing, stalking their every movement, has stopped.

'Oh, Nico, I'm sorry. I don't think she'll see it, no one will. Look. Look at the cameras. They're off!'

There is bewilderment written over all their faces as they check them out. Jackson goes right up to the closest lens, presses his face against it and moves from side to side, backwards and forwards. Nothing happens. It stays deathly still.

'Can't hear or see us now, guys. Guess it really is Isolation Island. Let's drink to that!'

As Nate speaks, he raises his goblet to them all. Lauren catches amusement in his eyes as he drinks and also a flicker of something else – is it calculation? Triumph? Or are the paranoia and alcohol going to her head? Either way she has a flash of anxiety. The gloves are truly off now; what will he do now the cameras aren't on? Is she safe? Are the girls safe?

'I guess they lost comms with us when the tower went down,' says Mac.

'Or before – pretty sure they stopped working hours ago. Surprised no one else spotted it.' There is an undertone of malevolence in Nate's voice and, to underline his point, he raises an eyebrow in Lauren's direction and gives the briefest of smirks.

Lauren feels sick. Fuck, fuck, fuck! When did the cameras go off? Was it when the tower went down, or before? Shit! The last time she knows they were on for sure was when she was supposedly locking up Mac. What happened after that? Had they been on when she was in Nate's room, when he made a pass at her? She can't be sure. In the heat of the moment, she hadn't thought to check, had just assumed. Oh God, how stupid of her.

'Bloody BRILLIANT, that is!' exclaims Mac, making Lauren jump. 'We can do what we like! We are FREE.'

With that he tears the microphone off his neck and throws it with abandon into a far corner. His actions are infectious: everyone except Lauren does the same, and moments later there is a tangled pile of seven abandoned mic packs. She takes hers off more slowly, still mentally kicking herself.

'God, Production would go mad if they knew they'd missed that show,' Nico says, laughing.

'That's not all they missed, is it?' Nate speaks over him. 'Like, Mac, how did you manage to get out of the gatehouse so quickly? I thought Lauren locked you in. That's what she told me, when she came to see me in my room afterwards. When the cameras had stopped working.'

He shoots Lauren another sly glance, which is enough to make her skin crawl and her heart sinks as she realises what he's insinuating. He'd known the cameras weren't on all along. That they weren't recording anything that happened in his room. She tries to reassure herself; maybe he's wrong, maybe it wasn't until the tower went down that they ceased working. But deep in her gut she knows. He would never have risked his reputation unless he'd been sure.

Not waiting for a reply to his question, Nate flashes her a Hollywood smile and pats Mac on the back, full of brotherly bonhomie, refilling his cup with whisky, saying, 'But let's not worry about that now, buddy, eh? Let's just agree, from here on, whatever happens on Isolation Island, stays on Isolation Island.'

He sounds icy as he says this. It is a command not a question, and to make sure they all know he is deadly serious he sweeps his gaze around the room, clocking each of them in turn.

'Agreed, everyone?'

There is a chorus of, 'Agreed' in response, and as a *frisson* of fear ripples down Lauren's spine. To counter it, she takes a large sip of her drink. The reality of the situation hits her. Without the cameras she has nothing: no proof, no evidence, no chance of a great exposé. Just her word against his, which she knows won't be enough. She put herself in his cross hairs to achieve absolutely nothing.

'Well, in that case,' Nico whispers in a low voice, leaning forward with a wicked gleam in his eye, 'I think we should play a game. Now that nobody's watching, who's up for a bit of Truth or Dare?'

Chapter Nineteen

With Nico's words, the celebratory atmosphere in the great hall changes, crackling with an unsettling charge. There is still laughter, and a few cries of, 'Yes! Truth or Dare!' but Lauren feels every nerve in her body sharpen. Even the haze of golden light round the candles seems to crystallise. Her journalistic instincts flick into red alert, as does her acute sense of self-preservation.

'No way,' Hollie says. 'I don't have any deep dark secrets. And even if I did, I'm not telling.'

'So choose Dare then, babe. Anyway, I'll go first,' says Nico. 'I choose Truth. Ask me anything.'

Lauren takes the initiative. 'All right, simple question. How did they get you on the show? What did they promise you as your Answered Prayer?'

There's a slight indrawn hiss of breath from someone, she's not sure who. This is the million-dollar question. The one they all want to know the answer to, the one they have not been allowed to ask. Lauren knows how precious her own prize is to her – she assumes everyone else's must be equally ambitious. And revealing. Because admitting what your prize is means exposing your deepest desires.

'Ouch. Going in hot, Lauren!' says Nate.

'Go on, Nico! Tell us, tell us, tell us,' Taisie chants, clearly more than a bit tipsy.

Lauren is worried she's gone in too hard. Her concern is misplaced, though, because Nico takes the bait. Taking another sip of his drink he steels himself to answer.

'You all probably know what happened to me on the talent show. All those vicious, hurtful rumours about me. None of them true, by the way. Xavi and I split up years ago. He dumped *me*, said I wasn't a good enough singer. And then, when he saw how well I was doing on the talent show, he was so jealous, he turned it all round, lied about everything. If he hadn't done that video, said all those horrible things, I could have won it . . . *would* have won it. Things would have been so different for me.'

His voice falters. He is holding back tears, and Hollie and Taisie rush to hug him.

'Babe, that's awful.'

'How could your best friend betray you like that?'

Clearly, they are convinced by his story, as is everyone else, but Lauren's bullshit detector is tingling. To her, these look like crocodile tears, not real emotion. He is playing to his audience. She says nothing, though. It's not Nico she's here to expose.

Bolstered by the girls' support, Nico carries on.

'So, what're they offering me? It's obvious, isn't it? The same contract I would have had: a three-album deal with all the backing, publicity, management, *everything*. That's why I'm here. So, I can get it all back.' There is a round of applause before he seems to sober up a bit and adds, 'I don't suppose that can happen now, can it?'

'It is never too late, buddy, never too late.' Nate slaps him on the back affectionately.

'So, who's next?' says Lauren, confidence bolstered by alcohol and

Nico's confession. 'What else have people been offered? How about you?' She turns to Hollie and Taisie. 'What brings you here? You seem to have the world at your feet.'

Taisie giggles at this, clearly not really wanting to answer. But Hollie frowns. 'Well, if you must know, it's a new business opportunity. A partnership with a huge fashion label who will add our make-up to their brand,' she says, sounding more like Jude than Taisie for once.

'Is that the best move right now?' Jude interjects. 'I thought you two were doing perfectly well on your own. You've got to check the small print on these things. These fashion houses will take a huge slice of the pie, then spit you out when you're no good to them anymore.'

Hollie's answer seems to have brought out the businesswoman in Jude, and Lauren can't help but think she's being slightly patronising. Hollie and Tasie have proven time and again that they are far more savvy than the others give them credit for.

'Yeah, we've thought about that, and of course we'll be careful, but the thing is . . .' counters Hollie, still trying to sound businesslike, though Lauren notices she is actually slurring slightly, 'this *particular* opportunity offers a platform through which we can diversify into markets where we our products are currently not the market leaders . . .'

Her words sound stilted, scripted; not like Hollie at all.

'She means America,' says Taisie, noticeably more drunk than Hollie. 'It's a bit of a secret. You mustn't, don't, don't tell *anyone*' – she puts a finger over her lips theatrically – 'but d'you know, they don't love us there like they do here. Or Asia. They love us in Asia. But America, not quite so much. America, they don't know us, our make-up. We're going to change that. Going to partner up with someone huge. That'll do it. But it's hush-hush. Hush. Hush,' she repeats solemnly, then lapses into a fit of the giggles.

'Taise . . .' says Hollie warningly, but Taisie continues.

'We wanna move there. Gonna go and live the high life in LA. Things we need to do . . .'

'What things?' asks Nico eagerly.

Taisie doesn't answer the question directly. She is mumbling, focused on the drink in front of her.

'I've always wanted to. Always wanted to ever since . . .'

Hollie reaches over and puts her hand on Taisie's to stop her, and tries again, reaching for some kind of formality: 'Well, if it comes off, if we win this thing, it could be a really exciting new development—'

'It's for me, it's because . . . because of my mum, because she told me . . .' interrupts Taisie loudly.

'Taisie,' says Hollie, quite sharply, 'shush. I don't think now is the time . . . Oh, babe, no. It's OK. I've got you.'

Taisie has dissolved into tears and the others all rush towards her, trying to comfort her. Nate curls an arm around her shoulders.

'Hey, look, I can help you out in the States. You girls can stay in my place in LA. I'll put in a good word with whoever needs it. You don't need some reality show when you've got Nate Stirling on your side.'

Nate's tone is kind and Taisie looks up at him gratefully. But Lauren's blood runs cold.

'Thanks, Nate. We'd love that,' Hollie replies, then whispers above Taisie's head, 'Sorry, she gets like this sometimes. She's had such a tough time. She'll be fine, honestly.'

There's an awkward pause as Hollie hugs Taisie, Nate still hovering far too close. It takes all Lauren's willpower not to physically insert herself and warn Hollie and Taisie to stay far, far away. This is not the time nor the place. Instead, to steady herself, she takes another sip of her drink. Jackson, clearly feeling it would be better for Taisie if they moved on, jumps in.

'I'm here because of my family too. My mum and dad have grafted so hard for me. Both of them, working two or three jobs, day and night, and then driving for miles all over the country to go to races, sleeping in the back of the car, going without so I could have the right kit, the best shoes. Without them, I wouldn't have had a chance to compete, let alone win two Olympic golds. So, I'm here to pay them back. To let them retire, stop working so hard and win them the house of their dreams. It is what they've always wanted: somewhere they can call their own.'

'What a wonderful thing to do,' says Jude. 'They must be so proud of you.'

'It's all I've ever wanted, to make them proud,' says Jackson, voice clogged with what Lauren can see is real emotion, unlike Nico's earlier tears. He collects himself and nods at Jude. 'How about yours, then?'

'Mine's quite simple really: a daytime TV talk show, with a political slant. Something like *Jude's Views* or *It's all Wright.* We're workshopping the title.'

'Nice! So, you want to do more telly then?' Nico says, nodding approvingly.

'Oh, I don't, not really' Jude says dismissively. 'Honestly, it's just a way to raise my profile. Ultimately, I want to go into politics. This country's in the gutter, and everybody at the top is too woke to do anything about it. We need proper good old-fashioned leadership, and I can offer that. But my recognition factor's not quite there yet. But a year or two of really consistent airtime, talking about the issues of the day, will help with that. People will really get to know me. What I stand for. I'll be well on my way then.'

It's said in such a tone of assurance that the others are struck dumb. Lauren has a brief image flash of Jude standing outside Number Ten, her perfect grey bob back on point, her red lipstick deployed like warpaint. She shudders a little. Even Nico, never lost for words, clearly can't think of much to say in response. And Mac, Lauren realises, has completely passed out, overcome by the whisky in his hand. Which puts either her or Nate next in the firing line. She steels herself and speaks quickly.

'What about you, Nate? What made you swap your glamorous Hollywood life for this tiny corner of Scotland? Must have been something pretty special to tempt the person who has everything.'

'Oh, it's not that interesting really,' says Nate modestly. 'It's a passion project of mine. I've been trying to get this documentary drama thing off the ground. It's about climate change – yeah, I know, everyone is doing it – but this is going to be different, ground-breaking. I mean, all my Todd Hunter stuff is great and everything, but it's not going to change the world, is it? But the documentary, well, it would be a bit like this show is for me, an opportunity for people to see the real me, get to know what I'm like behind the camera, talk about the things I really care about. But it's been a bit hard to get the green light . . .'

Lauren almost chokes on her drink. As if Nate Stirling would struggle to get the go-ahead for *the* issue of the day. And as for the real Nate, if only people knew. She can just imagine the horrified expressions on her fellow contestants' faces if they'd heard what she had, knew what a piece of shit he really is. If only, *if only* the cameras had been rolling earlier.

She watches as he holds court, riffing on the importance of public consciousness, on the difficulties of steering his ship through the choppy waters of development, on the great people he's working with. The others are grouped around him now, all nodding along in agreement, enraptured by him. She feels furious. Can't they see that he is talking utter rubbish? She takes another angry sip of drink. Fuelled by alcohol and adrenaline, her temper flares dangerously high, and her normal caution evaporates.

She can't stop herself from blurting out, 'Oh, come on, Nate, as if *you*, of all people, would struggle to get the green light for something like that!'

Her interruption comes out louder and more aggressively than she had intended. Everyone turns to stare at her. She can see they are all shocked by the ferocity of her outburst. Even Taisie, who had been resting her head on Hollie's shoulder, is rousing herself. The congenial sparkle that was in Nate's eyes only moments ago is extinguished, replaced by something much darker. He turns slowly towards her.

'Sorry, Lauren. Back up a bit. What do you mean exactly?'

'Well, it's ridiculous, isn't it? You don't need a British television company to sort out a climate change documentary for *you*! You've got plenty of money and plenty of contacts. It's rubbish. Bullshit. I think you're here for another reason entirely.'

Nate's eyes flash angrily, but Lauren holds his gaze. She may not know exactly *why* he's here, but she's willing to bet it's not for some documentary.

Nate takes another deep breath, and this time his voice is threatening.

'Who the hell do you think are you are, to challenge me like that? Are you calling me a liar?'

'Yeah, Lauren, what on earth . . .?' Nico is the first to come to Nate's defence, and he is not alone. Jackson mutters something under his breath, which Lauren doesn't quite catch but sounds like 'Calm down', and Hollie rolls her eyes.

Jude turns and looks pointedly at Lauren.

'Just ignore her, Nate. She's had too much to drink, like most people in here. I, for one, think your project sounds admirable. It's just what we need, someone like you, with your profile, taking the lead on climate change. If I can help in any way I would be delighted to.'

'Thanks, Jude. Back at you.' He seems placated but his eyes are still

161

focused like lasers on Lauren. It's clear to her that he's not going to let what she said go unchallenged. His voice is icy and she realises, unlike her, he appears to be stone-cold sober.

'And what about you, Lauren? You sure seem interested in other people's prizes, but you haven't told us yours. I'd say it's your turn, wouldn't you?'

Everyone murmurs in agreement.

Her heart skips a beat. The silence that follows Nate's question is laced with menace. Even the wind outside has halted its incessant whine. Lauren closes her eyes briefly, taking another large gulp of her drink. She has no choice; she is going to have to fill the void. When she opens them, she sees the others are still staring at her. The circle of expectant faces is wavering slightly, testament to the fact that she has had more than one too many.

'Er . . .' Lauren stalls, playing for time.

'What's the matter, Lauren? Happy to call out my dreams, pour scorn on them, but don't want to share yours?' Nate says, his voice as hard as steel.

The pressure is too much; she has to say something.

'Fine. I've been offered my own show. A series of investigative documentaries in a prime-time slot, once a week.'

She hurries the words out, hoping it's enough to divert their attention from her.

It doesn't work.

'Really?' says Jude. 'Seems strange you would need to come on here to land something like that, with your profile. Although now that I think about it, I haven't seen you on air for months now. What *have* you been up to?' There is more than a hint of challenge in her tone. Clearly, she is very much on Team Nate.

'Well, now, that *is* interesting,' says Nate snidely. 'Come on, Lauren. Do tell.'

All eyes are now on Lauren and, unlike with Nate, no one leaps to her defence. She holds his gaze a moment, trying to see from his expression what he knows. Is he just goading her, or does he know it's him she's been investigating? Her head is spinning slightly, but she has a sudden flash of clarity, of purpose. Whatever he knows or doesn't know, she needs to try to bring him down before he tries to discredit her completely. This is it: she has nothing else to lose. She puts down her drink and steadies herself, looking around at the now-familiar people who feel like a dysfunctional family. A captive audience who, if they believe her, could be powerful enough to take on Nate and his lawyers.

She takes a deep breath.

'I've been investigating a story.'

Chapter Twenty

A hush descends as everyone waits for Lauren to continue. When she doesn't immediately, Nico jumps in.

'What story's that, then?'

'It's about one of us in here.'

She can see the confusion wash over the assembled faces, as well as a flash of alarm on a couple of them.

'Don't worry, Nico. It's not about you. Or Jude, or Jackson, or Mac. And you girls, you have nothing to worry about.' She realises she is stumbling over her words slightly. Oh God, she is more drunk than she thought. She kicks herself for letting her guard down. But it's too late, she can't stop now she's started. Slowing down to focus, she lowers her voice.

'It's about him.' She raises her finger to point to Nate, horrified that her aim is slightly off.

He is as still as a statue. He hasn't taken his focus off her for a second since she first dared to question him. In the flickering candle-light, she sees his eyes narrow. He says nothing, but from the others there is flurry of comments tumbling over each other.

'Seriously? No way! You're investigating *Nate*?'

Nate remains silent, but Lauren addresses her response only to him.

'Yes, Nate. I know what you've done. I know about the women you've used. The women you have abused. The lives you have ruined and the careers you have destroyed. I've been investigating you for years. I have hours of testimony, and I *know* what they say is true.'

When he speaks his voice is more of a growl.

'What. Are. You. Talking. About?'

'You know exactly what I'm talking about. The real Nate Stirling my arse. *I* had first-hand experience of the real Nate Stirling when you lunged at me in your room earlier' – at this Nico gasps theatrically – 'and that's nothing compared with what you've done to countless other women.' Lauren pauses, letting her words land. To her consternation, Nate's expression of fury has been replaced by pity.

'Lauren, honey, c'mon. We both know that's not what happened. I wasn't going to tell anyone but if you're going to stand here spreading lies about me, well . . .' He looks at the others. 'She came on to me earlier, in my room, and got pissed when I said no. Then the siren went off and I was happy to let bygones be bygones . . .'

Lauren feels her face flush with rage.

'You *know* that's not what happened!' she snarls.

'Oh, yeah? You're the one who came to my room, wanting to "talk" alone. The worst thing is, I genuinely believed that's why you were there. I was shaken up, could have used someone to confide in but then . . . well, you know the rest. And I'm sorry, Lauren, I just don't see you that way.'

'Bullshit!' she cries, then turns to the others, imploring them to believe her. 'Yes, I went to his room, but only because I wanted to catch him out, show the world the predator he really is. He made a pass at me then tried to stop me from leaving. I thought the cameras were still on, but . . . he knew they weren't.'

From their perplexed frowns she can see that they don't quite believe her. Nate is too credible an actor and Mac, her only potential ally, is still passed out. It is details she needs, details to persuade them. In her head she rifles through the hours of heart-breaking interviews she has done. Ariadne is the first who comes to mind.

'Do you remember Ariadne, Nate? I am sure you do. She's only nineteen. Eighteen when you met her. She was an extra on your latest *Hunted* movie. A gorgeous, vivacious young girl until you got to her. You tried it on with her, in your trailer, and when she said no you got her sacked, didn't you?'

His response is immediate and deadpan.

'I have never met anyone called Ariadne.'

'Oh, come on, Nate! And she was just one of the most recent. You've been at this for years, using and abusing women since you first started in movies. Remember Lily-Ann? She was just a teenager when she worked with you on, what was it? *The Pearl*?'

For a gut-wrenching second Lauren realises she has forgotten the name of the film that Lily-Ann worked on. The alcohol has befuddled her quick-thinking skills. She blinks quickly and shakes her head to clear her train of thought.

'No, not that one. *The Final Escape*? No wait, you only had a cameo in that one. *Red Jackets*! That's it. You ALL know that one, don't you? Brilliant film, visionary. And Nate, you won an award for it. Best Actor. Lots of people won awards for it, but you made sure she didn't get one. You dumped her once you'd slept with her, then when it got back to you, she'd told someone, you spread such vicious rumours about her she never worked on a film again.'

'Lauren, you need to stop. You're making a fool of yourself. I don't know either of these women.'

His words are so commanding, his tone so serious, and the reaction from everyone else so muted that a small part of Lauren acknowledges this is not working. Her faith in herself falters. She is conscious she is letting herself down, embarrassing herself. But it is worse than that. Much worse. She is letting down all the women she has spoken to. The women who have opened their hearts and souls to tell her their stories, risked everything they have left in their lives by breaking binding non-disclosure agreements and furnishing her with the facts about Nate and what he had done to them. Too scared to go on record, they instead put their fate in her hands, trusted her when she said she'd get justice for them.

What hurts the most is that she is letting Allegra down: failing her most beloved friend. That thought persuades her to carry on. She swore to herself she would never mention Allegra's name, but the journalist in her knows that however painful, however revealing, the personal is always the most powerful. The others may not believe Nate made a move on her, but they will surely see that her grief for her friend is real. At this point, she has no other option: it is the only card she has left to play.

'And then there was my friend. Allegra. You know her. She's a set designer. Brilliant. Brilliant at her job, and this was her first time working in America. She was so excited. It was her dream gig. And it was all going great, until *you* got to her.'

She has to stop for a moment. To catch her breath. She is almost overcome with emotion, remembering how badly her friend has suffered. The image of her lying broken and sobbing on the floor of Lauren's flat, in floods of tears when she eventually divulged the whole story of what Nate had done to her, how appallingly he had treated her, sobers Lauren up a bit. She continues more fluently, with a renewed sense of purpose.

'You got her pregnant. But you wanted nothing to do with the baby, and nothing to do with her. You gave her no option, said you would go after her if she didn't have a termination. Practically forced her into it. Not the first time you've done that either. But then it went wrong, as you well know. Horribly, terribly wrong. She nearly *died*, all alone in a country she didn't know, and you wouldn't even return her calls.'

The memory of Allegra's distress is too much. She can't continue. She stops her tirade, breathing heavily and doing her utmost to hold back tears. She will not cry in front of him. The room is deadly quiet. No one knows what to say or how to react, except Nate. He sits up a little taller, rolls his shoulders, his chest rises as he composes himself. It is like watching a butterfly emerge from a chrysalis, as he transforms his thunderous expression to once of abject sorrow.

'Allegra,' he says softly, vulnerability carefully wrapped around every syllable. 'Yes. I'm ashamed to admit it, but . . .' He pauses and looks around the room.

Lauren's heart stills. Could this be the confession she's been waiting for?

'. . . we were in a relationship. My wife, Jen and I, we're . . . we're actually separated. Have been for a little while.' At this, Nico gasps dramatically. 'It's what we both wanted, and we're still on good terms. I'm sorry I didn't say anything, guys, but we agreed to keep it private for now. And you know how quickly news spreads in Hollywood . . .'

'You have nothing to apologise for,' says Jude fiercely. 'It's your business and yours alone.'

'Thank you,' Nate gives her a weak smile. 'I appreciate that. Anyway, I met Allegra after we split, but I still shouldn't have disrespected Jen like that. But I couldn't help it – I fell for her, hard. And she . . . she broke my heart. Really broke it. I hate to talk about this stuff. It's so raw, and she hurt me so deeply. But yes, Lauren, you're right. We were together. I was in love with her, deeply in love with her. And then she left. Just disappeared back to England. Not a word to me. She wasn't returning my calls, nothing. Eventually, after months of trying, when I finally got hold of her, she told me. Told me that she'd been carrying my baby, and that she'd got rid of it.'

'Oh, my goodness. How awful. I'm so sorry, Nate.' Jude slides over to him and puts an arm over his shoulder. The rest of his audience are mesmerised, transfixed by his words.

He waits a beat. Timing his last comment perfectly for maximum effect.

'I was devastated, utterly devastated. It is what I had always wanted. A child. Jen and I . . . it just never happened for us. This felt like a second chance. Probably my last.'

Lauren is utterly stunned. This is the last thing that she had expected: that he would admit to the affair but then twist its ending so grotesquely. It is masterful – an Oscar-winning performance by an Oscar-winning actor – and she can see by their expressions of sympathy and outrage that, to all the others, it is utterly convincing.

His words transport her back to a summer night when she returned to her flat to find Allegra sitting alone in the dark, staring unseeing at the mobile phone in her hand. 'I called him,' she whispered. 'I know I shouldn't, I know you said not to, but I called him. I just wanted to hear his voice. He told me . . .' She faltered. 'He was so . . . so cold. He just said it straight. Said it might be better if I . . . if I hadn't made it through the operation. He would prefer it, he said, if I was no longer here. I think he might be right, it might be better if I died.'

That was the moment that Lauren resolved to bring down Nate. The moment that had brought her here, to this island. The devastating thought that her best friend should think that her life was no longer worth living because of him.

The gulf between the two stories is insurmountable. White-hot rage surges through Lauren, as she realises she has been outmanoeuvred by a master of manipulation. He doesn't need his lawyers, his layers of protection; he is a consummate performer and a brilliant orator. With that speech he has turned around the narrative, just like he did about Lauren in his room. She can see there is nothing she can say that will change it back, persuade the others that what she has said is the truth. In that moment of realisation, she finally loses control.

'You LIAR, how dare you twist it like that?' Unthinking she starts towards him, not knowing what she is going to do. Jackson instinctively reaches out to her, in a movement intended to restrain, not comfort. But nothing can stop the tide overwhelming her. 'You absolute shit! How *dare* you!' Nobody moves to reassure her or take her side. Every head is turned towards Nate, arms reaching out to him, consoling him.

Jude rounds on Lauren. 'So let me get this straight,' she spits. 'Your friend feeds you a pack of lies about this poor man here and you go on a mission to "expose" him by, what, seducing him on TV? Making up a list of names of his supposed "victims"? I've always respected you as a journalist, Lauren, but you're just as corrupt as the rest of them. And when we get out of here, everyone will know it.'

Lauren has a ghastly sinking feeling as she sees Jude's disbelief reflected on the others' faces. Derailed by emotion and alcohol, she has completely messed this up. All those hours of anguished conversations with the women Nate destroyed have been in vain. Her investigation has come to nothing, and, after this, her career and reputation will be well and truly in the dirt. Meanwhile, Nate stands impregnable. She has used every weapon in her arsenal, including her own best friend's secrets, and has failed to land even the tiniest of blows. How will she ever face her parents, her niece, Allegra, all the other women she has spoken to?

Sick to her stomach, unable to escape into the howling wind outside, she stumbles away, making for the furthest corner of the room.

There, she crouches down and puts her head between her knees to hide her face. On the other side of the room, in front of the warming fire, the others are crowded round Nate. Jackson briefly catches her eye, expressionless, and then looks away. She curls up and turns on her side so the others can't see the tears running down her cheeks. It's over. However long it takes to rescue them, however many more hours they have to spend on this island, makes no difference. For her, whatever happens next doesn't matter. She has utterly failed.

Chapter Twenty-one

For a split second, Lauren can't remember why the air feels loaded with doom, but it only takes her first intake of waking breath for her heart to pitch downwards as she is shattered by an avalanche of mortifying memories. *Flash.* Her pointing finger, waveringly on Nate. *Flash. Flash.* The circle of uncomprehending eyes, lowering to look at the floor as she speaks. *Flash.* Her voice raised, incoherent with rage.

She can hear sounds – someone else is awake – but she is reluctant to open her eyes. She lies as still as she can, wishing for obliteration, but it doesn't come. Knowing that more sleep is out of the question, she is torn between a desperation to escape the room and the knowledge that any movement is going to bring a fresh raft of humiliation. Already she is having trouble fighting a rising tide of nausea. Her eyes are sticky, and half glued together, her tongue so dry it feels alien in her sandpaper mouth. A beat of pain reverberates every time her heart pulses. But none of it is as bad as the crawling awareness of what happened last night.

Eventually she can bear the rising tide of panic no longer and half-opens her eyes so she can see what is going on. Under the cover of her lashes, she can make out Taisie, Hollie and Nico sharing a makeshift bed on the other side of the room, limbs thrown across each other. Nico has one of the jester's capes pulled over his eyes to keep out the light and Taisie is using the other as a pillow. Both girls must have changed back into their habits sometime after Lauren hid herself in the corner. They are as dead to the world as teenagers after a night out. None of them is going to stir for a while.

She braves the pain to turn her head a little further. Jackson is lying on his own, balanced like a broken bird on the narrow wooden bench, the grooves of his shoulder blades anchoring him on to it. He is snoring soundly on his back, feet placed either side firmly on the ground to keep himself balanced. A bottle of red wine is still held in one outstretched hand, its spilled contents pooling like blood beside him.

The sounds of movement she can hear are coming from Mac. She can see his back, hunched over the fire, fiddling with the grate, and blowing in frustration on the ashes. It must have gone out some hours ago, and there is not even a single log left from the giant stack that was piled high before the storm.

The great hall is in utter chaos, a scene of a bacchanalian riot. There is not a tumbler or vessel that is upright. Dirty plates smeared with congealed food are upturned on every surface. A knife stands vertical, stabbed into a wooden chopping board. The candles are burned down to their wicks, wax has dripped off the side of the table, forming stalagmites on the floor. Smashed glass is littered like jewels.

There's no sign of either Nate or Jude, nor any empty mattresses, and the heavy oak doors are ajar. Lauren assumes that they must have slipped back illegally to the comfort of their own beds in the night, despite the Voice instructing them all to stay in the great hall. That is a relief, given that she wants to avoid any sight of Nate for as long as possible. What she needs is water and fresh air. Immediately. She staggers upright, trying to ignore the onrush of nausea, and heads for the door. She doesn't care that they have been told not to leave the great hall. She needs to be outside.

The wind hasn't fully abated, but she is at least able to stand now, buffeted by the erratic gusts. More devastation greets her. It looks as though a vengeful giant has been on a rampage, hurling around the monastery's ancient masonry. There are gaping holes in the sloping slate roofs, like missing teeth punched out. She sees that one of the colossal yew trees that guard the entrance to the graveyard has been pulled in two, its red bark indecently ripped apart, sap coagulating from its open wounds. It has crashed through the stone walls of the north-east corner, tearing a hole in the enclosure and exposing the view.

Lauren can see for miles, across a raging sea where furious white horses gallop towards the island. Clearly it is still in the grip of the storm, and the clouds to the north-west are ominously dark, signalling the weather is going to get worse again. It exacerbates her feeling of dread. With the sea raging like that, no one is going to be able to come for them. They are utterly alone.

There is no water in the jugs by the sinks so, stepping over the detritus, she makes her way over to the well to assess the damage there. The pitched housing that protected the water has been destroyed, lying in ragged pieces on the grass. The wooden posts that held up the axel and winch handle so they could lower the bucket to draw water have cracked into splinters. As for the bucket itself, it is nowhere to be seen. She presumes it must be lost to the depths. What are they going to drink? Her own thirst has become a pressing problem, and there is nothing for it but to go back inside and face the others.

She stops for a moment to focus. Then she takes a deep breath and walks in. It is worse than she had feared. Not only are the sleepers now awake, up and sitting along the benches of the long table, but Nate is among them, not at the head this time, but at the dead centre of the bench, Jude on one side, Nico on the other. He looks up as she walks in, fixing her with a stare as she breathes out shakily. Despite everything that has happened, he looks no worse for wear. He is a little more dishevelled, has more than a five o'clock shadow, but even Lauren has to admit that adversity suits him. He looks like the hero triumphing in the final minutes of a movie, bruised but victorious.

It's clear from the hush that descends that she has been the main topic of conversation. Her legs shake under the weight of the silence, and the distance from the door to the table seems to lengthen in front of her: a true walk of shame. She steps forward like an unwilling sup-plicant, her normally quick brain deserting her. No words come to break this awful moment.

Nate waits until she is a couple of feet away from the table before he finally speaks. 'Lauren,' he says, then allows a pause to develop. 'OK,' he says, on an outward sigh, signifying an elaborate, wounded patience. 'I've thought about what you said all night, and I can't let this stand. Those lies you told, here, in front of everyone, they could be seriously damaging. It's slander. I can't fathom what made you say what you did. Maybe you really thought you were helping your friend Allegra, who is clearly very disturbed. But what I am certain of is that I am deeply, deeply hurt.'

The others, clustered around him like acolytes, nod in sympathy. Jude is actually stroking his forearm. It is only Mac who ignores him, shoulders bunched, head down.

'What I need you to do, so I can move forward, so we all can, is to apologise. Admit that you were wrong.' His voice is purposely meas-ured, he is making it sound gentle, but from the way his eyes bore into her she knows what he is saying is a threat.

He leaves it a beat for her to say something and, when she doesn't, carries on with added menace, 'I can see you don't want to apologise now. So, I will give you time. But I can't let this go. Before we leave this island, you need to take back your words and consider carefully how you will make amends.'

Lauren still doesn't respond, and Nate smiles malevolently as he carries on, 'Turns out it is your lucky day, from what I can see, it looks like Production are making the most of the storm, taking a while to get here, so you have time on your hands. Take my advice and use it wisely.'

And with that he stands back from the table and sweeps out of the great hall. Lauren hears his footsteps heading for the Abbot's quarters. Jude is hot on his heels, her shorter steps pitter-pattering after him in the stone corridor.

There is a painful pause after he leaves, nobody willing to look Lauren in the eye. Mac is the only one who talks directly to her and, when he does, he doesn't address what has just happened.

'Food?' he asks in a grunt.

Lauren can't contemplate food yet but silently points to the coffee, grateful to be able to sink her face into the rough metal beaker.

Chapter Twenty-two

The next hours pass inexorably slowly and Lauren is tormented by her thoughts. Ignoring the Voice's final instructions, people come and go, braving the outside, only to return soaked and windswept.

A foray to the Sinners' dormitory reveals it to be uninhabitable – so much rain has come in through the unprotected windows that the floor is an inch deep in water. The Saints' dorm isn't much better: a stray branch has smashed through one of the panes. Everything inside is sodden. The only places that are dry and warm are the great hall or Nate's chambers, and there is no way she is ever going to step in there again.

It's Jackson who starts tidying up the evidence of last night's feast, joined after a while by Nico and then Hollie and Taisie. Lauren knows she should muck in, to show penance, but she feels incapable both in body and mind. She is relieved when her half-hearted offer to help is rebuffed. Apart from that, nobody really speaks to her. Mac is also slumped in isolation, poking the fire from time to time.

Lauren finds a mattress and closes her eyes. She hears Jude come back in after a while, apparently setting to with a brush and attacking the floor with vigorous, angry-sounding strokes and grumbling about why it is taking Production so long come to their rescue. Then there is the sound of Nico and the girls putting together some make-shift lunch out of leftovers. The others sit down together. Lauren waits till they have finished and dispersed, then cuts herself a slice of stale bread.

It is only once she has eaten that Lauren feels fortified enough to try to speak.

'You all right?' she says to Mac.

He grunts in reply, then takes a deep breath. 'Ach, I guess so. Just . . . well, heavy night, eh?'

Lauren nods, unsure how much he even knows about her own dis-grace. But it appears he does.

'Heard you put him in his place,' he says. 'Or tried to, at any rate. They're all a bit shook up by it. Me? I couldn't give a stuff. Not his greatest fan, to say the least.'

Lauren can see this is an opening and knows she should ask Mac what's bothering him, but she just can't summon the right words. She looks outside.

'It looks like the rain has stopped for a bit,' she says. 'I'm going to try and get some fresh air.'

Mac raises a hand, seemingly quite relieved not to be interrogated at this time, and Lauren steps outside. In the centre of the courtyard, she can see Jackson clearing away the broken housing of the well. Beyond him, Nico, Taisie and Hollie are giggling by the lavatorium. Their heads are close together and Nico is smirking, leaning in as though sharing some gossip. She wonders what the odds are that she is the main source of it.

She crosses past the broken yew tree into the graveyard, where Jude is wandering, lost in thought among the gravestones. Wherever Lauren looks, there seems to be another person she would prefer not to speak to, though to her huge relief there is no sign of Nate. Putting her head down, she heads through the kissing gate away from the monastery. Without consciously seeking it out, her feet find a lightly worn coastal path. She can imagine the monks that lived here centuries ago treading the same route, seeking solace, locked in prayer. She tries to take inspiration from them and settle her mind, concentrating only on the rhythm of her feet through the soaking heather, trying to stop the dark thoughts from seeping in.

But her mind won't stop desperately, fruitlessly, rehearsing the opening lines she might use on Nate later. For a start, she has decided, she is definitely not going to comply with his demand to apologise. Not today, not ever.

She knows he is trying to trap her into an admission that her accusations were lies. The minute he has that, then he can go after her with all the legal might he can bring. She has accused him, in front of witnesses, of career-derailing acts. She has failed to back them up. If she admits any fault on her side, the consequences will be dire for her, and his victims. The only thing she can hope for is that he will do all he can to avoid any public denunciation. But what pressures will he use to muzzle her now? She shivers at the thought.

If only they could get off this island. Then she could get some advice, get some help. She scans the sea, hoping that the horizon might be clearing, but as the path reaches the cliff edge, she realises that the wind is picking up again, too strong for her to be up there safely, and an ominous curtain of dark rain is heading in from the Atlantic. She turns back and, as she does so, hears the high, tinny clanging of the small cloister bell.

She braces herself as she enters the hall, then a wash of relief runs through her as she sees he is not there. A reprieve.

'Thought I'd better ring the bell and get everyone back here,' Jackson is saying to Jude and Nico. 'Looks like the storm is coming back pretty quickly. It's going to be dark soon, and I don't think it's safe to be out there anymore. We'd better stick together and stay inside again from now on.'

Mac comes in behind them, carrying jars full of water in his huge hands. It seems that Jackson has succeeded in fixing the well. At the other end of the hall, Nico and Hollie are coming up from the store-room stairs, carrying more supplies, and an instant later Taisie rushes in from outside, slightly out of breath.

'What's going on?' she says, alarmed. 'Why's the bell ringing?'

'Just wanted everyone back here,' repeats Jackson. 'For safety, you know.'

Nico looks around. 'Where's Nate?' he asks. 'I was with him in the Abbot's quarters earlier, but I just came past there and it's empty. Jude, do you know where he is?'

'No, why would I?' she says sharply. Lauren catches Nico and the girls exchanging amused looks, and sees Hollie turn her head away and smile at Taisie, who responds with an almost imperceptible raise of her eyebrow. Lauren catches the shared moment and is annoyed with herself. She's been so focused on Nate that her instincts have been off, and she's missed something.

'Anyone else seen him?' asks Nico.

Everyone else mumbles a negative, including Lauren. It seems Nate hasn't been in the great hall since this morning.

'Think I saw him come into the courtyard after lunch, when I was fixing the well,' says Jackson, 'But not since then. Anyway, not sure it was him. Bit hard to tell who's who when everyone has their hoods up.'

At least another ten long minutes go by, and there is still no sign of Nate.

Nico begins to look concerned. 'It's kind of weird, isn't it? Where could he be? I mean, I'm sure he's fine, but what if he's tripped or something, hurt himself? Could he be trapped somewhere? I think we should maybe go look for him?'

Jackson nods. 'Yeah, I reckon you're right. But we have to be careful; it's almost dark out now. Tell you what, why don't we each take a different direction, look for him for ten minutes, then meet back here? I'll ring the bell.' The others murmur in agreement, glad someone else is taking charge. 'We don't all need to go. Taisie and Hollie, could you guys stay here and get some food on the go?'

Lauren is sure she sees a flash of irritation in Hollie's eyes at being relegated to the kitchen again. She'd be frustrated too, if everyone kept underestimating her. Still, both Hollie and Taisie nod their assent.

'Mac, how about you go out towards the woods, and I'll head down to the jetty?' Jackson continues. 'Jude, you look inside the buildings and, Nico, maybe head towards the cellars and check the stairs to the cave? Lauren . . .' here he stumbles a bit, no doubt remembering the last encounter between Lauren and Nate, 'just check outside a bit, could you?'

They disperse, but only Jackson seems intent on the task, leaving the great hall with purposeful steps.

Watching Jude move reluctantly away from the warmth of the fireplace, Nico giggles and raises an eyebrow at Hollie. 'Don't think *she* really wants to find him, does she?'

Hollie shushes him with a grin, turning her attention to Taisie, who is gathering the cooking utensils. Soon the two of them have their heads together over the fireplace, whispering urgently.

Nico waves at Lauren as he heads towards the storeroom stairs. 'Don't think *you* want to find him much either, do you, babe?'

She doesn't deign to reply.

Lauren feels lightheaded as she heads across towards the gatehouse, unsurprised to find it empty. This wild-goose chase feels like another moment of respite. The doom that has enveloped her all day is lifting; the others seem to be softening towards her. The bigger consequences of her tirade, well, she won't think about that again until they are off the island.

For now, she is just anxious that it shouldn't be her that finds Nate. Wherever he is, let one of the others find him first. The last thing she needs is a twilight showdown in the midst of an approaching storm. She will do a quick circuit of the graveyard, perhaps a glimpse into the tower and the belfry, and then she will head back to what, after even a few days spent on this desolate island, she has to admit feels a bit like home.

In the fading light, as she picks her way through the sculpted outlines of the gravestones the unwanted images of the ancient inhabitants beneath her feet make her shiver, and she flinches at the haunting shriek of a gull in the distance. She is not normally one to get spooked, but the last few days and the extraordinary sequence of events have rattled her. What will happen if she finds Nate and they are alone again? She has a word with herself. 'It's fine, I'll be fine. There's no way he'll be here. I just need to be able to say I looked.'

Her route takes her to the belfry next. Conscious of the gaze of the gargoyles perched menacingly on each corner, she notices that the ancient oak door, the only entrance, is very slightly ajar. Jackson must have left it open when he had been searching in vain for Frank. She is reluctant to go in and part of her wonders if she should just say she checked, but she doesn't want to lie. When she pushes against the door, at first it doesn't budge, and she's not quite small enough to squeeze through the gap, so she braces herself and shoves her shoulder against it. With some effort, it gives way, just enough to let her in.

Inside, it is much darker. Only small shafts of oyster-grey light filter through the narrow windows in the thick stone walls. Once her eyes adjust, she can make out a set of cantilevered stone stairs winding once, twice, three times around the edges of the walls, leading to a wooden platform suspended about forty feet above her. It must be the mezzanine where she landed during the Leap of Faith.

She calls out into the space above her. 'Hello? Is anyone in here?'

The only sound that comes back to her is the echo of her own voice.

That must be how Frank got out of here, she thinks as she gingerly puts her foot on the first step and presses her hand against the rough wall so she can feel her way upwards. In the gathering gloom she can only just make out where she is going. She wishes that she had her phone with its torch to help show the way.

This is ridiculous, she thinks. Why on earth would Nate have come in here? It's freezing, and he would have no reason to. With that thought in mind, motivated more by her curiosity about how Frank disappeared than any hope of finding Nate, she persuades herself to stop being such a wuss and to keep moving upwards.

As she climbs, breathing in the pungent mix of damp and dust, she shouts up again, 'Hello? Anyone there?' The only sound in return is her muffled footsteps and her ragged breath. She is aware that what she is doing is dangerous. How precarious the stairs feel beneath her ill-fitting slippers.

She takes a few seconds on each corner to gather her courage and it feels like an age passes before she finally reaches the mezzanine, where she stops to calm her nerves. Inhaling deeply, she glances back to where she has come from, towards the fading light at the open door. She stops dead in her tracks. She gasps and puts her hand to her mouth. There is something wedged behind it.

'Help, HELP!' she screams at the top of her voice. 'Someone help, *please*!'

It takes her a second to realise her screams are futile; no one is going to hear her entombed in the thick stone walls. With no thought for her own safety, Lauren flies down the stairs, taking three at a time, trying to make sense of what she can see: a crumpled heap of dark brown fabric, feet protruding from the bottom of a hem, limbs splayed out at wrong angles.

It is not *something* lying behind the door, it is *someone*. And from where she is she can't see who. She screams again.

'Is that you, Nate? Frank, *Frank*? Please MOVE.'

There is no answer. No movement. Just a deathly stillness.

She skids to a halt beside the body. Whoever it is, they are lying on their back with their cowl covering their face. She falls on to her knees, scrabbles at the rough cloth to rouse them, to try to find a hand, to find a pulse. She recoils when she touches them and feels how cold their flesh is compared to hers. Desperate for signs of life, she places her hand on their chest to feel for a reassuring rise and fall. But there is no answering movement.

'No no no no . . .' She is already crying as she pulls back the cowl to reveal the face, and then she is screaming louder, her ears full of a piercing noise that she barely registers is coming from her. Her eyes are squeezed shut, to block out the horrifying sight in front of her. It is Nate, and he is unmistakably dead.

Chapter Twenty-three

She will never be sure how long she kneels beside him, holding his lifeless hand in hers, only that her throat is raw and every muscle in her body rigid with tension before she hears footsteps running up the path.

Before she knows it, she is enveloped in Mac's arms, and he is saying over and over again, 'Hush, Lauren, shhhh. Lauren, it's OK, it's OK . . .'

It is only then that she is able to open her eyes, to look up at him imploringly, hoping what she has seen is not real, that this is not happening. But he is staring in horror at what lies before them: a body bent and broken at the bottom of the belfry steps.

Slowly, he lets her go and kneels, placing a hand on Nate's neck, feeling for a pulse. Shaking his head, he lowers his ear close to Nate's mouth. His ashen face confirms what she already knows.

'But he— How did you . . .? What happened?' he asks.

Silent now, screams extinguished, Lauren's teeth are chattering too much for her to form a coherent answer. 'I – I . . . the door was open, so I thought, thought I should check in here. Oh God. Oh my God. I didn't see him, didn't see where he was until I was up the stairs, and I turned round, and then I saw . . . then . . . I found . . . found him,' she stutters, until Mac pushes himself up to standing and once again braces his arms around her.

'Hush,' he says again, and for a second, she feels her muscles relax, before they judder again in cold and shock. She is trembling so much that even Mac's arms can barely contain her. They hear the creak of the graveyard gate and then, seconds later, Hollie and Taisie arrive, skittering in close formation beside Nico.

'What's going on? We heard someone yelling,' Nico is asking as they burst in. 'Was that you, Lauren? What are you—' His words come to an abrupt halt as Mac points downwards. 'What the hell? Is that . . . is that . . . *Nate?*' His voice is high and rises to a shriek on the last word. He steps backwards, raising his arms from his sides to shield the girls from the sight. But he is too late. They are already wailing.

'Oh my God, is that . . .' '. . . Nate?' 'Oh my God, oh my God. What happened?' 'Did he fall?' they howl in unison, indecipherable from one another.

More footsteps, at first sedate and then faster as whoever it is approaches the open door and in steps Jude. There is a sharp intake of breath, and then a sharper volley of questions as she goes down on her knees in front of the body, rubbing Nate's hands between her own.

'What are you all *doing*? Come on, people! Why are you just standing there? Why is no one helping him? *Come on.* We need to – you need to . . .' She leans into Nate's face, ear to his mouth, listening for breathing.

'It's no use, hen,' Mac says. 'He's gone. I'm sorry. I checked. He's not breathing, he has no pulse. Lauren did too. There's nothing we can do.'

But Jude is determined, locking her arms in front of her and pressing on Nate's chest, her mouth set in a grimace.

'Jude,' repeats Mac softly. 'Jude. You need to stop. He's gone. Nate's gone.' And then, as the rhythms of Jude's counting become faster and more panicked, he speaks more loudly. 'Jude. He's dead. Please stop.'

Only then does Jude look up, wide eyed and staring. 'But he can't be,' she says. 'He can't be dead. How could it . . . how could that happen?'

Something in her words snap them all out of their trance-like state, and they look around at each other wildly, then up into the darkness above them. There is nothing to see, beyond the flight of the first stair and the blackness beyond.

More quick footsteps, then Jackson is there, holding a lantern that throws the scene into sharp relief. Where before there had been a cloak of darkness to mute the reality, now Lauren can see the body clearly. In the flickering light she sees that Nate has one arm twisted under him, the other braced across his chest, hand spread against the cloth of his habit. His legs are splayed awkwardly, his long robe pulled above his ankles, halfway up his shins. Somehow, he still has one slipper on, but the other has fallen off and his foot is clothed only in a woollen sock. It looks oddly vulnerable. But worst of all is his head, twisted back at a violent angle, his neck bent. There is no blood, but there is no doubt that all breath has left his body. Even in the low light there is a grey-blue tinge to his skin, and his eyes are wide and staring.

Jackson takes in the scene. 'What the fuck?' he says, the light swaying as he nearly drops the lantern. 'This can't be real.'

Mac takes the lead. 'It looks like he's fallen,' he says. 'I'm afraid he's dead, probably has been for a while. He's stone cold.'

The strange words ring out into silence, and then Hollie breaks down.

'Nooooooo,' she wails. 'No! No, he can't be. Not dead . . . You must be able to do something, please, Mac? Please . . .?' Her voice trails off into unintelligible sobs. Taisie hugs her as tightly as she can. Her eyes are dilated, and she is shaking, clearly in shock.

Nico stands beside them, motionless, his eyes fixed uncomprehendingly on Nate's body. Jude is still on her knees, her head bowed over Nate as if in benediction, her face frozen, anguish etched deep. Mac and Jackson stand reverently at his head and feet.

In the lamplight, the strange tableau looks like a scene from a nightmare. A suffocating blanket of paralysis seems to have dropped over each one of them, robbing them of the ability to move or speak, as if by moving, they will make it real. The silence is broken only by the sound of Hollie's increasingly hysterical sobs and the wind outside beginning once again to whine.

Eventually Mac shifts, bending down to gently lift Jude off the frozen stone slabs. As he does so, she leans against him, and it is that small gesture, the sagging surrender from the always upright and redoubtable Jude, that brings home to Lauren the magnitude of what has occurred. A Hollywood star has died in the midst of a violent storm during a reality TV show and the seven of them are, for now, the only witnesses. Not friends, not family, not loved ones, not the people who make up the landscape of Nate's life. Just this ragtag group, in this strange artificial reality: the people who happened to share Nate's last days. It is utterly horrific.

Lauren's mind refuses to comprehend it. She hated him, what he'd done, and after last night she started to fear him too, but there is no feeling of relief, no hint of retribution. The finality of it is unfathomable; now there is no way of Nate repenting or making amends. No vindication, no next chapter. She wanted justice, wanted him punished, but not like this.

There is a rustle of movement. Mac is handing Jude over to Nico, who guides her towards Hollie and Taisie. And then, wordlessly, Mac and Jackson nod to each other.

'We have to bring him back,' says Mac quietly. 'Nico and Lauren, I'm afraid we may need your help. Jude, can you take the girls back ahead of us? It may not be pretty.'

Jude stiffens and, still in silence, takes Jackson's lantern, shepherding the whimpering girls outside. Jackson and Mac lean down at each end of his body, Mac cradling Nate's shoulders and his lolling head, Jackson at his feet. It is unwieldy, and they stagger under the weight of him as they lift him through the door. Once on the pathway, Nico and Lauren take an arm each, doing what they can to ease the burden.

As the macabre procession makes its way, Lauren fixes her eyes on the bobbing light ahead, desperate not to think about the arm she is holding, or the unnatural coldness that seems to seep through Nate's robes.

She can hear Hollie and Taisie moaning as they make their way in slow motion through the graveyard. Gusts chase them as they are swallowed by the dark stains of the yew trees, and around the corner into the shelter of the cloisters. How much further? Lauren's arms are burning, and she can hear the effort in Mac's breathing, but it feels wrong to put Nate down, even for a moment, so wordlessly they brace themselves and set their footsteps in time, marching in silence down the cloisters, as perhaps the monks did with their dead long ago.

Determined to carry him with respect, they reach the courtyard without stopping and mount the steps towards the Abbot's quarters. As they reach the doorway, the others part before them into an impromptu guard of honour. A vision floats into Lauren's mind: Nate as he was only days ago, taking possession of this room, the purple ring flashing on his hand, the Abbot's rulebook held aloft in delight as he threw back his head and laughed. And now he is coming back to his bedroom for the last time, with only the sighing of the wind outside as a lament.

As carefully as they can, they lie Nate on the high wooden bed, and

Lauren and Nico fold his arms across his chest. Mac reaches out to close his eyes while Jackson covers him with the rich eiderdown, they had all so jealously coveted. The others file in quietly behind them, bowing their heads, the lamp casting shadows on the wall and bathing Nate's face once more in golden light, a last glimpse of his former charismatic self. Is it one minute or ten they stand there? Still, no one can think of what to say to break the silence, until there is a muffled moan from Hollie, and she flees the room, Taisie following hard on her heels.

Taking it as a sign, the others turn back to the body once more, bow their heads instinctively, and then file out one by one, first Nico, then Jackson, then Lauren, then Mac. And, finally, Jude, who turns and pauses on the threshold for one last look, before quietly closing the door behind them.

Without conscious decision, they follow the girls back into the hall, and sink on to the benches next to them. It is as though they have been robbed of all thought, all ability to do anything practical. The only light is a dull red glow from the dying fire. It casts malevolent shadows, like living spectres mimicking their every move.

Lauren feels shaken to her very bones, and almost everyone is shivering. But nobody moves to add logs to the hearth, or to get food. The girls, who would normally be bustling round the fireplace, are instead hunched up together at the end of the bench, not entwined in their usual embrace but so sunk in individual misery that they have wrapped their arms around themselves. Every single one of them has taken up a similar pose, searching for some scrap of comfort in themselves. But no comfort comes.

Chapter Twenty-four

'I want to go home. I want to go home. I *want* to go *home*.'

It is Hollie who breaks the excruciating silence.

Her words are almost unintelligible, each phrase forced out on a sobbing wail. Her hands are covering her face and she is repeating the same thing over and over into her palms. Taisie presses up against her, arm around her shoulders, but is unable to stop the shudders racking her friend's body. Nico does the same from her other side. Despite their efforts to comfort her, she doesn't stop trembling.

Taisie looks up. 'She's right. We have to get away from this place. Wh-what are we going to do? When are we going to be rescued? Nobody else *knows*.' Her voice breaks on the last word, and she buries her face in Hollie's shoulder.

At first, no one answers. The girls have put into words what they've all been thinking. How are they going to escape this nightmare? From the sound of the rising whine of the wind outside, and the creak and crack of old timber under strain, the brief lull in the weather is well and truly over: the storm is back with a vengeance.

Mac is peering out of one of the tall windows, eyes scrunched up, hands against the frame. 'One hundred per cent they are not getting to us tonight, maybe not even tomorrow. It's pitch black and that wind is ferocious. Any boat would be a deathtrap. I've seen some storms in my lifetime, but never known anything as bad as this one. You've seen the damage it's done here. I can only imagine it's worse on the mainland. I imagine the power is down, which will mean communications are down too.'

'He's right, no chance they're coming for us.' Jackson has joined Mac by the window, which is rattling ominously against its rusty frame and looks as if it might give way.

'I think we'd better stay back from the glass,' Mac warns.

'Maybe we should see if we can put something up against it, to protect us, stop it caving in?' Lauren says in barely more than whisper, her throat sore from screaming.

'Good idea. Give us a hand, Mac.' Jackson starts dragging a bench towards the windowsill. As he does so, Lauren speaks again, desperate to focus on something rational, anything to distract herself from the horrifying memory of Nate's body imprinted on her brain.

'They don't know what we know, so if you think about it from their point of view, they think we're safe here. What did the Voice say: that the monastery has been here for hundreds of years? Kind of makes sense to leave us here until it calms down out there. They know we have enough food for days.'

'But we're not safe, are we?' Jude interjects. 'One of us is dead! We are cut off from everyone, all on our own in a record-breaking storm. We've been in danger since we got here. Look what has happened since then. Remember the portcullis? That nearly killed Nate days ago.'

'Jude, hen, that was an accident.'

'But an accident waiting to happen! Nico could have died too, if Lauren hadn't spotted his harness wasn't secure. He could have ended up like Nate! Dead! Smashed to pieces!'

'She's right. You are *so* right, Jude. I could have died!' Nico voice is almost as shrill as Jude's.

'That's my point. Someone should have been here looking after us. We are not safe, and we never have been. I have said so all along. Production put us all in danger right from the start. Remember Kez? They didn't give her the things she needed most. It was inhumane. And how about your back, Mac? You should never have had to do that idiotic Leap of Faith, sleep in those ridiculous beds. It's been all wrong from the moment we stepped on to this island, and I think this is what they wanted to happen. Someone wanted one of us to *die* out here.'

In response to Jude's tirade, Hollie's wailing reaches a crescendo. She is hysterical now.

'This can't be happening. What if we all die here?'

In a quiet voice, Taisie tries to reassure her that they will be OK.

Lauren steps in. 'What happened to Nate is horrific. And I agree it's all felt unsafe. But they would never have wanted anyone to get hurt, to *die*.'

'How do you know?' Nico challenges her.

'Because it's a reality TV show, entertainment! Not an episode of *Black Mirror*. I know we're in an extreme situation, but no one is out to murder us.'

'How can we even be sure that we're on the island alone? Maybe someone is here with us. Lured him out there. Did something to him?' Jude is spiralling. 'Do we even know where Frank is? Is he here? Is he safe?'

'If only we'd followed their instructions,' says Hollie, struggling to get her words out again. 'They . . . they said . . . told us not to go out in the storm. They said it was dangerous. And they were right. We should have stayed inside, stuck together. Not gone wandering all over the place. If we'd just been together . . .'

'What the hell was he thinking anyway, climbing up towers in the middle of a storm?' Jude carries on, ignoring Hollie. 'Why would he go there on his own?'

'Guess you'd know. Better than we would,' says Nico. Lauren senses a note of spite in his tone as he turns his gaze towards Jude. She watches as Jude compresses her lips, clearly biting back a retort.

Beyond the obvious – Nate's death – there is clearly something else going on here, something that is being left unsaid.

'M-m-maybe he just wanted some space,' says Hollie between sobs.

'I guess he thought it was a good place to be alone for a bit. After . . . well, you know . . . last night . . . what was said.' Taisie picks up where Hollie left off.

Everyone's eyes flick towards Lauren.

'But why *there*? That place is creepy at the best of times, and Nate had his own bedroom. He was quite happy to hang out there when he wanted to be alone,' Nico says.

There are murmurings from everyone apart from Mac, who steps in to break up the conversation.

'Look, this isn't going to get us anywhere. The fact is, we don't know why he went there or what he was doing. He is the only one who does. Speculation won't help. What we need to do now is stay safe and get some sleep. I strongly suggest no one leaves this room. Tomorrow, we'll make a plan of how to get out of here.'

Jackson, who for the last few minutes has been holding his head in his hands, looks up, encouraged by Mac's suggestion of some sort of plan of action. 'I agree with Mac. If they aren't here by morning, we need to send out an SOS or something. A signal. I'll find a way to do that if anyone wants to help.'

No one volunteers, but Mac and Jackson's words bring their speculating to a close. Too exhausted to talk any more, one by one they climb into their makeshift beds. Lauren takes the furthest spot, in what feels like the relative safety of a corner, and lies down. Finally able to be still, she can't stop her mind from whirling, can't stop thinking about the moment she found Nate's body. And the fact that he is lying in the room next to them, cold and lifeless in the Abbot's bed.

Her mind keeps going back to what Nico said: 'Why *there*?' Why there indeed? Despite her better judgement, there is a kernel of guilt seeding itself in her gut. Had she driven Nate to do something drastic? It seems completely implausible, and yet . . .

She can't stop imagining the possible sequence of events. Nate, humiliated and furious, drawn to the solitude of the belfry. Trying to find a spot to compose himself, replay her accusations. Climbing those stairs in the fading light, standing on to the edge of the platform, and then . . . and then what? Surely, he wouldn't jump . . . would he?

She stops herself there. No. No way would he do that. Every single part of such a scenario rings false to her. In every conversation she has ever had about him, with the dozens of women whose lives he ruined, never once had he shown any regret. Contrition is not part of his DNA. Nor would he have feared the consequences of her outburst. He knew all too well that he had the upper hand.

No. Nate wasn't full of remorse or fear, he was full of revenge. She pictures him as he was the last time she saw him, confident that he could control her like he had everyone else, force her to take it all back. If anything, he seemed gleeful, far from a man intent on harming himself. This is not her fault.

So, what happened? How did he fall? Why was he there?

And as much as she doesn't want to give in to the hysteria – Jude's wild accusations that Production has it in for them – she can't stop the thought that comes next.

What if he wasn't on his own? Could someone have been with him? And, if so, who?

Chapter Twenty-five

'Is there any hope at all that any of the comms might work again?'

'I seriously doubt it. You saw the tower go down – we all did. But we can take a look later, when it's safe.'

Lauren must have dozed off during the dark hours and wakes to hear Mac trying to placate Jude. The weak light tells her it is still before dawn, but they are all awake and restless. No one knows what to do with themselves. The girls have made a paltry breakfast, but their enthusiasm has been extinguished. They are just going through the motions, not even speaking to each other, let alone anyone else.

'How much longer can this go on? It is beyond a joke. How can they not have left us any way to communicate in emergencies? Is there really nothing? Have we double-checked?' Jude is relentless.

'Look, I know as little as you do,' says Mac, patience wearing thin. 'We just have to hope they can get here today. But it's still hellish out there, can't you hear it?'

After a while, Jackson pipes up, 'We've got to do something. Try and communicate with the outside world. I could light a bonfire on the landing beach. Where they burned our stuff that first day. Like an emergency signal?'

This only seems to add to Jude's irritation. 'What good is that going to do? They know we're here. It's not exactly a secret. Even if you did manage to get a fire going in the driving rain, are they going to decode a plume of smoke and realise it means "Help! Come and get us! We've got a dead film star on our hands!"?' Her voice is shrill.

For a moment nobody speaks, and the usually unflappable Jackson looks chastened. Mac steps in, trying to bring the temperature back down a notch or two.

'Look,' he says, 'let's focus on getting through today and keeping ourselves safe. But we can't just sit here. We'll drive ourselves mad. So, what do we need to do? We're OK for wood for now. But we need more water . . . Hollie, Taisie, could you and Nico sort out the plates and jugs and things, and also go down to the stores to get more food? Lauren, maybe you could help me with the water? We need as much as we can carry, and it'll take a couple of trips. Jude, you get the fire going – it's freezing in here. And, Jackson, why don't you check if we can even get down to the beach?'

Nico stands up from the table, jittery. 'OK, girls, come with me. Let's go to the stores first. See what we can find.'

Contrary to Hollie's hysteria last night, both she and Taisie are now circumspect and withdrawn. Neither has said a thing.

Taisie looks doubtfully at Hollie for a moment, as if wondering if she's up to helping. When she doesn't move, Taisie tugs gently like a child at her sleeve and they set off slowly towards the stairs that lead to the storeroom. Jude starts to bustle about the fire, clearly pleased to have something to do, while Mac and Lauren pull their hoods over their heads, pick up the pitchers stacked near the great hall doors, and prepare to step out into the storm.

Something is hovering on the edge of Lauren's consciousness. She feels an echo of the tingle she always feels when there is a story to be investigated – something awry, something very slightly strange about some of the reactions round the table. She can't get a handle on it, but she feels it like grit in a shoe. She admonishes herself. Of course something feels wrong. Nate has died and there's no reaction that could ever feel normal in this situation.

Lauren gasps as the rain hits her full in the face. It is almost horizontal, and so strong that the force of it billows her robes. She struggles the twenty yards or so towards the well, crouching to get shelter as Mac hooks a rope to the handle of the bucket and lowers it down. Once they have filled it, she grabs the end of the rope to help with the weight, and together they haul it up.

Back in the Hall, they find that Jackson has got the bit between his teeth about his bonfire idea and is trying to work out what he could use as fuel. He presses Mac to go outside again and help him gather heather and gorse, in spite of Mac's protestations that it will be too wet to burn. Eventually, realising that Jackson needs to be doing something practical, Mac gives in, throwing a look towards Lauren to apologise for leaving her. She waves him goodbye, finding a spot at the far end of the hall away from the fire, away from everybody else. It's cold over there, but it gives her time to process the last twenty-four hours.

No one comes to talk to her, and as the long minutes tick away, thoughts about Nate keep creeping into her mind. Images revolve in her head, each one worse than the last. Time crawls, and the powerlessness she feels makes her skin itch. It is a relief when a shadow falls across her and she looks up to see Mac, returned, standing in front of her.

'I've persuaded Jackson not to go down there. It's impassable in this weather. He's trying to find some dry logs for this fire now. Mind if I sit down?' he asks.

She gestures at the bench next to her. 'Go ahead.'

'I . . . I wanted to,' he says, then lapses into silence. A minute passes, then he tries again. 'It must have been tough, you finding him there, all on your own, in the dark.'

'Yeah,' she answers, unable to find the words to conjure the horrible chasm that seemed to open up under her during those moments.

'Especially since – well, I didn't hear it myself, but obviously you'd had words, the night before, you and him.'

Immediately, Lauren is on the defensive. 'That had nothing to do with what happened to him.'

'No, no,' he says soothingly. 'Of course not. That's not what I mean. I just mean it's hard. When you're on bad terms with someone, and then they die suddenly, when you haven't resolved things, that's tough to take.'

'Oh,' says Lauren. 'Yeah. You're right. He wasn't a good person, I know that better than anyone. But I didn't wish him dead. And now, now it's all screwed up. It's just so horrible.'

She feels tears prick the back of her eyelids, and swallows hard to stop herself crying. She hates crying in front of anyone, prides herself on keeping it together, and hopes Mac hasn't noticed she is struggling to keep her emotions under control.

If he has, he graciously shows no sign of it. 'I wasn't in the best mood with him myself,' he says, after a pause, and Lauren can see he's trying to tell her something. 'That's what I wanted to say. That I kind of know how you feel – when someone who's wronged you just . . . dies . . .'

He peters out, then clocks her confused expression and continues, 'Look, I know you notice things. So, you probably noticed I wasn't in the best mood yesterday. That is, even before all this, before Nate . . .'

'Yeah,' says Lauren, smiling weakly. 'Hunger or hangover, I reckoned, maybe a mixture of both?'

Mac looks her dead in the eye, not returning her smile. 'Exactly,' he says. 'Well, hangover mostly.' He lets a pause go by and then sighs.

'I wasn't really going to tell people, but after what's happened I feel like I need to talk to someone I trust. And that someone is you, I'm afraid. Sorry.' He takes a deep breath. 'Thing is, I've been struggling with addiction for a while. Ever since I retired, really, on and off. In fact, that's kind of *why* I retired. It started with painkillers – I had to have them for my back, a few years ago. And then I couldn't do without them. So, the club gave me a chance, gave me some space so I could wean myself off them. Trouble is, I kind of replaced them with alcohol, and that's when things got really out of control. I mean, it's OK,' he says, seeing Lauren's expression. 'I was close to retirement anyway. It just moved things along a bit. And then I went into rehab, and I've been clean and sober for six months. Well, till the night of the party anyway . . .'

Lauren thinks back to that evening, shifting the perspective off her own behaviour, and looking at things from a different angle. There, in the candlelight, a memory of Nate passing the whisky bottle to Mac, and Mac passing it on untouched. But then, another memory, this time Nate is hovering the neck of the bottle over Mac's goblet. And then one more: the two of them raising drinks at each other, yelling, 'Cheers!'

Now she thinks about it, Nate did the same to everyone. Right from when he opened that first bottle of whisky, he was on a mission to get them all drunk. Yet Lauren remembers how sober he still seemed by the end of the night. Had that been intentional? She shudders when she imagines what might motivate someone to do that. He would have known it was the quickest way for him to expose all of their vulnerabilities, not just Mac's, and take advantage of some of them. She thinks of the slurring Taisie, passing out on Hollie's shoulder. Lauren knows her imagination is running wild, but she wouldn't put it past him.

'I shouldn't blame him, I know,' Mac is saying. 'That's the whole point: I've got to take responsibility for it myself. Only I can control it. But all day yesterday it was playing on my mind, the way he was that night. The way he kept passing the bottle back to me. The way he was almost needling me into it: "Come on, Mac, just a small one, great big guy like you." It was almost like . . . like he knew. Like he was trying to make me break. But then, who would do that? And how would he even know I was in recovery? It must have been my imagination. Just the comedown paranoia, I guess. But I was so angry, so ashamed. And the only place I could put it was on him. I was just feeling . . . well, murderous. Right up till when you found him. And now he's dead, I feel terrible. Like I somehow wished it on him.'

Lauren starts to say something, then stops herself. She's sure it was well within the bounds of Nate's personality to take Mac down a peg or two, for standing up to him, making him look bad. Maybe he knew Mac's secret, or maybe he guessed, and out of pure malevolence encouraged him to break his sobriety just for the Machiavellian fun of it. But what use would it be to tell Mac that now?

'You shouldn't blame yourself,' she says instead. 'For any of it. Not for the drinking, and not for your thoughts yesterday. You know you weren't really wishing something bad on him. Neither was I, not in that way.'

She pauses to gather her thoughts.

'I mean, believe me, I wanted him to be punished for the things he'd done. It's what I've spent nearly two years working on. But I didn't want it to end like that. That's not justice.'

Mac is silent for a moment, then says, 'Do you mind me asking . . . what did he do? The others said a friend of yours got rid of his bairn, fed you a pack of lies, but I'm guessing that's not the whole story?'

At his words, Lauren feels the old fury rise up.

'No, that's just *his* story. A lie. Allegra is my best friend. I saw what it did to her. What *he* did to her. He slept with her, then threw her away, just like all the others. And then he forced her into an abortion that nearly killed her, and he made her sign an NDA. He makes them all sign NDAs. They spoke to me, the other women, but they refuse to go on record. They're too scared of him. He destroys people: mentally, physically, financially. He's a monster. Or was.' Lauren's voice catches in her throat as she remembers the awful truth. 'He made a pass at me in his bedroom the day before yesterday too, got angry when I said no. I thought it was on camera, that I had finally caught him, but he knew, he knew that nothing was recording. Then he taunted me in front of everyone. Said I'd come on to *him*. And I just . . . lost it.'

Mac looks appalled.

'Jesus. I'm so sorry, hen. I shouldn't have asked.'

'I've already lost my job over him, you know.'

It is the first time Lauren has admitted the severity of her situation to anyone but her agent. She's not even dared to tell her mum or dad yet, knowing how proud they are of her, how devastated they will be when she tells them the truth.

'Oh shit, Lauren. When?'

'My boss gave me a final warning weeks ago. Told me to stop investigating, that I was obsessed. I guess, in a way, I was. I was so determined to bring him down, I couldn't let it go. He told me if I didn't stop asking questions about Nate Stirling, then I would lose my job. But how could I? Stop, I mean. And my boss was true to his word. So now, here I am, stranded on an island with the man I have been pursuing for months, dead in mysterious circumstances. Doesn't look great, does it?'

'Lauren, none of this is your fault. Or mine. It was an accident. He fell. Simple as that. All right, hen?' he says, reaching out one of his huge hands and placing it over hers. 'We just need to get off this god-forsaken island.'

There's a long pause, then Lauren breaks it. 'Too right. I think people were starting to lose it even before Nate died. At least since the storm started, maybe even before. Look at Jude. She's been paranoid about our safety since day one. And she's not been herself the last couple days. I mean, I guess that's normal given the circumstances . . .'

Mac lets out a snort of laughter, so loud and inappropriate that Jude, who is fiddling with the fire and tidying up, glances at them. 'Well, I can think of another reason!' he whispers, leaning forward so only Lauren can hear. 'Sorry. No laughing matter.' He sees Lauren's confusion and lowers his voice. 'Ach, you don't know, do you? Nate and Jude spent the night together.'

'*What?*'

'Yeah. I missed it all, of course, passed out in a stupor like a fool. And I guess you had your own troubles. But Nico told me yesterday – the two of them went off together after the feast. Very lovey-dovey. Hand in hand and everything. That's where Jude spent the night – in the Abbot's quarters.' Lauren shivers inadvertently, thinking of what lies in that room now, and then Mac continues, more seriously, 'It feels wrong to gossip about it now, especially after what you've just told me. But she spent the night there, and then, according to Nico, she went there again after breakfast and Nate more or less kicked her out. Nico ran into her in the cloisters as she was coming out of his room. He said she looked absolutely gutted. Poor woman. No wonder she's in a bit of a state.'

'Poor Jude,' Lauren echoes, glancing down the room to where she is fiddling with the oil lanterns. So that, then, was the detail she'd missed, why the air in the room had felt so charged yesterday. It wasn't just because of her; everyone else knew that Nate and Jude had slept together. God, he was utterly insatiable.

But Nate and Jude . . . it's just so *bizarre*. She knows Nate's usual type – beautiful, vulnerable, young. Hollie or Taisie she could more than believe, and he'd made it pretty clear in his room he had no qualms about their age. Jude has a certain magnetism, no doubt, but surely she'd be too much of a challenge for Nate, too much of a risk? Or maybe that was the point. Maybe he wanted to prove he could humiliate anyone, even the indomitable Jude Wright. She remembers Jude's harsh words towards her the night of the party, but feels no sense of vindication. She knows how easy it is to fall under Nate's spell, and Lauren can only imagine how nasty he must have been to knock the stuffing out of a woman like Jude.

For a fleeting moment, Lauren feels a small spark of optimism. If Nate was cruel to Jude, surely she can get Jude on side, fire up her sense of justice? Then her shoulders sag as she realises that none of it matters any more. There can be no more investigation, no more search for evidence. Nate is gone.

But, in the back of her mind, a small note is made. She isn't the only one here who knew Nate had a dark side. Who might have wanted to get revenge.

Chapter Twenty-six

The hours drag. Those who can face it eat lunch. Lauren stays where she is at the cold end of the Hall. Only Nico seems in the mood to talk and starts slightly jumpy conversations with anyone who strays into his orbit. He seems more hyper by the minute, breaking into bouts of laughter, chatting constantly. The girls, normally his best audience, keep their eyes down, still barely speaking. Occasionally one of them, usually Hollie, bursts into a fit of crying. At first when this happens she is surrounded by a forest of sympathetic arms. But eventually it is only Taisie who continues to comfort her.

'Shush, babe,' she keeps saying. 'Just shush, Holls. Come on. It'll be OK.'

As one of these rounds of tears passes, Nico becomes more and more agitated. He can't sit still, jiggling his right leg and bouncing on the balls of his feet as he casts evermore pointed looks towards where Lauren is sitting.

He mutters something under his breath.

'What's that?' says Mac.

'Just saying,' says Nico, 'the whole thing's quite strange, now I think about it. Nate's accident, I mean. Because in a way, it's very *convenient*

205

for her, isn't it? For Lauren. We all saw what happened, what she accused him of. No way was he going to let that lie. He would have really gone after her. Lawyers, the lot. He said as much. He told me things, too, afterwards. How she'd been stalking him for months, stirring things up, talking to all his ex-girlfriends, spreading vicious rumours about him. And now, well, she can say anything she likes about him, can't she? Can't slander the dead, can you? Seems to me she's at *least* one of the people here who might have wished him gone.'

Everyone in the hall freezes. The silence seems louder than words.

Taisie looks horrified. 'Nico!' she says sharply. 'What are you saying?'

Hollie's sobs increase again.

'Listen, pal, you better—' says Mac, dangerously quietly, but this seems only to spur Nico on.

'No, I mean it. I've been thinking. Like, who here benefits from Nate dying? I mean, I know you didn't exactly like him, Mac – we all saw you threaten him. And I don't know *exactly* what went down with you and him, Jude, but it didn't end well, did it? But Lauren, you seem the most obvious to me . . . you came here with a vendetta against him. And now he's dead. The ultimate punishment for what you *say* he's done. Though I, for one, don't believe a word of it.'

Lauren feels the blood pound in her ears. It's the accusation she's been dreading, far worse than any fears she had about him taking his own life.

'What exactly are you saying, Nico?' She strains to keep her voice calm, even.

'Well, he won't be able to come after you now, will he? To ruin your reputation, your career, just like you wanted to do to him. You're safe because he's dead. So what I guess I'm saying is, well . . . I would just like to know where *you* were when he went to the belfry. When he supposedly fell.

206

With that, Nico raises his eyebrows and glances round at Taisie and Hollie for corroboration. They nod in unison.

'Supposedly? Are you trying to say that I was there? That I *pushed* him? Are you serious?'

'I am . . . very!' He looks round at everyone else. 'Come on, guys, you heard her. Throwing wild accusations all over the place, refusing to apologise. As if he'd let that slide. You're a reporter, you knew the stakes. Seems to me you're the only person who'd want him dead. Who's to say you weren't with him when it happened? And you *were* the first to find him after all. I can see the headlines now: "Loony Lauren cracks . . ."'

He tapers off as Mac gets up and strides towards him in three quick steps. He towers over Nico ominously.

Nico cowers, taking a step backwards, away from Mac, and in his haste trips over a mattress, landing sprawling on the floor. But Mac doesn't stop.

'Would you like to repeat that, pal? No, I didn't think so. You talk about wild accusations – perhaps you should watch what you say.'

But the damage is done. Four pairs of eyes swivel between Lauren and Nico, where he lies spreadeagled on the floor. It's as though she can see the wheels of their minds turning, landing on the awful possibility that Nate's death might not have been an accident. Worse, that *she* might have had something to do with it.

Her only instinct is to get away. Rising from her seat, she makes for the door, trying to pull together the threads of her dignity by walking, even though everything in her is screaming to run as fast as she can.

'Lauren,' calls Mac behind her, and she can hear him starting to follow her, but even his sympathy feels as if it's too much to bear.

Chapter Twenty-seven

Head down, unshed tears stinging her eyes, Lauren makes for the kissing gate, her feet speeding under her. All she wants is to get as far away from everyone as possible.

Automatically, as she exits the graveyard, she turns away from the belfry door, walking past it as she tries to block the memories of Nate's body lying there. Before she knows it, she is heading into the watchtower and up the vertiginous spiral staircase.

As she climbs skywards, she feels she is moving through the layers of a recurring nightmare, unable to escape its clutches. Echoes of the laughter and chatter they shared before the Leap of Faith swim in her head. It feels like a scene from another life, the camaraderie she had felt then distorted with hindsight.

Round and round she goes, and by the time she makes her way up to the trapdoor in the roof her breath is ragged. It is only when she gets to the top and climbs through the small doorway on to the para-pet that she realises why she felt compelled to come up here: it is a desperate attempt to get some perspective.

She leans her hands on the edge, gazing at the tiny world below in an effort to collect her thoughts. The sea is still furious, uniform regiments of giant waves, crowned with glistening plumes of white, marching towards the island. The crests surge on to the rocks, roiling around boulders, slithering and sliding between the rocks.

So much has changed from the moment when she first stood there. The storm has destroyed everything Production had painstakingly installed to make it a set for a reality TV show. The satellite platform is beyond repair, toppled on to its side. The zip-wire, which carried them over the space between the two towers has snapped, its thick metal cables coiled snakelike in the scrubby grass, and no doubt the cave beneath the monastery is a surging mess of foam.

From what she can see of the sea and sky, there's no hope that anyone will come to their rescue today; it's too dangerous. Like the day before, the rain has abated, with some sunshine even poking through, but the wind is still high, and Lauren can tell from the clouds in the distance that it is just another temporary reprieve.

And if by some miracle someone *does* come, what does that mean for her? If things were bad before she stepped on the island, they are considerably worse now. She may have already lost her job, been taken off air and ostracised, but if Nico makes his accusations public and they stick, her reputation will be unsalvageable, even though there's no real evidence. His cruel words ring in her ears: *Seems to me you're the only person who'd want him dead . . . Loony Lauren . . .*

Is that what she will have to face, once the world crashes back in? An accusation of murder?

It's so outrageous that she cannot comprehend it. But, given the circumstances, will Nico be the only one to think it? She saw the looks on the others' faces. They may not be convinced yet, but they could be. And there *is* something strange about Nate's death. She has felt it herself since the moment she found him. There was no logical reason for him to be alone in the belfry. The facts don't fit. And facts are what she deals in, so what are they? What does she know? And how can she use them to clear her name?

A crashing realisation comes to her. *They moved the body.* How could they have been so stupid? She knows that when Production finally comes for them, police will be called in to investigate. And that by moving Nate's body, by touching him, they will most likely have destroyed crucial evidence.

A feeling of dread overwhelms her. The thought that had seemed absurd moments before, that she might become a murder suspect, takes root. There may not be any concrete evidence, but she has covered enough criminal trials to know that, if this were ever to make it to a court of law, the prosecution could build a credible case against her. She had a clear motive – an attempt to seek retribution or justice – and had ample opportunity to get to him. Nico is spot on: she has no alibi for when Nate went missing and, equally damning, she was the one who found him. Only she knows what she was doing at the time he died and she has no way of proving it. She had been on her own most of the day, walking along the cliff path, replaying the events of the night before. If only the cameras had been working, they would have seen her. But, of course, she has no witnesses.

She frantically tries to work out the possible scenarios that would have enabled her to kill him, ludicrous as it seems. Would they say she lured him to the belfry somehow, maybe to discuss her apology in private? Then, what, pushed him off the mezzanine? Took him by surprise? That would surely be more difficult to prove, though her heart sinks when she remembers that she might have provided the evidence herself. Not only was she the first to find him, but she alone went up the stairs. She was the one who first removed his cowl so she could see his face. She had held his cold lifeless hand for those long desperate minutes when she was screaming for help. He is covered in her DNA.

But then, didn't everyone else touch him too? Her brain whirrs with all the potential evidence against her until she sinks her head into her hands.

Oh God. *What am I going to do?*

She casts her eyes again over the island, searching for answers. It's suddenly blindingly obvious: she is going to do what she does best. She is going to investigate. She came here to tell the truth about Nate, to reveal his real story to the world, and that is what she is still going to do. The story has changed, horribly so, but she will find out what happened. If Nate's death was just a tragic accident, she needs to do whatever she can to prove it. And, if it wasn't, well, she needs to unmask the real killer if she wants to clear her own name.

Chapter Twenty-eight

Lauren tries to put her emotions aside and focus instead on using the logical, reporter's part of her brain. The best place to start, she reasons, would be where it had ended so disastrously for Nate: in the stairwell at the bottom of the belfry. It feels almost illicit, investigating a situation that others think she might be responsible for. But it also feels like a relief to actually do something, to have a purpose. She heads down, back to the belfry.

Making her way up the worn steps to the heavy oak door, which has been left wide open, she has an overwhelming sense of *déjà vu*. She is retracing the exact path she took to look for him yesterday evening, and even though it is bright sun at her back now rather than the foreboding half-light of dusk she is filled with dread.

The dust sparkles in the wedge of sunshine streaming through the open door and, where there were shadows before, the light illuminates every crevice. The space at the bottom of the stairs is far larger than it had seemed in the twilight, as is the void above her. Even in daylight the space feels oppressive and suffocating, and the musty smell of it catapults her back into the terrible long minutes that passed in the dark, holding Nate's hand and trying not to look at his face.

Much as she doesn't want to, she forces herself to look at the corner where she found him, where she had knelt beside him, desperately feeling for a pulse. A casual glance would reveal nothing untoward about it but, knowing where to look, she sees the drag marks Mac and Jackson left as they picked up Nate's body, some scuffing on the dusty floor where they struggled to lift him.

She moves towards the spot where his body fell, then stops herself, conscious that she shouldn't get too close for fear of disturbing something important. What is she even looking for? An anomaly perhaps? Something out of place that might give her an insight into Nate's final moments? She drags her mind back to the image of him lying there broken, splayed on his back. What did she notice? What did she see?

She remembers the cowl crumpled over his face, and that he had one hand on his chest, the other twisted behind him. She remembers that his habit was pulled up over his shins, that his feet had been protruding grotesquely. She stops there, rewinds a little bit, and replays the image as far as she can recall it. She is sure there is something odd about it. Yes, she can picture it exactly. His feet had been sticking out from the burnt hem, and he had only been wearing one slipper. She had thought it strange at the time. So where is the other?

Without stepping on the space where his body lay, she peers as best she can into every corner, every nook and cranny, but there is no sign of it. Then, she steps backwards, looking upwards again. If she can find the missing slipper, it might tell her more about how he fell. She glances up the stairs. Could the slipper be there, at the top? Perhaps that's what happened. Their badly fitting slippers were treacherous at the best of times – perhaps it got stuck on the wooden boards, made him lose his footing so he tripped and fell into the void. Was his death as simple as that, a terrible accident?

Conscious she must do her best not to add to the evidence against her and contaminate the scene more than she and the others already have, when she gets to the first step she looks carefully to see if she can follow exactly in her own footsteps. She can see several prints in the dust and grime. She tries to count them: one, two, three pairs going up, and are there three sets coming down? It's hard for her to be one hundred per cent certain; the prints overlap in places, scrubbing each other out.

God, she wishes she knew more about forensics, but surely three is one set too many? She stops to work it out. One set going up must belong to Nate. She pairs them with a descending set, which Frank would have left as he made his way down during the Leap of Faith challenge. Then there is her own set, the prints she would have made going both up and down when she was looking for Nate yesterday. But the third set? Who could they belong to? As far as she knows, no one else has been up and down here. Jackson ran into the belfry to look for Frank, but he was only in there a few seconds. Not enough time to go up the stairs, surely? She wishes desperately she could narrow it down by shoe size, but of course all their slippers are the same. A nuisance in more ways than one.

She places her foot as carefully as she can into an existing print and starts to climb, looking around guiltily. The feeling of being constantly watched hasn't quite left her, in spite of the cameras being long dead. She hugs herself into the left-hand side, staying as far away as she can from the edge while checking every inch she can see for Nate's missing slipper. It is a relief when she finally reaches the relative safety of the mezzanine again, but when she looks down to where Nate came to rest, she registers with a swimming head and sudden vertigo how high the drop is, how far it is to fall.

She takes a breath to steady herself and to register what she can see there. The black foam crashmat they had landed on during the Leap of Faith dominates the ancient space. It looks modern and incongruous, as does the shiny lens of a camera fixed high on the wall, perfectly placed to focus on their terrified faces as they flew through the open window. She spots a discarded safety harness, which must have been Frank's. And then . . . *there*. Her sharp reporter's eyes catch sight of something in the far corner: the slipper. Lauren feels a jolt of triumph as she leans over for a closer look, but her joy is short lived. What, really, does the slipper prove? There's no way of telling when or how it came off. That Nate lost it when he slipped is perfectly plausible. She leaves it where it is, unwilling to compromise evidence the police will need to examine.

Next, she makes her way gingerly to the edge, standing as close as she dares. She tries to imagine, without falling herself, how Nate's body had ended up wedged behind the door. Was he sitting on the edge or standing? Would that have made a difference? She tries to rationalise it. If he had been sitting, and pushed himself off, given the distance between the walls he would almost certainly have fallen into the middle of the void, not behind the door. To land where he had on the far side, he would have needed momentum and more height. So, she deduces, he could only have been standing.

She pictures him where she first saw him lying on the floor. He had been on his back, hadn't he? Surely if he had tripped, wouldn't he have fallen forwards, landed face down? Did he twist in the air in a desperate attempt to save himself? There are so many questions, and no clear answers. Frustrated, and no closer to knowing what happened, she turns to go back down, taking care to tread in a descending set of footsteps. One more question to add to her mental list: who else besides herself has been both up and down these stairs?

When she is safely back on the ground floor, she slips out of the door, breathing a sigh of relief, hoping never to have to go back in there again. The freshness of the air outside feels like a blessing, but she notices it is almost dusk again and her shoulders sag at how quickly the dark is falling. Another day gone, left to their own devices on this godforsaken island. When will this living nightmare end? The last thing she feels like doing is going back to the great hall, to see the condemnation or pity on her companions' faces. But with the claustrophobic blanket of night beginning to close in, and the wind starting to howl again, it feels reckless to stay outside.

Chapter Twenty-nine

In the great hall, the mood is still tense.

Nico gives her a filthy look and tosses his head away from her, but Mac raises a hand in greeting. Supper preparations are under way. Hollie and Taisie are peeling and chopping vegetables wordlessly, knives flashing expertly in their hands.

Lauren knows she should offer to help, but she can't bear the awkwardness of breaking into their mutual silence. They are focused, intent on their task. Everybody else seems to be busy, stacking the logs, fetching the crockery in from the outside sinks, laying the table, ferrying water. It's a distraction technique, Lauren recognises. But she needs distraction as well.

'What can I do?' she asks Mac, desperate to occupy herself in some way.

'We thought we'd move the mattresses closer to the fire for tonight. Can you help with everyone's things?' he answers, picking up the top blanket from a muddled heap and shaking it out.

Lauren joins in, picking up the next one and smoothing it, then taking one end of the long table under Mac's direction and moving it to one side. They line the mattresses up in the space they have made.

'You've got this now, right?' says Mac.

'Sure,' she says, picking up an armful of cotton bags and distributing one on to each mattress, careful to ensure that her own is placed as far from Nico's as possible.

Once she's finished her task, she glances over at Jude, still occupying her place by the fire. She thinks about what Mac told her earlier, how different Jude now seems from the no-nonsense, outspoken woman she met on the boat. Of course, none of them is him- or herself since Nate's death – how could they be? But Lauren detects something else undercutting Jude's miserable demeanour. Fear, perhaps. Or guilt?

She hears a clatter and looks up to find that Hollie and Taisie have placed an enormous cauldron of soup in the centre of the table, flanked by loaves of bread. There's a confused shuffling towards the table as everyone gathers, but nobody seems to know how to behave now that Nate, their dynamic master of ceremonies, has gone.

The girls reach across the table, silently handing each person in turn a wooden bowl. It seems to occur to everyone simultaneously how hungry they are, and they bump elbows and proffer awkward apologies as they crowd round, passing the ladle from hand to hand, helping themselves to soup. The warmth and nourishment provide some comfort, but it feels wrong to gather like this, while the chair at the head of the table is so conspicuously empty.

Even after they have finished eating, still nobody can think of a good way to start a conversation. Pantomimes of elaborate politeness break out: Jude courteously cuts a slice of bread for Nico to mop out his bowl; Mac stands and goes round the table like a waiter to offer everyone water or mead, making sure he sticks to water; Jackson ostentatiously doles out seconds. Apart from Mac, who makes sure she has everything she needs, Lauren feels as though everyone is deliberately ignoring her. Her own attention is fixed on Jude, whose expression is closed, her eyes mostly downcast. It is impossible to guess what she is thinking.

As much as Lauren wants to talk to her about what happened with Nate, she stops herself. To get to the truth she needs to talk to Jude alone, not in front of everyone.

Of course, it is Jackson who eventually tries to break through the awkwardness, standing up and raising the mug of beer he is drinking. 'I think we should raise a glass,' he says, 'to Nate. A legend. Here's to you, mate. Rest in peace.'

'Rest in peace,' they all mumble. There's an expectation in the air that someone else should speak, but instead they lapse into another painful silence. Eventually, Nico stands, trying to turn up the wattage of his energy. He looks pale and hollowed out, but he does his best.

'To Nate,' he says. 'Jackson's right. A total legend. The way he left us, well, it's just awful, terrible. I still can't believe it .'

Is it Lauren's imagination or did his eyes flick in her direction when he said that?

'Here's to you, big man,' he finishes, draining his mug of beer. 'I know I'll never forget you.'

'To Nate!' there is only a faint chorus in response. Nico and Jackson's efforts to lift the mood have fallen flat. Nothing can distract the group from the reality that lying next door is a corpse, and that they are trapped here, unable to do anything about it. The temperature is dropping, and a weariness is overtaking Lauren that she sees mirrored in every face around her.

'I think I'm going to—' says Hollie, and as soon as she does, other voices cut in over her.

'Me too.'

'And me.'

'Let's just tidy up a bit first,' says Jude, ever practical.

By the time they have cleared the table, putting the dirty bowls and cups next to the door to be washed in the morning, and snuffed out all but one of the lanterns, exhaustion has crept over every one of their faces. One by one they turn in. The girls are side by side as ever, sharing a blanket, whispering in the firelight. Mac lies just to the right of the fireplace, with Jackson beside him. Jude and Lauren are on separate mattresses next to them, in front of the huge hearthstone. Nico doesn't take his place next to the girls right away. He sits up, his robes pulled tight around him, cowl over his head, so close to the fire he is almost sitting in it.

'Not going to bed yet?' asks Jude.

'In a second. I'm just really cold. Banging headache too. I'm just gonna sit here for a bit – put another log or two on the fire, warm myself up. Won't get to sleep otherwise. And it will keep you lot a bit warmer too.' He manages a weak smile.

''Night, then,' says Jude.

'Goodnight.'

Lauren is woken by a weak, milky light, her limbs rigid from the cold. Her mind feels fractured; she has hardly slept a wink. Every time she closed her eyes she had been assaulted by a flood of traumatic images: Nate's head lolling backwards as they picked him off the cold stone floor, Hollie's pitiful howling, Nico's vicious accusations. Add to that the conundrum of the footprints on the stairs, her growing suspicion that someone had been with Nate when he died, and sleep was nigh on impossible.

There are so many things to process, to unpick. She needs to talk to everyone, find out where they were and what they were doing in the hours before she found Nate's body, but without making herself look more suspicious. It's Jude she wants to speak to most urgently. What exactly happened between her and Nate after the party? And what did he say to her the next day? How did they leave it? Maybe they went to the belfry later, to continue their row in private, away from prying ears.

She looks around the now familiar room, their new sleeping quarters. Given the circumstances, it is a peaceful scene. Jude is deep in slumber on the mattress beside her. To her right she can see that Mac and Jackson, too, are both still out for the count. To her left, the girls are nothing more than a tangled heap under a pile of blankets.

Sitting up, she sees that Nico has managed to fall asleep slumped but upright, propped up against the fireplace, the embers of which are now nothing but papery white ash.

Reckoning that the sense of discombobulation will only leave her if she starts doing something, she stretches her creaky joints and levers herself off her mattress. Tiptoeing softly to let the others sleep, she heads towards the hearth. The hall is tomb cold but there is still a meagre pile of logs. If she builds the fire up now, the others will wake up to that small comfort, at least.

She hesitates before waking Nico, not wanting to face his jibes and insinuations again so early in the day. But she has to get past him if she wants to light the fire. She takes a deep breath.

"Morning, Nico,' she says, and reaches out to touch him on the shoulder. It is only a gentle nudge, but, to her horror, rather than waking, his body pitches unnaturally towards the embers, his head landing face-down in them. His eyes stay closed, his body twisted at an uncomfortable angle. Puffs of ash float up preposterously around his head.

Her scream is so loud that the force of it throws her backwards, stumbling away from the fireplace.

'Nico!' she screams. 'Nico, wake up! For God's sake, *wake up!*'

Her shouts have woken the others. She wheels round to see Mac and Jackson both sitting bolt upright, staring at her open-mouthed.

'What's happening?' says Jackson.

'Wake him up! Wake him up!' she shouts, grabbing at Nico's robes and trying fruitlessly to drag him upright. 'Help me wake him up!'

Jackson and Mac are by her side in an instant, their muscles straining, lifting Nico's motionless body out of the hearth and lying him down in the recovery position. Lauren is dimly aware of the girls behind her, sitting up from their tangled covers, and Jude rushing to kneel beside him. She feels rather than sees the tiny head shake that Mac gives to Jackson, and then Mac draws her away, shielding her vision with his body and holding her hands in his own.

'Lauren, it's hopeless,' he says. 'He hasn't got a pulse. He's gone.'

Lauren hears a loud buzzing in her ears, muffling all other sounds. The world swims in front of her. Black curtains draw across her vision and her legs crumple underneath her. Then she is falling helpless to the ground.

Chapter Thirty

What feels like an instant later, she wakes to find she too has been laid out on the cold floor, in a grotesque parody of the pose that Nico is lying in, not ten feet away. Mac is bending over her.

'Lauren, are you OK?' he says, 'You fainted.'

She looks at him wildly. 'OK?' she gasps in a strangulated half-laugh. '*OK?* How can I be OK? Nate is dead and now Nico is too! I am *not* OK.'

She scrambles upright, running through the doors to the courtyard without heeding the fact that she is dressed only in her unbelted habit. The bitter cold of the flagstones smarting the soles of her feet is almost welcome. Anything to stop her mind trying to pick through the tangle of consequences that lie before them. She flies at breakneck speed across the courtyard to where the portcullis still guards the entrance and grips its bars, the iron biting into her palms. She shakes the gate, desperately pleading for someone to take her away from this place.

'Please, please!' she finds herself screaming, without conscious thought. 'Somebody help us. Help us!'

Even as she wails, she knows it is hopeless, that no one can hear her, but she only stops shouting when her throat is raw. Sobbing and still holding on to the bars, she presses her forehead against them, allowing only one thought to enter her mind: she is not going to go back into that hall. She knows what lies in there: the shock, the crying, the horrified denials; Mac and Jackson's attempt to take control in the midst of mounting hysteria. She cannot face any of it, not until she can wrap her head around what's happened. Nate dead, now Nico. Two corpses in two days. It is utterly unimaginable, worse than any nightmare.

Lauren has no idea how much time passes before the door to the great hall opens, and a figure comes out. It is Jackson. He looks changed. The animation and joyful enthusiasm she is accustomed to seeing in his face replaced by a deep frown, he looks pale and wrung out. When he sees her, he beckons to her across the courtyard.

'Lauren, it's freezing out. Mac says you should come inside.'

'I can't,' she says, not moving, then finds herself backing off slightly as he approaches her across the grass, holding something in his hands.

He shrugs. 'He guessed you might say that. So he made me bring these out for you.' She sees that he is holding her slippers and a blanket. 'Here, put this over your shoulders. It might help.'

When he leans over to hand them to her, she shudders, but not from the cold. His tall frame and powerful shoulders, which have always been so reassuring, suddenly make her feel vulnerable and small.

'Thanks,' she says. 'Sorry. I just can't face it in there. Is he . . . are you sure he's . . .'

'Yes,' he says quietly. 'He's dead. Mac checked him over. Thinks he might have been for quite a while. He's trying to work out what happened. He thinks maybe carbon monoxide, from sitting too close to the fire. He reckons we'll have to stop lighting it now, just in case. It's just . . . just . . .'

'Unbelievable,' says Lauren shortly. 'It's unbelievable.'

'Yeah. I know.'

He can't seem to find any more words, so looks at her for a moment, 'I can see why you don't want to be in there. It's horrific. Everyone is crying. Hollie and Taisie are a total mess. But I'm gonna go back in, help Mac move him. The plan is to put him next to Nate. Seems like the most respectful thing to do. Do you want to help?'

'No. God, no. I can't face seeing him again, I just need to be out here for a bit, process what's happened,'

Just as he turns to leave, Lauren stops him.

'Hey, Jackson. Did you see Nate go to the belfry the day he died?'

He looks bewildered by the question, but after a moment he answers.

'Nah, 'fraid not. I had my head down that well all afternoon, trying to fix it. There were lots of people coming and going, but I didn't see who. Kept hearing the gate bang, though – you know, the kissing gate? Sounded like a few people went in and out. Why do you want to know?'

'Just trying to work something out. Whether someone might have been with him.'

Jackson looks a little uneasy now, no doubt recalling Nico's accusation that Lauren herself was with Nate when he died.

'Not as far as I know.' He pauses for a moment, then goes on, 'As far as I can remember, the only people I saw together were the girls. But then they always are, aren't they?'

'Yep. Thanks, Jackson.'

'Anytime. Sure you don't want to come back with me? I know Mac wants you to keep warm, at least.'

She shakes her head. 'No thanks, I'm going to wait out here a while.'

She watches him as he turns to go. Even his gait has changed, the athletic spring now gone. It is more like a shuffle. Once he has shut the door behind him, she sits on the low wall of the well, her back to the portcullis, and puts her slippers on, wrapping the blanket around herself like a protective shawl.

For the first time in what seems like days the wind has died down. The storm seems to have finally vented its fury. Surely, she thinks, surely, they must be rescued soon, today, within hours. Surely this hell can't go on any longer.

She sits there for a long time, thinking. Two people dead in two days. If Nate's death *is* suspicious, does that mean Nico's is too? He was vocal about his own suspicions, after all, although Lauren was the main target. Good God. What if they think *she* silenced him somehow? She shakes her head, won't allow the dreadful thought to take hold.

But what the hell *did* happen? A young man who seemed to be in peak health, dying noiselessly in his sleep, while his companions slumbered on, unaware, beside him. It is too macabre, too disturbing, for Lauren to comprehend. What did Jackson say? Possible carbon monoxide poisoning? But then why are the rest of them fine?

Out of the corner of her eye she catches a shadow, a fleeting glimpse of dull brown fabric. Someone is heading towards the portcullis. Perhaps, like her, they are desperate for solitude. She turns to see who it is, but by the time she has looked up, they have disappeared. Presuming they must have gone to the graveyard, Lauren gets up to follow them. She can't face going into the great hall yet, but maybe this person can give her some answers. As she stands, her joints feel stiff and achy from the cold and sitting on the low wall for so long.

The graveyard is deserted when she gets there, apart from a pair of scruffy looking ravens on the far side, pecking insistently at the base of a Celtic cross. They take off in fright as Lauren opens the gate and it bangs behind her. Intrigued by what the birds were so focused on, she steps off the well-worn gravel path and walks gingerly over the wet grass, the damp soaking through her slippers.

She is picking her way between the lichened gravestones when her gaze catches a hint of something shiny and out of place, lodged under the cross. She hurries over to investigate. At first, in the filthy mix of mud and leaves, she can't make out exactly what it is. To see better, she gets down on her haunches and lightly brushes away the mulch with her fingers. When her hand bumps up against cold hard metal, her heart skips a beat. She clears the earth more carefully, to confirm what she fears already. The purple stone encased in gold is unmistakable. This is what the ravens have been pecking at: they have found Nate's ring.

Chapter Thirty-one

Blood thrums in Lauren's ears. She can hardly believe what she is seeing. She has found Nate's ring, hidden from view on the far side of the graveyard where, as far as she knew, none of them has ever been. She sits down to take it in.

How on earth did the Abbot's ring end up here, and what does it mean?

She's certain it couldn't have just been dropped where she found it, crammed into a tiny crevice so far off the well-worn path. Why would Nate have even been there? It doesn't make sense.

Even though the graveyard is deserted, she still can't help looking over her shoulders, scanning the area to see if anyone is watching her. The feeling of panic rises, as if she is trapped in a maze and the walls are closing in.

'Breathe,' she says to herself, making a conscious effort to steady her jangling nerves. 'Breathe slowly and think.' She sits completely still in an effort to focus. First things first: can she remember the last time she saw Nate wearing the ring?

She pictures the self-satisfaction on his face when he first placed it on his finger, in the flickering firelight of the Abbot's chambers. She sees him at the head of the table, laughing during the feast, his fingers lifting a goblet to raise a toast to her, flashing her a malicious smile. He was wearing it then. She thinks back to the last ghastly encounter she had with him over breakfast, him gesturing emphatically, pointing at her in accusation, demanding an apology. She hadn't wanted to look him in the eye, and instead had watched his hands gesticulating. It was there, glinting on his right hand.

What about when she found him? She catapults her mind to the moments spent with his body in the belfry, shivers as she feels the sensations again, his cold fingers clasped in hers. It had been his right hand, his arm twisted awkwardly across his chest. And his fingers? She searches her mind. His fingers were bare inside hers. She is sure of it. She flashes forward again: the bedroom, Jackson gently folding Nate's arms on top of the burgundy cover. Yes, his hands were bare. Somewhere between breakfast and his death, he had lost the ring.

She kicks herself for not noticing before, when she was holding his hand, or when she realised his slipper was missing. How could she have missed it? The emotional rollercoaster of the last few days has clouded her sharp mind, but she needs to get it back, to think logically, work out what the hell is going on.

She hesitates before she picks the ring up, knowing that she shouldn't; it is valuable evidence. And they have already destroyed plenty. But despite her initial reluctance, she leans over to grab it, reasoning that the ravens could come back and steal it. And she has a feeling she just might need it. As she slips the ring into her pocket, she flinches as the sharp edges scrape her palm.

She continues towards the gatehouse. If the person she glimpsed running past her hadn't headed to the graveyard, that must be where they are. The ring she will keep under wraps, for now, but she has a renewed sense of purpose. She is more convinced than ever that someone is hiding something about Nate's death. And she intends to find out what it is.

Chapter Thirty-two

The low arched door is locked from the inside when she gets there. She rattles the latch to double check, and then knocks twice.

'Hello, is someone in there?'

She receives a curt, angry response from inside.

'Go away!'

The voice is unmistakably Jude's.

'It's me, Lauren. Please let me in, I just want to talk.'

'No.'

'Please, I promise it won't take long.'

Lauren hears the bed springs squeak and light footsteps coming towards the door.

'Are you on your own?'

When she confirms that she is, the key scrapes in the lock and Jude opens the door a fraction. She grabs Lauren's arm, pulls her in with surprising strength, then shuts it quickly behind them. The key clicks again, locking them both in.

'I've been saying it all along, haven't I? That we're not safe. And now look. First Nate, then Nico. Two of us killed in the space of two days,' Jude hisses, her eyes wide with fright.

'Calm down, Jude. It's OK. We are OK.'

'But they're not, and neither are we! I kept telling everyone this place was dangerous. And now I've been proven right!'

'I know, Jude. It's horrific, unthinkable, what's happened to them. But you need to calm down. And, look, I need to talk to you about Nate. Mac told me some things . . . about the night of the storm,' Lauren says quietly.

'Did he now?' Jude's tone is accusatory, and for a moment her panic is replaced by the steel she is known for. 'He had no business doing that.' Now her face is reddening, her voice is rising, even more shrill than before she unlocked the door. 'And I don't know why you think it's your business either, coming over here, poking your nose in where you're not welcome. Given what happened between *you* and Nate, I don't think you're in any position to be asking questions. There are two people dead, after all. Leave it to the police.'

'Look, I know something happened with you and Nate, and I'm trying to piece together his last day. I'm not trying to catch you out, or humiliate you. I just need information. You heard what Nico was saying about me, you know what he was implying. And now he's dead too. What if . . . what if people think I killed Nate, then Nico too? You know I didn't do this, Jude. I can't let anyone else believe it either.'

Jude eyes her warily. Lauren recalls again how quickly Jude took Nate's side. Does she, too, think Lauren is capable of murder? But then her eyes cloud ever, unshed tears threatening to spill over.

'Christ, that poor, poor boy. So young. I know he was a dreadful gossip, liked to stir things up, but I don't think he meant any real harm.'

'And Nate?' Lauren asks tentatively.

'Nate is a different story.' Jude's tone is suddenly angry. 'But you already knew that, of course.' Jude pauses, seeming uncertain whether to elaborate or not. Lauren says nothing, waiting a beat to see if she will continue.

'As you no doubt already know,' spits Jude, 'we spent the night together after the party . . .' As she trails off, different emotions pass over her face so quickly that Lauren finds it hard to read them. Anger, embarrassment, regret?

'Yes, Mac said,' confirms Lauren, then waits again for Jude to tell her side of the story.

'Oh Christ, it's all so fucked up,' Jude bursts out suddenly, her voice far too loud in the small room. 'I was so angry with him – and so repulsed by myself. Humiliated. So horribly, horribly humiliated. He made me feel small, and stupid. I felt like I would do anything to get back at him. *Anything.* And now he's dead and I can't feel any of the normal feelings about that. I hated him after that night, but now I keep remembering how I felt before that. He was charismatic, charming. So handsome. For all of that to be extinguished . . . it just makes me feel sick. And now Nico's dead too . . .'

Jude is openly sobbing now, and Lauren's mind is reeling. This is definitely not the Jude she is used to, but then, will any of them be the same after this? She pats her back in an effort to comfort her.

'It's OK, I understand. I feel the same way. You can talk to me. Maybe if you tell me what went wrong, it will help you process things.'

After a while Jude's breathing returns to normal and she continues more calmly, still looking at her lap.

'I should have listened to you, of course. I just thought I knew better. All those Hollywood starlets and wannabes, piggybacking on his coattails, and then trying to pretend they hadn't. And you? You'd fallen for it, hook, line and sinker. Ranting away about all those wronged women. Pretending he'd stopped you leaving his room . . .' Even Jude has the good grace to look shame-faced here. 'I'm sorry I

232

didn't believe you. But I just thought, a man like that – so attractive, rich, *charming*. Of course all those women fell for him, then felt bitter once he'd ended it.'

Lauren feels a surge of righteous fury. It's exactly this kind of view that stops women coming forward, that lets men like Nate, and worse, get away with what they've done. But she realises that Jude is acknowledging her mistake, and she bites back the angry words she longs to say.

'So what happened after I went to bed?' she asks instead.

'I got chatting to him and, well, I was a little drunk, but that wasn't it. You don't know what it's like yet, to have men pass you over simply because of your age. But trust me, it isn't fun. And then there he was, this handsome, powerful Hollywood actor, paying attention to me, *flirting* with me. I have to admit I was flattered. Anyone would leap at the chance. It wasn't like I thought we were going to ride off into the sunset, but I thought we'd have a good time while we were here, get through this thing as a team.'

Lauren waits out the pause, and Jude sighs a heavy sigh. 'I can't believe I was so stupid. I can read people usually, you know – it's one of the reasons I'm so successful. And what I was getting from him was friendship. A genuine connection. Someone who respected me, who saw me as an equal. So, yes, we slept together, and I felt good about it. Buoyed up. Until the next morning.'

Jude falls silent. It feels almost cruel to press her, but Lauren needs all the facts.

'What happened the next morning?' she says softly.

Jude doesn't answer directly, not at first. 'I just don't know what compelled him to talk to me like that. There wasn't any need, I wasn't asking for anything. We'd had a bit of fun, that's all. He was a bit quiet in the morning, but we got up, went into breakfast. Everything was fine. We even talked a little bit about you. He was very, very angry with you, you know.

'And then, after breakfast, after you'd run away, we went back to his room again. I was trying to be supportive, said I was sure you'd apologise. I tried to give him a hug – God, I feel so stupid – and that was it. He turned on me. He told me . . . he told me to stop pawing at him, that the night before had been a huge mistake. That he was revolted by me, and had demeaned himself by sleeping with a woman my age. Then he went into details about what it was like for him, sleeping with someone as' – her voice shakes – 'someone as old as me. As if he wasn't two years older than me himself! It was just so . . . vindictive. So cruel.'

She takes another deep breath. 'You should have seen his eyes. They were so cold. I could tell a part of him was enjoying himself, as if he was almost getting off on seeing me humiliated. He went on and on, commenting on my face, my body, my . . . sexual prowess. He even went after my money, accusing me of making it off the backs of the poor. I just froze. I couldn't speak. Couldn't stand up for myself. I saw a glimpse of the monster you'd described the night before and I wished, I *wish* I had listened to you.'

The words ring in Lauren's ears and, for a moment, the relief of hearing someone validate her outweighs the circumstances they are in. Someone who will back her up. Without thinking, she turns and hugs Jude without restraint, eyes closed to fight back her emotions. And then the harsh reality comes back to her as she realises it doesn't matter. None of that matters now, not with Nate and Nico dead.

Jude laughs softly through her tears.

'I was thinking of coming to you. Eating humble pie. Seeing if we could team up to bring him down. But what use is all of that to us now? When I saw Nate was dead, I was horrified, just as horrified as anyone else was. I didn't want him to die. Of course I didn't. It's awful. And maybe all the more awful because now he's just got away with it all, hasn't he? Nobody's going to listen to your

stories now. He'll be the Hollywood hero and philanthropist, idol-
ised for ever.'

Lauren has no answer for this and nods despondently. She knows
Jude is right, yet she can't let go of the hope that she might still be able
to expose Nate for what he was, as well as uncovering the truth behind
his death.

'Was that the last time you saw him?'

'Yes, when I rushed out of his room in tears. That's when I ran into
Nico.' Jude's voice hardens. 'He was smirking. I could tell he'd heard
every word, every little detail. He had a habit of that, you know, listening in on conversations. He enjoyed finding out things about
people and using it against them. I begged him not to say anything,
and he said he wouldn't. But sure enough, I know he told everyone he
could. Anyway, I left him going into Nate's room. I don't know what
his business was there, probably to have a good laugh at my expense.'

Lauren sighs. 'Did you stick around long enough to hear any of
what they said?'

'God, no. I wanted to get as far away as possible. I went for a walk.
Then on my way back I saw the girls giggling together with Nico. I
guessed what they were laughing about, so I took myself off again.
I just needed some space.'

'And you didn't see anyone?'

'No one, not until I got back.' She pauses for a second, remembering. 'I did hear something, though, just as I was going back into the
cloisters. The kissing gate, clanging open and shut. As if someone was
going through it – you know how it bangs when you shut it. But it did
it twice over, as if there were two people. Hadn't thought of it before.
Probably just the wind, though.'

Didn't Jackson also mention the kissing gate? Lauren makes a
mental note, but she still has questions for Jude.

'Do you think Nate wanted some time out too? It's just, I can't work out why he would visit the belfry in the middle of a storm. Don't you think that's odd? Do you think someone was with him?'

'God only knows. Maybe he was tormenting someone else.'

'Right, so . . . if someone else was there . . . do you think he just fell? Or could someone have pushed him?'

There is a stunned silence.

'Like who?' Jude's voice has turned hard again; she sounds more like her old self. 'What exactly are you suggesting, Lauren? Surely you're not implying *I* had anything to do with it?'

'All I know is what you've just told me. That Nate was vicious to you, and Nico was a witness. And you were on your own when Nate went missing. It doesn't look great, does it?'

This pushes Jude over the edge. There is venom in her tone. 'So you're accusing *me* now, are you? Have you seen the size of me compared to him? How could I possibly have the strength? Besides, I may be known for being tough, but I'm not some twisted killer. And anyway, what about you? You had far more reason to go after Nate than I did, maybe even Nico, if he was getting too close to the truth. Trust me, Lauren, you do *not* want to make an enemy out of me.'

Lauren raises her hands in a conciliatory measure. Jude's right, whether ally or suspect, the last thing she wants is to make an enemy of her, especially now they share an understanding about Nate.

'I'm sorry. I didn't mean to accuse you. I know better than anyone how damaging that is. I'm just so confused. I just want to work out what happened. I *know* you didn't do anything, and you know *I* didn't. So I suppose my real question is, do you think someone *else* might have pushed him?'

Jude shakes her head in disbelief. 'Another contestant? No way! I just don't buy it. Can you really imagine one of the others doing it – Mac, Jackson, the girls?'

'No, but . . . it doesn't mean it's not possible.'

Jude shakes her head again. 'Look, Lauren, you're a great journalist, and I'm sure you have good instincts, but I think you're way off. If you want to look at anyone, look at Production. I've always said the health and safety is negligible, but what if it's something more sinister? Maybe one of *them* is playing some sick game, nearly killing Nate with the portcullis, tampering with the harness so one of us would fall. Maybe we were never really alone at all. For all we know, someone might have been hiding on the island the whole time, taking us out one by one. Either way, I am staying right here until the police arrive and I suggest you do the same.'

Clearly, Jude's paranoia is back, but as hard as Lauren finds it to believe that a hidden assailant is toying with them, Jude's words still make her shudder. She certainly won't be locking herself away in here, though. She looks carefully at Jude, trying to discern if she's hiding anything. Could her wild accusations about a Production member gone rogue be an attempt to divert attention away from herself? Lauren's not sure, but she knows she won't get anything more out of Jude, and she doesn't want to risk angering her again. There are no more answers to be had in this room.

As she makes for the door, one last thought crosses her mind.

'Weird question, was Nate wearing his ring when you last saw him?'

Jude looks perplexed and takes a moment to answer.

'Yes, he was. He never took it off. Not sure he *could*, actually. He mentioned it was quite tight. Although, really, I think he just loved what it represented, the power it gave him, even if it was just brass and glass. I am sure he was wearing it when I left his room. Absolutely sure of it.'

So how had it ended up half hidden at the back of the graveyard? Despite the confessional nature of the conversation they've just had, Lauren is not going to ask Jude, nor tell her where she found the ring, until she knows the answer herself. As she opens the door, Jude takes her parting shot.

'Leave it alone, Lauren. No good can come from interfering.'

With that, the door shuts and Lauren hears the key turn in the lock. So, what now? An unwelcome thought crosses her mind: perhaps there is something to be gleaned from examining the bodies? As ghastly as it sounds, she knows this is the next logical step.

Chapter Thirty-three

With Jude's final words playing on her mind, Lauren makes her way to the other side of the cloisters, trying not to think about what she is going to do.

She has seen dead bodies before, a necessary but gruesome part of her job, but it is quite a different experience to examine the corpses of people she knew, two men who up until a couple of days ago were living under the same roof as her. She may have had her reasons to dislike them, especially Nate, but it doesn't change the onslaught of emotions she feels when she thinks about seeing them dead. Her mouth is dry and her heart beating audibly as she approaches the closed door of the Abbot's room, and she has to steady herself on the threshold.

One breath, two . . . she reaches out and pushes the thick oak door, which swings open into the cramped space. As her eyes adjust, she sees the bed where Nate is lying. There's something ghastly in the very fact that he has not moved, of course, from the position in which they placed him. He is lying peacefully, one hand clasped over the other on the purple eiderdown.

Far worse is what, or who, lies next to him on the floor. The others have taken as much care as they can, putting a pillow under Nico's head and covering his body with a tartan blanket. As with Nate, they have left his head and shoulders uncovered, perhaps unable to bear the finality of covering his face, so that at first glance it looks as though he is simply sleeping. But Nico's face is utterly changed. Where Nate's patrician features were often still and arresting, even in life, everything about Nico's face was mobile, mischievous, filled with expression. The stillness of death has cast a mask over his features that leaves him somehow unrecognisable, his spirit undoubtedly extinguished. His eyes are closed and his mouth is set in a straight line. There's no emotion in it, nor any pain, she is relieved to observe. In death, his cheekbones are more pronounced, and he looks aged beyond his years. As she thinks this, it's as though she can hear his voice saying, 'Babe, as if I'd *ever* allow myself to look old. *So* not my style . . .'

All at once the tragedy of it hits Lauren, her stomach dropping so quickly that she puts her hand over her mouth, nausea rising. Her skin feels cold and clammy, sweat prickling along her hairline. She has to concentrate on her breath so she doesn't faint again.

She shuts her eyes and then opens them, trying to look at the bodies objectively, as if she hadn't known them. With Nate, she has a very specific purpose. She wants to look at the ring finger of his right hand to see if there is any sign that the Abbot's ring was removed or pulled off by hands other than his own. If she's lucky, there might even be signs of a struggle.

Leaving the door open behind her to let in some light, she steps forward and bends over to look at Nate's hands where they lie folded in the dark covers. His left hand is covering the fingers of his right one. Carefully she reaches forward and pushes the offending hand slightly, covering her own hand with her robe and touching it as fleetingly as she possibly can. Even so, she can't help her fingers recoiling a little; through the rough cloth of her sleeve she can still feel that Nate's hand is icy cold.

In response to her light touch, it flops downwards, leaving his right hand exposed. She looks at his ring finger intently, not daring to touch his actual flesh or move it again. There is a clear indentation at the base of it, where the ring would have sat, encircling his finger. Jude was right, for that to be noticeable days after his death the ring must have been tight.

But it is his knuckle that draws her attention. It doesn't look right. There is a deep cut across the top of it, about a centimetre long. The skin is puckered where it has been pulled away, and there is a crust of dried blood tracing a line through it. How did that happen, and when? Before or after he fell? Her scant knowledge of biology and forensics means she can only guess, but then she remembers she does have something that could help.

Her fingertips search for Nate's ring where she has stored it, in the depths of her pocket. She examines it and rubs her thumb around its circumference. It is sharp – sharper than it looks. Even though she knows it is already covered in her DNA, she feels reckless as she slips it on to her finger. It doesn't fit – it is several sizes too big – but even though it is too large for her the metal grates uncomfortably against her skin.

She pulls it off again, dragging the side of it against the joint of her own finger. If she pressed it hard enough, it would scratch her, but not badly enough to pierce her skin. To have a cut like Nate does, it would have to be ripped off violently. No one would do that to themselves – it would hurt too much. Oh God. The implications of what she is seeing sink in. It's more than enough to convince Lauren that someone else was there when Nate died.

And what of Nico, lying so still beside him? Is his death linked in some way? It seems so unlikely, so unnatural that he could just die quietly right beside them. Could it really be as simple as carbon monoxide poisoning? Sure, he'd been sitting close to the fire and had complained about a headache, but that could be anything.

She tries to mine her memory for what she knows about how carbon monoxide kills. It is not much. All she can vaguely remember is that the poison brings a quiet death, unexpected and painless. She looks at his face carefully. Is there something strange about the lips? A tinge of blue that seems unnatural? She would like to believe that he died peacefully in his sleep, and though she is no expert, this seems to fit the picture in front of her. Nothing in Nico's face reveals any kind of struggle or violence.

But is it the only explanation? Gently, she lifts up the sheet that covers him, exposing his feet. His legs are visible where his robe has been pulled up his shins and, incongruously, he is still wearing his socks and slippers. Apart from that, he is wrapped in the rough brown wool of the habit. What is she looking for? Had she expected bruises, some sign of struggle? She tries and fails to think of other things that could have caused his death, the tell-tale signs of asphyxiation, or some other kind of poison, dredged up from too many hours watching CSI boxsets. She can see nothing obvious.

Could there be a tiny puncture wound on him somewhere? Might somebody have taken a needle from the medical supplies and administered him an overdose? Theoretically, it seems plausible, but when she tries to picture the steps involved, she falters. Wouldn't Nico have noticed the sting of a hypodermic needle? Wouldn't he have cried out? And, as far as she knows, only Mac has the keys to the medical supplies.

Mac might know. He's a paramedic. He would know what to look for. And then the thought bounces back, slightly twisted, like a distorted echo. *Mac would know . . . only he has the keys for the medicine cupboard . . .*

She shakes her head, not allowing that thought to settle. She stops herself from uncovering Nico further and potentially contaminating the scene. She'll have to leave this to the experts.

As she lifts the blanket to cover his body, one of her happier memories of him flashes before her: Nico smiling and laughing, his white-blond hair shimmering in the candlelight as he led them through song after song that night of the party. He might have said awful things to her later, but he didn't deserve to die like this, out of the blue, away from his home and his family.

She steps back to take one last look at them together and a deep sense of desolation washes over her. This is all wrong. She stands for a long moment in vigil, as a small mark of respect for the dead, then turns for the door just as a huge shadow falls across it, startling her.

'Jesus!' shouts Mac in return, his bulk framed in the small doorway. 'Lauren! What the hell are you doing? Christ, you nearly gave me a heart attack!' Then, as though realising how inappropriate that sounds, he drops his voice almost to a whisper. 'Sorry. Just you gave me a shock, is all. What are you doing here?'

The blood has drained out of Lauren's face with fright. 'Never mind me, what the hell are you up to?' she snaps.

Mac returns her gaze evenly. 'I was coming to check on the temperature of Nico's body, if you must know. Didn't think to do it before, and I thought it might be useful later for the post-mortem. I want a sense of when he might have died.' He pauses. 'But seriously, Lauren, what are you doing here?'

Still shaken she doesn't answer and instead darts past him, back down the passage towards the great hall.

'Lauren, come on,' he says, following. 'Please. I didn't mean to give you a shock. Talk to me. I've been worried about you since you ran out this morning.'

Reaching the hall, Lauren tries to keep her eyes away from the spot where she last saw Nico alive, but she can't help it, her focus is inexorably pulled to the fireplace, the image of his inert body toppling forward playing and replaying in her mind.

'Oh God,' says Mac, seeing where her eyes are resting. 'Lauren, come here.' And once again he pulls her into his massive arms, his chest obliterating everything else from her view.

Releasing her after a moment, he gently steers her towards the table, gesturing to a seat deliberately facing away from the hearth.

'Sit down,' he says. 'Firstly, you need to eat. You must be famished.' He lifts the lid on a steaming pot of porridge, chatting away idly. 'I made this before we put the fire out,' he says. 'The proper way, Scottish, with salt and water. None of that sweet milky stuff that the girls make for us.'

She wrinkles her nose at the thought of it, but he persuades her to try it. 'Seriously, you have to eat. You'll make yourself ill otherwise. And we can't have you keeling over. We need to look after ourselves, and each other. Stay safe until we're rescued.'

Lauren nods, heart rate slowing, and takes a bowl of porridge. She glances around the great hall and is surprised to see it's just her and Mac. Clearly they've all decided to disregard the Voice's last plea for them to stay inside.

'Where's everyone else?'

'Jude disappeared not long after you did – no idea where she's gone. Jackson and the girls are down on the beach. He's still obsessed with the idea of building a fire, sending up a signal of some sort. Says he'll burn everything he can find. Not sure how much difference it'll make, to be honest, but I think he just needs the distraction.'

Lauren forces herself to have a mouthful of warm oats and, to her surprise, it tastes delicious. For a few minutes she thinks of nothing else but the food in front of her. Mac busies himself with tidying up, and when she has finished, he asks her again why she was in the Abbot's quarters.

Lauren hesitates before answering. She's not sure she wants to admit her suspicions out loud. But this is Mac she is talking to. Mac, who she knows better than anyone else in here, who has been nothing but supportive of her even when she was an outcast. And who also knows a lot more than the rest of them about medical matters.

'I wanted to examine the bodies. For evidence.'

'Why? Evidence of what?' he says, looking appalled.

'What do you think?' Lauren realises her voice is rising, but she doesn't care. 'Two people have died in two days! That's not normal, is it?'

Mac sits beside her.

'OK, back up a bit. You're saying, what, that you don't think their deaths were accidents?'

'I don't know. Maybe. There are things that don't add up about Nate's death. Something doesn't feel right.' Lauren wants to trust Mac, but decides to keep her cards close to her chest for now.

'Well, yeah, none of this feels right. We're trapped on an island, two people are dead. But it doesn't mean there's something sinister going on, hen. Nate tripped and fell. It was a God-awful accident, but there's nothing more to it than that.'

'How do you know? How can you be *sure*? Why was he even there in the first place? What if he wasn't alone? And Nico – people don't just drop dead for no reason! What if their deaths are connected?'

'I have no idea why Nate was up there, but this place, this island, the storm, it's a lot to deal with. The pressure was getting to all of us. Maybe Nate just wanted a breather. And Nico – again, I can't be sure but it looks like carbon monoxide to me. You saw how close to the fire he was.'

'Come on, Mac. Really? How much closer was he than the rest of us? We were all in the same room, for God's sake! And we're still alive.'

'It's tragic, but strong young men *do* just die sometimes. It happened to someone I knew once, on the pitch, younger than me. It's one of the reasons I became a paramedic, because I didn't know how to save him. Look at the conditions on this island: the cold, the lack of sleep, the stress, the lack of food and water. Maybe it was simply dehydration. You know he wouldn't drink the water from the well.'

'Seriously? You can't believe it's just a coincidence, both of them dying in such a short space of time.'

'There could be other explanations, lots of them. Nico was a last-minute addition, remember? Maybe Production skimped on his medical? One thing we do know is that they have been careless about our welfare right from the start. Who's to say he didn't have an underlying health issue? It's horrible. But both deaths have straightforward explanations.' He pauses. 'Occam's razor, you know?'

Lauren nods reluctantly. She knows, often refers to it herself when an investigation gets complicated.

'Yeah, so by that logic, Nate fell, and Nico was taken ill. No one else was involved, no one *killed* them. You'll go crazy thinking they did,' Mac adds.

'I'll go even more crazy if I don't try and figure out what happened. Especially if I'm the one in the firing line when the police eventually get here.'

'No one is going to think you had anything to do with their deaths, Lauren, because they were just accidents. I know what Nico said, but he was just mouthing off. Trust me, you need to leave this to the professionals, otherwise it *will* start to look suspicious. Who else have you spoken to about this?'

'Just Jude, after she told me what happened with Nate,' she says. 'She's holed up in the gatehouse. Seems to think someone from Production is out to get us. She's scared too.'

'Christ, Lauren, have some sense! Do you actually think someone from Production has been creeping around, picking us off one by one? Jude has been spiralling since that bloody portcullis fell. But I know you know better. I mean, do you really believe someone here could have murdered not one, but *two* people? Jude had reason enough to dislike Nate by the end – maybe it was her? Or what about me? It's no secret I didn't like him. Do you think *I* killed him?'

Lauren decides not to mention that the thought did briefly cross her mind less than half an hour ago.

'No, of course not. I'm not even saying someone did kill him. But I'm pretty sure someone was with Nate when he died. And I need you to help me prove it.'

Mac looks sceptical. 'What makes you think that?'

'Well, firstly, there are three sets of footprints going up to where he fell from, when there should only have been two. Mine and Nate's.'

'How can you be sure someone else didn't go up another time? I know you're good at your job but, with respect, you're not a forensic scientist.' Mac is beginning to sound exasperated.

'I counted them carefully, and I've checked with everyone else. They all said they hadn't been up there. Did you go up?'

'I certainly haven't, but people's memories are funny things. Especially in circumstances like these. Anyway, even if someone had gone up there, it doesn't prove anything. It could have been any time, for any reason. For all you know it could have been someone from Production going to get Frank. Look, hen, I don't mean to pour cold water on your theory but I just don't think this is helping—'

'That's not the only thing I found. Nate's ring was in the graveyard, wedged into a crevice on the far side. There is no way he could have dropped it there by mistake, and he never took it off. I think there was a struggle, that someone ripped the ring off. And I think whoever did it must have hidden it there, trying to cover up that they pushed him.'

'Please, Lauren, stop. This is too much. You're seeing things that aren't there, conflating things that aren't related.'

'I'm not, I'm sure I'm not. Look, here's the ring.' She scrabbles in her pocket for it and holds it up triumphantly. 'See how sharp it is? And if you look at his hands you can see where it must have been pulled off him.'

Mac looks stunned. 'For God's sake, Lauren. Please don't tell me you *touched* the bodies?'

She nods almost imperceptibly.

He thumps both hands on the table, making her jump.

'Jesus, how could you be so *stupid*? That's tampering with evidence. You know better than that! If their deaths *are* suspicious, you've just put yourself at the top of the list of suspects. Never mind playing havoc with the investigation. You need to stop this, for your own sake and everyone else's! I'm warning you—'

'*Warning* me?'

'Telling you, advising you. Say it how you like, I'm just trying to protect you,' he says under his breath, glowering at her. 'Give me the ring.'

Hating herself for doing it, she backs away from him as far as she can without actually moving the bench. She knows Mac has a temper – he has never tried to hide it – but it's the first time she's considered what he might be capable of in the heat of the moment. Is he really trying to protect her, or protect himself? Trying to muster her courage, she pulls herself up, straightens her back, and asks the question she dreads the answer to.

'Where were you when Nate went missing?'

Mac tenses, his eyes flashing with unbridled fury.

'What the *fuck*?' His voice is dangerously low, almost a growl. The bench he was sitting on screeches in protest as he pushes it away, standing up and planting his vast clenched fists on the tabletop. He stares at her menacingly.

For the first time, she truly feels their difference in size – his height as he towers above her, the immense strength of his muscles. Proud at how calm her voice is, she says again, 'Simple question, Mac. Where were you?'

'Are you out of your mind? I'm not even going to dignify that with an answer.' He lashes out with his left foot and kicks Nate's chair over with a bang, then storms out of the hall, slamming the double doors behind him.

Lauren trembles as they reverberate with the force.

Chapter Thirty-four

Moments later, Lauren follows in his wake, shouting as loud as she can, 'Mac, wait! I'm sorry, I didn't mean that!'

He doesn't respond and keeps his head down as he strides though the cloisters. She speeds up, running now, but he is too fast and has crossed the graveyard before she even reaches the gate. Should she even be following him? Part of her hates herself for even considering he might be involved. He's always been the one person she could rely on, has always supported her. And having a temper doesn't make you a murderer, but why is he *so* adamant that Nate – and Nico's – deaths were accidents? Why is he so keen she stop investigating?

She forces herself to sit down, perching on a raised stone monument and mentally apologising to its occupant. She feels further away from the truth than ever. And, she has to admit, she is scared. If someone on the island really *is* a murderer, who's next? She closes her eyes, trying to pick her way through the labyrinth, but her thoughts are tumbling over each other and coming back to the one question everything hinges on: who? Who was with Nate in the belfry?

Whoever it was, they have tried to cover their tracks. Did that include killing Nico? He was always good at eavesdropping, stirring the pot. Did he pay for that with his life this time?

On reflex she reaches into her pocket for her phone, intending to note down her thoughts like she would in any investigation. Her hand twitches in frustration when she feels the only thing she has in there: Nate's ring, yet another piece of this ghastly puzzle that she is no closer to solving.

Instead, she picks up a fallen twig that is lying next to the path. Using it like a pen, she sketches out lines in a pathway to make a rough map of their strange little kingdom: an enclosed square for the courtyard, a long rectangle for the great hall, an octagon for the chapter house. A small circle marks the footprint of the watchtower, a square indicates the belfry. She stands up and drags the stick right round it all to mark the moat and, further out, a ragged line that indicates the shoreline and the sea beyond it.

Next, she grabs a handful of stones to represent each of them as she moves them around her makeshift map. First, the great hall, that terrible morning after the party, the last time they were all together. So much has happened since then. She cringes, remembering the mortifying way Nate spoke to her, the way the others backed him up. But that is not important, she thinks. What is important is what happened next. Where did everyone go?

Nate swept out to his quarters, Jude hot on his heels. And then there was Nico, listening outside Nate's room. The others? It's harder to know. She stayed in the great hall while they milled in and out. But Nate did not come back in, and nor to her recollection did Jude.

Lauren remembers going for a walk, leaving Mac alone in the hall, passing Nico giggling with Hollie and Taisie in the cloisters. But she has no idea how long they stood there, or where they went afterwards. The next time she saw them was in the great hall when they were summoned by the bell.

Jackson was fixing the well, and Jude was just here, wandering among the gravestones. She remembers thinking how odd it was at the time. What was she doing?

If she takes Jude's testimony at face value, there were about three hours from when she stormed out of Nate's room to when they realised he had disappeared. Three hours during which any one of them could have knocked on Nate's door, asking him to come with them to the belfry. Why the belfry? For privacy, surely. It was practically guaranteed that nobody else would disturb you there, that you wouldn't be overheard.

She was walking for around an hour before Jackson summoned them back. Now she puts all the stones in the great hall, except for Nate's, which she holds in her hand. That was the first time they noticed he was missing. And then they scattered in search of him, and she found him, just there – she sets Nate's pebble down lightly – at the foot of the belfry stairs.

She considers the other pebbles in relation to each other. So many hours passed, and everybody's movements were so disparate that it is hard to get a handle on them. She knows that Jackson succeeded in fixing the well, because it was working later. But how long would that have taken him? And who is to say that he didn't take a brief break from the work to lure Nate up into the belfry? For what, though? Once again, her imagination fails her.

Finally, Hollie and Taisie. Always together, but where? No doubt they could have tempted Nate into the belfry, but Lauren finds it hard to believe that even two of them would be a match for him, with their slight frames. And it always comes back to the same question: why? Why would they, or Jackson, or even Mac have any reason to want Nate dead? That just leaves Jude, who certainly had more motive, but Lauren just can't see it being her.

Exasperated, she scuffs the lines of her sketch with her slippered foot, kicking the stones out of place. The truth is, there was more than enough time for anybody, over the course of the afternoon, to make their way unchallenged up the belfry steps. The weather was closing in again and, after this length of time, there is simply no way to plot out the intricate back and forth of anybody's movements.

Her train of thought is interrupted by hurried footsteps. It's Hollie, walking at speed, her face grim, followed three or four steps behind by Taisie, who is out of breath.

Lauren stands up, hoping that her robes will cover the lines of her sketch, and tries for a natural tone.

'Hi, girls,' she says. 'Are you OK?' even though they are clearly not.

In response, Hollie ducks her head down to her chest, lets out a strangled sound, and bolts towards the gate to the courtyard.

'Hollie,' Taisie calls, looking distressed. 'Hollie! What are you doing? Come back!' And then to Lauren, 'Sorry. She's really not coping . . . it's been . . . well, you know.' Her face is full of anguish.

'Sure,' says Lauren. 'Of course.'

'Well, I'd better go after her,' says Taisie, her forehead twisted in concern. As she turns to go, she glances down at Lauren's feet, and the lines and shapes marked in the path, the stones lying next to each other in the dust.

'What's that?' she asks, then when Lauren hesitates. 'Drawing pictures?'

'Ha, yeah . . .' says Lauren. 'Just doodling, really.'

Taisie squints at the ground. 'Looks like some kind of map. Oh, I see it! It's, like, the island, right? What's it for?'

Cornered, Lauren feels her face reddening. 'Oh, just thinking about the last few days, trying to process. It's really to get things straight in my own head. It's so frustrating not having a phone, somewhere to make notes.' She takes a breath, aware she's babbling. 'I just feel like I'm going to forget stuff, and that feels wrong, you know? Disrespectful somehow to Nico and to Nate. Guess it's my journalist side coming out.'

Taisie looks at her as though concerned for her wellbeing, then smiles a bit blankly. 'Yeah, I guess. I miss my phone too.' She makes a sweeping gesture at the ground. 'What are the stones for?'

'Oh, they're . . . us,' says Lauren. 'One for each of us.'

'Cool,' says Taisie a bit uncertainly. 'But you're missing one.'

'What do you mean?' says Lauren.

'Frank. It's not like we ever saw him leave. Came sailing in at that window up there . . .' she gestures, 'and then, like, never seen again. These shows, they love to play tricks, right? What if he never left?'

A shiver runs through Lauren. Could he have been hiding out all this time? Taisie's right: they don't know for sure that he left.

'Yeah,' Taisie continues. 'It's sort of creepy, right? The idea that he could have been here all this time, without us knowing.'

'Why wouldn't he have just come and found us when the storm hit?'

'I thought that too,' says Taisie. 'But what if he was, like, trapped, or something during the storm? Couldn't get food and stuff?'

Lauren feels sick. It doesn't bear thinking about.

'The show wouldn't let that happen. If they'd had Frank squirrelled away somewhere, I'm sure they would have told us to go find him.' Lauren is reassuring herself as much as Taisie.

'Yeah, I'm sure you're right. Anyway, I'd better go after Hollie. Don't want her to be alone. She's a bit freaked out after everything that's happened.'

'I'm not surprised. We all are.' Lauren watches her leave, and now all she can think about is Frank. What if Taisie's right? Could he have been here all along? If they stashed him somewhere with his own supplies, might he have just hunkered down to wait it out? It seems unlikely, but you never know. And how much did she really know about Frank? Only that he was fun, a bit reckless, friendly. He didn't like Nate, that was clear. And he'd heard the rumours too. Could he have had some kind of confrontation with Nate in the belfry? He certainly would have had the opportunity to go up unseen.

She picks up an extra pebble for Frank, then hesitates, unsure where to put him on her map. What does she know of Frank's movements on the day he disappeared? He went into the belfry, and nobody saw him come out. Nor did he leave any trace back in the Saints' dormitory. If he had actually left the island, most likely would have gone down the passage to the sea cave, the one that they explored together on that first day.

Out of other options, she heads towards the outside wall of the chapter house and slips through the small door that leads to the secret tunnel to investigate.

Chapter Thirty-five

Lauren shivers as the temperature drops. The familiar smell of brine and rotting fish assails her senses. The narrow path is slick and far more slippery than before – clearly the rain has been pouring in here from the ground above. Even the walls are wet, she notices, putting her hand out to guide her.

She props the small door open to let in as much light as possible, and wonders if she should go back to the hall to get a lamp. But she doesn't want to run the risk of encountering anyone else and having to explain what she's up to. 'Just do it,' she says to herself, stepping into the spiralling passageway.

It is eerie in here, like entering a tomb. She tries to bat the thought away. Keeping her right hand on the cold wall to steady herself, she twists downwards. Just as before, the tunnel seems endless, though this time she doesn't have Frank to lighten the mood. She picks her way carefully, so as not to stumble, and it feels like an age before she hears the swell and grumble of the waves. Another turn, and she can sense the darkness thinning. She speeds up, anxious to get out of the gloom enveloping her, is about to step out of the tunnel when she is blinded by the light from a lantern shining straight into her face. It is like an interrogation beam.

'Who's there?' says a familiar voice.

Lauren stumbles backwards in fright. The heavy swell of the sea throws her off balance. She feels adrift for a moment, the rocky ceiling above pinning her down and the water below confusing her senses, making her feel claustrophobic. It's not Frank. Of course it's not.

'Wh-what are you doing here, Jackson? And get that light out of my eyes.'

'Came down to get some more fuel for my fire. What are *you* doing here?'

Her mind stutters, unable to think of a good answer. The truth – that she is looking for evidence that Frank never left – suddenly seems so absurd she doesn't want to admit it out loud. Instead, a wave of irrational anger surges through her.

'For God's sake, Jackson, your fire isn't going to help! Jude's right, they already know we're here. Meanwhile, there are two people dead and I'm trying to find out who killed them.' It's the first time she's been so explicit and immediately she regrets it.

'*Killed* them?' He leans towards her; she can feel his hot breath on her face. Alarm bells flash when she realises no one knows she's down here. The two of them are completely alone, buried under hundreds of feet of rock. She takes a step away from him, the wet stone slippery under her feet. She sees him notice.

'Lauren, why are you looking at me like that?' He moves forward and, as his mass fills her vision, all rational thought escapes her. She turns and runs, her feet slipping. Then she's scrabbling on her knees when she falls. As she gets up, she feels his fingers close on her arm and she wrenches it from his grasp.

'Where are you going? Come back!' he shouts after her as she charges blindly upwards, round and round the tunnel until she feels dizzy. Her thighs are aching and her lungs almost bursting, but adrenaline forces her to keep going, no thought in her head but the need to get away. She doesn't stop even when she can't hear him behind her any more, doesn't stop until she bursts out of the doorway beneath the chapter house. Even then, she pauses only for a moment while her eyes adjust to the light.

Then she is off and sprinting again, through the courtyard and down the slippery slope into the moat. Blindly she runs, until her legs give up, then she sinks down on to the grass, her breath coming in deep gasps, her legs aching.

She folds herself up, her head on her knees, eyes closed, doing her best not to think of anything at all, trying to control her fear.

Chapter Thirty-six

Crouched into a ball, knees pressed into eye sockets, Lauren tries to imagine that she is anywhere else in the whole world other than on this island. It doesn't work. Even her knees themselves, clad in the scratchy, and now filthy, wool of her habit, remind her that she is still a prisoner in this place. She tries to calm down and think logically, annoyed at herself for being led by fear, not facts. Christ, maybe she is as paranoid as Jude. Only moments ago she was running for her life from Jackson, of all people.

She cannot afford to crumble now. They must be only hours from rescue – please God – and she needs to understand what happened here. She can only imagine the chaos that will ensue once the outside world descends. Even if the deaths are ruled accidental, accusations will be hurled. The blight will spread like wildfire, across the papers, the TV, the internet. It will cling to all their names for ever. Especially hers. She's no fool, given the circumstances she knows she has the most to lose. She thought the stakes were high when she arrived on the island, but that's nothing compared to what she faces now. Unless she can find out the truth.

She breathes out and sits up a little straighter, consciously unfolding herself. She is just stretching her legs when she hears the squeal of a window opening in the gatehouse.

'Lauren! Are you OK? What on earth are you doing down there?'

Jude peers down at her, looking mildly irritated as she pushes her face through the small gap in the window. Embarrassed, Lauren gets to her feet quickly, hoping Jude hadn't seen her hunched over her knees.

'Oh, nothing, just having a bit of a rest.'

Something about the way Jude is having to peer through the gap and is banging her hand against the frame, trying to open the window more, reminds Lauren of the moment she first arrived at the belfry, before she found Nate. She had thought it strange at the time that the door was slightly ajar and remembers how she had to use her shoulder to push it wide enough for her to get through, because, as she knows with hindsight, his body was wedged behind it.

She has a flash of clarity, a moment of breakthrough. There are only two other people on the island slim enough to squeeze through that gap. Only two people who, if they had been with him when he fell, would have been able to get out of the door past his body. Either Hollie or Taisie was with him when he died. She is sure of it.

'Have you seen Hollie and Taisie?' she shouts to Jude, who is still gazing out of the window.

Scrunching up her eyes, Jude looks to her left, towards the beach.

'I can see Hollie. She's down on the jetty.' She looks again, momentarily thrown. 'Taisie's not there, though. Strange, that, seeing one without the other. They're normally joined at the hip. Like twins. What do you want them for? I hope you aren't planning to interrogate those poor girls. They wouldn't hurt a fly.'

'No, no, I'm just checking where everyone is, making sure they're safe. I'll be back in a bit,' says Lauren distractedly, heading up the other side of the moat and down towards the cliff path as quickly as she can.

She pauses for a moment in the gorse at the top. The beach below is unrecognisable, utterly transformed from the pristine canvas they landed on what seems like weeks ago. In place of the white sand is a glutinous grey paste, punctured by sharp rocks. The high waterline, which only days ago was marked by a trail of delicate shell fragments, is strewn with torn roots and branches ensnared by a net of slimy green seaweed. Right at the end is Jackson's bonfire, built on the ashes of the fire that burned all their things that first day. It is burning, but its low flames are hardly the roaring beacon he'd no doubt been imagining.

She can see the jetty where the ten of them first arrived, laughing with nervous excitement. There is a solitary figure, standing poised and still at the far end of the dilapidated wooden boards, the dishevelled hood of their monk's robe pulled over their head.

Lauren begins to pick her way down, the track more treacherous than ever after the storm. She has to concentrate on keeping her feet steady. Twice they nearly slide out from under her on the rain-soaked grass. She has to grasp the heather that clings to the steep slope to stop herself falling, an electric shock of fright shooting from her wrists to her elbows. Her haste to get to the beach is making her reckless.

Heart racing, breath ragged, she forces herself to slow down and concentrate on the placement of her feet. As her pulse slows, something Jude said comes back to her: *Strange, that, seeing one without the other. They're normally joined at the hip.*

Yes, it is strange. What did she say? *Like twins.* Lauren's mind flicks rapidly through everything she can remember about Hollie and Taisie since they arrived on the island. Sure enough, they always seem to be together. From the moment they were reunited on the beach they have been inseparable, an impenetrable team of two. But so what? They're friends, aren't they? Childhood friends. Why wouldn't they spend all their time together on this inhospitable island? That's what she would have done in their place.

And yet . . . and yet . . . there's something. Something about that phrase Jude used. *Normally, they're joined at the hip.* Yes. Apart from one time. They're not together now, but there was one other time. One time when subconsciously Lauren had clocked that the two of them were separated.

She comes to a dead halt, desperately trying to remember. She closes her eyes, playing the movie of the last few days on fast forward in her mind. There. That's it. She sees again the lull in the storm, the moments before they realised that Nate had disappeared. Everyone summoned back to the great hall by the tolling of the cloister bell. Her own dull headache and sense of dislocation in the wake of the previous night's disaster. Hollie was there before her. She was seated with Jude, Jackson standing by the fire. It was only after the rest of them were gathered that Taisie appeared in a flurry through the doors that led to the cloisters, moving quickly to Hollie's side and giving her a hug.

Lauren plays the scene in her head again to be sure. Taisie, coming in alone from the direction of the courtyard out of breath. Hollie's quick concerned look. Taisie sinking her head on to the familiarity of Hollie's shoulder.

A tiny snapshot. Barely anything. Is it possible it could have some meaning?

Lauren glances down the beach to where the lone figure still stands at the end of the jetty. She doesn't yet know the answers, but finally she feels that she is asking the right questions.

Chapter Thirty-seven

By the time Lauren has picked her way down the cliff face, her mind is racing. She tries to recall every interaction she's had with the girls.

She sees Taisie as she first met her on the boat, picture-perfect but almost mute, until she flew into her friend's arms on the beach. She sees the two of them finishing each other's sentences as they talk about their work. She sees them moving together, perfectly in sync as they cook. She sees Taisie, always the quieter one, looking quickly over at Hollie before speaking, in a way that started to grate on Lauren's nerves a little. And she sees them – here she catches her breath at the memory – laughing with Nico, the three of them always giggling together at a private joke.

'It's impossible,' she says to herself out loud. There's no way that gentle, reserved young woman could have had the means, or motive, to harm anyone, surely? But then she thinks of the belfry door, the narrow gap through which only Hollie or Taisie could have fit. And hasn't Lauren constantly under-estimated them? Hasn't everyone? Just because they seem innocent doesn't mean they are. And they've proven time and again how resourceful they are, how loyal to one another.

Something in her gut twists and Lauren finds herself sprinting full tilt across the sodden sand, curling her toes into her cursed slippers to try to keep them on her feet. By the time she reaches the base of the jetty the figure at the end hasn't moved.

'Hollie!' she calls. 'Hollie!'

As she is scrambling on to the wooden planks, slowing down to catch her breath, she realises belatedly that she hasn't formulated a single coherent question, not even as an opener. She just wants to talk to Hollie, she thinks, that's all. Ask her, perhaps, where Taisie is, and take it from there.

She knows that something isn't right. That something is amiss between the girls, and she suspects it is connected to Nate and Nico. She just needs to look Hollie in the eye. Look her in the eye and see what comes.

But as the figure turns round, alerted by the creak of rickety wood, Lauren sees that the eyes confronting her are not greeny-brown, as Hollie's are. Rather it is Taisie's startling – and startled – blue-grey eyes that peer up at her from under the cowl. Did Jude get them mixed up? Or had Taisie finally caught up with Hollie, only for Hollie to run off again?

Taisie is visibly distraught, her whole body trembling. Salty tracks of tears have made an ugly path down her pink cheeks. Her eyes are sunken, the deep bags under them made darker by the shadow of the cowl.

'Oh my God. Thank God it's you. I've been so scared.'

It's such an unexpected opening and Lauren is so surprised to see her that she comes to a halt, trying to take it in.

'Taisie! Hi . . . Taisie, what is it? What's wrong?'

As Taisie begins to sob, she moves forward to hug her, feeling her sharp shoulder blades and her body shaking through the rough cloth.

'It's OK. Everything's OK. I've got you. I've got you. Come on, Taisie. Take a breath. Just take one breath.'

But Taisie doesn't stop sobbing, dropping through Lauren's embrace on to her knees.

'It's not OK. It's not. I'm not safe. I'm never going to be safe. Never again.'

'Of course, you're safe. Production will be with us today, I'm sure of it. It'll be over soon. It'll all be over.'

'It'll never be over,' says Taisie, quietly. 'It'll never be over for me.'

Her hood slips back and she gazes up at Lauren with wide, imploring eyes, pupils dilated like a frightened animal. As Lauren looks down, she recalls seeing those eyes before.

Nate's eyes, as he looked up at her from the sand after Mac had felled him during the coracle challenge; Nate's eyes meeting hers over the fire after the portcullis fell, mouthing 'thank you'. She has a flash of insight. Unless she is grossly mistaken their eyes are the same colour, have the same unusual, charcoal ring around the outside of the iris, the same slightly upturned shape.

She shakes her head, trying to dislodge the thought. Surely not. But when she speaks, her voice is sharper than she means it to be. She grapples to lift Taisie to her feet, and her mind is whirring as she tries to think of the most comforting thing to say, rather than blurting out her thoughts.

'What do you mean, it will never be over?' she says. 'What will never be over?'

But even as the words are coming out of her mouth, Lauren is remembering the night when they shared their stories over the feast. Taisie's words about her childhood come rushing back to her: a single mother. A mother who had been a make-up artist, worked on films. Who had brought up her daughter alone in London with no sign of her father. She thinks, too, of their prize, their desire to go to

LA. Hollie made every effort to be businesslike, but clearly it was deeper than that for Taisie. Things they needed to do. Things to do with her mum.

She takes a deep breath. 'Taisie,' she says, 'did you know Nate before? Before we got here?'

Taisie's eyes are full of scorn. 'No, I did not know him,' she says, shortly. And then, emphasising each word, 'And he did not know me.'

Lauren looks at her for a long moment. As with so many of her investigations, she reasons that silence is the best tactic here. She holds her body still and keeps her face neutral, giving Taisie a chance to fill the void. Inside her mind, the broken pieces of the picture begin to move into place. It's only a tiny corner of the full image, but it's something.

Still Taisie is silent, head bent. Very quietly, Lauren leans towards her. It doesn't matter that they are at the end of a creaking jetty, the waves crashing below, the gulls crying above. They could be any-where: the world has shrunk to just the two of them.

'But did you know who he was?' she asks, her voice as calm and low as a breeze. 'When you came here?'

For a minute it is as though Taisie hasn't heard her, but then she looks up, fury in her eyes. 'No, of course not. It was *you* who made me realise. All this. All of it. It's your fault.'

Lauren takes a step back. 'My fault?' she says. 'What did I do?'

'With all your *investigations*, and . . . and your *prying*. And *calling out*. If it hadn't been for you . . .' She lapses into silence again, and then her voice rises, the words tumbling out faster. 'It was that night. The night of the party. Before that, I knew who he was, obviously. I mean, I knew he was, like, some big movie star, but no more than that. I don't really watch action movies. But even though I'd never seen him in a film, he seemed somehow . . . familiar. Hollie felt the same, like we knew him, but we couldn't work out where from.'

She takes a breath and seems poised to say more, when suddenly her head whips round to look up the beach as though she has heard something. Seeing nothing, she drags her eyes back to her feet. 'And that's it. You can't make me say any more. I promised I wouldn't tell anyone. I wouldn't say a thing. I swore I wouldn't . . .'

She's almost sobbing, and part of Lauren wants to just let it go, leave it there, wait it out until someone else arrives on the island to unravel the pieces. But she can't.

'But there was more, wasn't there? Was he your—'

Before she can say the word, Taisie cuts across her, fear replaced by rage.

'Father. Yes. *Father.* If you can call it that. I told you, I had no idea till that night. It's your fault I even figured it out. And I wish – oh my God, I wish so, so much – that I hadn't. I'd give anything not to know. Everything was all right before that. But it was when you were shouting at Nate, going on and on about this girl and that girl. And then . . .'

She goes quiet, flicking her eyes up and down the beach for a millisecond before continuing, her voice so low that Lauren has to lean towards her.

'Then you mentioned *The Final Escape*. How he had a small part in that. And it was like a light went on. Because my mum worked on that movie. She was a make-up artist on it. It was the last film she ever worked on.'

'So, you think—'

'I don't think, I know. The minute you said he had a part in it, I suddenly understood. I never knew why Mum gave up her career when she had me, why she never went back to it. She would never talk about it, but from everything I read online, she'd been smashing it – moving to Hollywood, doing make-up for the stars. But then she gave it all up, moved back to the UK to have me. But she was still so young, she could have gone back. I've always blamed myself, you know, for ruining her life. I could tell she missed her work. It's why I wanted to go into make-up – to make her proud. But after you said about Nate, about what he did to your friend . . . I get it now. He must have got her pregnant, then dumped her and trashed her reputation. He ruined her life. And now he's ruined mine.'

'But why didn't you say anything when you realised? If you'd said that night that he was your . . . your father . . .' Taisie gives a tiny grimace in acknowledgement, 'then . . . then I could have helped you. Got some kind of justice for your mum. For you.' Lauren pictures an alternative reality, a world where she and Taisie took Nate down. A world that didn't end in two corpses and the pair of them alone on this jetty.

'You'd have loved that, wouldn't you?' spits out Taisie venomously. 'If I'd helped you prove your point. Been living, breathing evidence that Nate knocked up his make-up artist then dumped her. But no. Unlike you, I don't just *blurt out* that kind of thing. I needed to think. It would have had consequences for me, for us.'

She sees Lauren looking blank. 'For me and Hollie. For our *careers*,' she says patiently. 'What if he came after me, threatened me with lawyers, like he was going to do you?' She looks terrified again. 'You can't tell anyone. You can't tell anyone I told you this. If you do, I'll just deny it. I promised . . .' Fear is back in her face.

'Promised who?' says Lauren. 'If you promised Nate, then, surely . . . I mean, he's . . .' Suddenly the penny drops. 'Hollie. You promised Hollie, didn't you? That you'd keep quiet. Look, I'm sure she'll understand. You had to tell somebody.'

A sob tears through Taisie's body. '*Understand*? You have no idea. No idea at all. Of course she won't understand. She told me – made me *swear* – that I wouldn't talk to anybody. And you've no idea what she's like. I can't do or say anything . . . anything *at all* unless she tells me it's OK.'

Lauren thinks again of the two girls, thick as thieves. How the quiet, circumspect Taisie seems to thrive in the company of the more outgoing Hollie. But, also, how Taisie looks to her before speaking, checking that she can, looking for validation. What had appeared to be a tight bond suddenly seems like something different. Claustrophobic. Suffocating. Controlling.

And still, she realises, she is no closer to understanding what actually happened. She is trying to frame a question, one that will penetrate Taisie's fear and unlock some answers, when Taisie gives a strangled half-laugh.

'Funny thing is, I didn't even tell Hollie, for once. Didn't tell her what I'd guessed. 'Cause just for once I wanted to do something on my own. I wanted to tell him I knew who he was, hear his side of the story without her interfering. I wanted to do it by myself.' She looks down again, a tear falling on her hands and mingling with the salt spray. 'Though look how that turned out.'

'So, you spoke to him yourself? You decided to tell him?'

Taisie nods. 'Yes. The day after the party, when he asked you to apologise. It was already such a weird day. After the night before, no one knew what to do with themselves. You disappeared – don't blame you – and so did Nate and Jude for a bit. I was helping with the food as usual, and then I saw Nate leave in a rush. I followed him and asked him if we could have a word in private. It was gross. He gave me this look and said, "Sure thing, sweetheart." For a second it was like he thought I was hitting on him. I should have stopped then, but I wanted to wipe that smirk off his face.'

'So you took him to the belfry?'

'He took me. Said he wanted to be a hundred-per-cent sure that no one would see or hear us. So, I went with him, and I just followed him up those stupid stairs. I was so desperate to talk to him, tell him what I knew. Like I didn't think, did I? I just did what he said.'

Lauren pictures the two of them, the tall muscular man and the slight figure of the girl, moving up that open staircase in the gloom of early evening. She has a horrible feeling she knows what comes next.

'When we got to the top, to the platform, he wanted us to sit down. But I felt uncomfortable with that, so I kind of leaned against the wall, in the corner. He was all puffed out but smiling. Leering at me. Kind of towering over me. So, I just got straight to it. I told him my mother's name. The film they met on. Everything. And yeah, for a second or two it did get rid of that stupid smile.

'And then he laughed. But, like, a furious laugh. It was like a switch went off in his head. You've no idea. His eyes went kind of dead, even though he was grinning. And then he . . . he went for me. He said he didn't believe a word of what I was saying. That I was a lying gold-digger. That I was deluded. That I was making the whole thing up to get his money. Like I would need it! He was yelling, like actually screaming. Saying he was only on the show to remind the world what a great guy Nate Stirling was, whatever his "bitch ex-wife" might be threatening to say. Yelling about lawyers, needing to get away from all that mess.'

A-ha, thinks Lauren. So that's why he was really here. 'On good terms' indeed. Had Jennifer finally got wind of what he was really like? Or had she always known and had finally had enough?

'H-he said if Jen found out he had a child, when she was never able to have one of her own, she'd stop at nothing to ruin him. That he couldn't let that happen. And that's when I realised I was at the top of that tower with him. On my own. And nobody knew we were there. And there was like zero chance anybody would hear us.'

Taisie hiccups, and Lauren fights an urge to put an arm around her, in case it stops her talking.

'Then it got worse. He stopped screaming, and his face changed. And his voice went all quiet, kind of like he was hissing. And he said, really quietly, that my mother was a whore. That she would sleep with anyone. And that looking at me, the way I paraded myself online, well, maybe I was the same . . .' Taisie trails off, leaving Lauren fighting a rising tide of horror.

'And he got this look in his eye, kind of wild, but with a sort of creepy smile. He started coming towards me.' Taisie's voice drops so low that Lauren barely catches the next words.

'He just didn't stop. Before I knew it, he was like grabbing at my robe, pulling me towards him. It was horrific. I didn't know if he was trying to kiss me or kill me. I was so scared, I couldn't even scream. And then I, like, just pushed myself away from the wall, anything to get away from him. But by mistake I pushed him away too, too hard. I didn't mean to. And then for a second, he was balanced on the edge, tipping over, and I grabbed for his hand. I caught it, held on for as long as I could, but I wasn't strong enough. His hand slipped through mine. And he just . . . he just toppled backwards, his other arm kind of waving around, and then he was gone. All I was left with was his ring. It came off when I was trying to stop him falling.'

She stops and swallows, tears pouring down her face. 'Then . . . then I ran down the stairs, in the dark. Oh my God, it was so frightening. And when I got to the bottom he was . . . he was . . . he wasn't saying anything, he wasn't moving. He was dead.' She chokes, unable to get any more words out.

'And then?' says Lauren gently, after a pause.

'I ran. Out the door, into the graveyard. It was so cold, so dark. I wasn't really thinking straight. I was still holding his ring and I panicked, stuffed it behind a grave. And then I ran, ran all the way back to find Hollie.'

Chapter Thirty-eight

A silence descends. Lauren is intensely aware of the water beneath them and the sky above. It's as if the two of them are floating in a void, untethered from reality.

'So then you told Hollie what happened,' she says. It's not really a question.

'Yeah. I told Hollie, when you were all out trying to find him.' Taisie shivers, as though trying to shake off a memory. 'She went mad, at first . . . and then she did what she always does. She took control. Once she'd calmed down. We knew we didn't have much time, that one of you would find him sooner or later. Hollie said we had to make a plan. And her plan was just . . . say nothing. Not a word, to anyone.'

A shiver runs down Lauren's spine as she remembers the desolate minutes she had spent holding Nate's lifeless hand, screaming for help. How could Taisie have just left him there? It is unthinkable.

'Do nothing? Seriously? You might have been able to help him. Mac might have been able to save him.'

Taisie starts wailing again. 'No, no it was too late. He was dead, I promise he was dead.' She hiccups, then continues. 'Nothing anyone could do would have made a difference. I'm sure of it.' Her next words are stilted as she struggles for breath. 'So, so, Hollie said, she said it would be best if we kept quiet, then no one would know what happened, and . . . and because of where he was, the way he was lying, people would think he'd fallen, or maybe jumped, 'cause of what you said.'

Taisie's words bring back the guilt Lauren felt after discovering his body. Guilt that threatened to engulf her when she thought she might be in some way responsible for his death.

'And you agreed, did you, to say nothing?'

'No, no, I didn't. Not at first. I wanted to confess. I'd killed someone! I told Hollie I needed to tell the truth. And she got, like, really angry. Said he had got what was coming to him. That he deserved it. Said he'd probably have killed *me* if I hadn't done what I did. She said if I told the truth, the scandal would ruin our careers, destroy us, destroy everything we had worked so hard for, just like he had destroyed my mum and those other women you knew about, like your friend. I couldn't argue with that, could I?' She shrugs and gives a small, hopeless smile.

'Taisie, that wouldn't have happened. You didn't kill him – not on purpose, anyway. You were trying to protect yourself. You didn't do anything wrong. I know I messed up, confronting him like I did, but you could have come to me. I could have helped you. I *would* have helped you.'

'Yeah, maybe. But he was still dead, wasn't he? And that was my fault. Hollie convinced me. Said that keeping quiet was the best option for us, for our future, and by the time you found him, it was too late to do anything else. We had already lied to you all, and you all thought he had fallen, like she said you would.'

In truth, Lauren doesn't know that she could have helped Taisie. The weight of Nate's superstardom, even in death, might have crushed the girl, as it had crushed Lauren herself. Looking at the tiny, beaten figure in front of her, Lauren feels another wave of fury rising in her. Nate's final action, his legacy, was to destroy yet another young life.

But, she thinks slowly, it wasn't just one more life, was it? There's a glaring void at the heart of this confession. She pictures three young heads together, bent over the lavatorium, deep in talk, their constant giggles. What about Nico? If her hunch is right and Nate and Nico's deaths are connected, Taisie is not telling the whole truth.

She looks up slowly to find Taisie watching her, her expression unreadable for a second before it crumples again in tears. She's clearly guessed what Lauren's thinking.

'Nico?' asks Lauren flatly, careful not to betray any emotion in her tone. Nico, who liked to listen, who hung around near doorways, hoping to overhear whispered conversations and people's secrets.

'That wasn't me! I wouldn't . . . It was her. I promise. I swear. It was all her. All of it. She took it too far. She always does.'

'What did she do, Taisie? What did she do to Nico?'

Taisie whimpers. 'He heard us when we were talking by the fire. We didn't realise he was there, but then the next day, after breakfast, we all went down to the storerooms together, do you remember? He said he'd heard everything – what I'd done to Nate, that we were covering it up. He was kind of smiling when he said it. Made it seem like it was all OK, like he was on our side. And I believed him. I mean, I was terrified, thought I was going to be sick, but I thought he was our friend, that he understood.'

Lauren feels sick herself. From what she knew about him, there's no way Nico would be able to keep something like that to himself, not unless there was something in it for him.

'I'm guessing that wasn't the end of it?' she says softly.

'No,' Taisie continues sadly. 'He started talking about how much money we make, how we couldn't possibly need it all.'

Lauren can see where this is going. 'He was planning to black-mail you?'

'Yes, he wanted us to pay him to keep quiet. We didn't agree to anything, obviously. Hollie said we would think about it, tell him our decision later. But then he started having a go at you, saying it was your fault Nate died, I think he was trying to divert attention away from me, from us, but he was just making it worse. Making what happened seem suspicious. Until he started saying all those things, throwing around accusations, you all thought Nate had fallen. It would all have been OK.'

Taisie, having finally reached the end of her confession, lets out a wail and buries her face in her hands. Lauren feels wrung out. Her limbs are freezing and her teeth have started to chatter. She is both shocked and disgusted by what she has heard, especially given what must have hap-pened next. Ignoring Taisie's distress, she opts for bluntness.

'So, he said he would blackmail you, and you and Hollie killed him. God, Taisie, how could you? He didn't deserve to die.'

'No!' screams Taisie. 'I never did it. I never touched him. It was her, all *her*. She told me that she'd, like, take care of it, that's all. We barely had time to talk after that, and I just told her I had to confess, or we'd all be ruined, every one of us on the island. She said no. She said leave it to her, that she'd fix it. I never dreamed . . . never for a second dreamed she'd do something so horrific.'

Lauren is remorseless. 'It was the meal, wasn't it?' She pictures the two girls, such a familiar sight next to the fire, handing out bowls for the soup, the liquid sloshing into the bowls. 'But how did you do it? We all ate from the same pot that night.'

'I told you. It wasn't me. It wasn't *ME*!' sobs Taisie. But Lauren's mind is busy, freezing the memory, holding it up to the light. 'The same pot . . . but you guys handed out the bowls, didn't you? You gave them all out individually. It wasn't in the soup at all. It was in the bowl.'

Taisie nods, once, before Lauren continues, 'But what on earth . . . what did you put in it?'

'You never listened to us that carefully, did you?' says Taisie. Her voice is muffled, but calmer. 'I could tell you thought we were air-heads, judging us before you even knew us. But if you'd been paying attention, Hollie was actually talking about it just the other day. Our historical beauty piece – what people used to use for make-up, what they grew in their gardens. Physic gardens, they called them, not just for make-up, but for medicine too. We've visited loads of them. We even went to a Poison Garden, way up north. Annick Castle. Alnwick? Something like that. That's where they told us about yew trees, how deadly they can be, how even a tiny part of it can kill someone. That's how she knew what to do.'

Lauren shivers. 'Of course. There are yew trees all over the graveyard.'

Taisie nods. 'Exactly. Their leaves are kind of spiky, they look a bit like rosemary. You see now, don't you? I had forgotten all about it, but Hollie didn't forget. I mean, whatever you think, she's *not* stupid. Once she's learned something, she never forgets it. She must have remembered how dangerous it was and slipped a bit into Nico's bowl. She wouldn't have needed much of it – a couple of leaves. He never would have seen it or smelled it; wouldn't have even known it was in there.

'And then we had, like, two seconds on our own before we went to sleep last night, and I tried to talk to her then about what were we going to do. Would we pay Nico off, or what? And she just said not to worry. That she had thought of something, and it would all be OK. We couldn't talk any more, not with everyone around. And then I woke up this morning and Nico was . . . was . . . well, the minute I saw him, I knew. I knew she had killed him.'

The last words are a shriek, and the flood of words isn't stopping.

'And now, what do I do? What do I *do*? I've told you now. We're both in danger. She killed Nico and now you know the truth she'll probably try and kill you too.'

Lauren tries desperately to pick apart the threads of this story. She can see it all too clearly: Taisie terrified. Hollie ambitious and controlling. Nico, chancing his luck. She's seen for herself that Hollie is no fool. Whatever Taisie thinks, it's been a while since Lauren has thought of either of them as an airhead or underestimated their intelligence. She sorts furiously through everything Taisie has told her, trying to see where the gaps lie.

'When did you talk to her?' asks Lauren, suspiciously. 'When did you get all these details?'

'Just before I saw you. We were down on coracle cove together. We told Jackson we'd go there to see if we could get those boats round to the bonfire. Stupid idea, obviously, but we needed time alone. I needed to find out what exactly she had done, but we had a row, and she ran off. That's when we met you, in the graveyard. I told her that as soon as help arrived, I was going to tell everyone the truth, and that's why I'm here now, waiting, just waiting for them to come so I can tell them everything before she can hurt anyone else.'

As Taisie pauses for breath, Lauren's mind is accelerating through the details. That Nate was Taisie's father – yes, now she knows, she can see it, should have spotted it before. Nate's terrifying rage – she has no problem at all believing that, or the manner of his death; a young woman just trying to protect herself. Nico's attempt to blackmail them – that too rings true. But Hollie? Lovely, bright Hollie, with her quick smile, her thoughtfulness. Is she really capable of all of this? Coercion, cover up and cold-blooded murder?

But then Lauren thinks of how close she and Taisie are, the fierce loyalty between them. Is that all it is? She has suspected for a while that the glossy shine of the girls' glittering career is not all it appears.

Their image is so tightly controlled, so unified, it has to be drawn by one hand. It makes sense that only one of them is in charge, and from the way Taisie defers to her, Lauren had always guessed it was Hollie. That under the softness and smiles there was ferocious ambition there. But murder? That's something else entirely.

Of all the questions running through Lauren's head, one rings so loudly that she has to ask it.

'How on earth does she think she'll get away with it? There will be evidence, surely.'

'Don't you remember? She sent Nico out last night, to get some rosemary for the soup. She put some shreds of yew in the pocket of his robe this morning, so it looks like he picked some by accident. Even joked with Nico last night about whether he'd ever seen rosemary in the wild. So if they find any traces in his blood they'll probably just think he made a mistake, poisoned himself.'

'But there must be more,' says Lauren, horrified. 'What about the bowls? They would analyse those, surely?'

Taisie gestures down the beach, to where Jackson's bonfire is still burning. 'You know Jackson's been burning everything he can find? Hollie came down here and put all the bowls on the bonfire. They're long gone by now.'

She is right. At the far end of the beach Lauren can see Jackson's fire now burning brightly, flames leaping. If the bowls are on it, there will be nothing left of them or the yew leaves now. Finally, Lauren knows the truth, but what can she do it about it?

'They'll catch her,' says Lauren with conviction. 'All you have to do is tell them what you've told me.'

At this, Taisie's eyes go wide, and her breath starts to come in shallow bursts. 'No,' she says. 'No. No way. She'll get to me first. She'll . . . you have no idea what she's like. You see what she's capable of. If she knew I had breathed a word of this . . . I've put you in danger too.'

Taisie's distress is so overwhelming that part of Lauren just wants to take her in her arms and console her. But another, more rational, part of her brain is whirring, trying to connect this murderous version of Hollie with the guileless young woman she's come to know this last week.

'Taisie, honestly, what do you think she'll do? Do you really think she'd come after me? After *you*?' she asks, but a wild look is coming into Taisie's eyes, her sobs increasing. Lauren gives up trying to reason with her. 'Come on, Taisie, calm down. We're safe here. Help will be coming soon,' she says, hoping she is right. Taisie seems to give in and steps towards her, clearly ready to sink into an embrace.

Out of nowhere a streak of movement catches Lauren's eye. Hollie is hurtling towards them, thundering forwards like a rampaging bull, fury distorting her features, screaming at the top of her voice, 'Stop, *stop*! Stop now!'

Chapter Thirty-nine

Everything happens too fast. Before Lauren can stop her, Hollie slams into Taisie, fists flying. There is a thud as a punch connects, and then the two of them are a whirl of motion, limbs flying ungainly in their voluminous habits.

'Get off her! Get off!' Lauren yells, reaching out to drag Hollie away from Taisie, but she is pulled into the mêlée of grasping hands and flailing limbs. She winces as sharp nails dig deep into her soft flesh, and she feels a merciless tug on her hair, a handful being torn from the roots. Her brain is struggling to process what is happening and how to end it. Desperate to free herself, impose some kind of order, she tries to pull herself away from them and, as she does so, looks down to see that the three of them are teetering perilously close to the edge of the jetty. They are only inches away from the freezing sea, and the treacherous pull of the current.

She braces her feet as best she can against the boards, curling her toes to grip, to save her from the maelstrom of limbs and the swirling water below.

'Watch out! We're going to fall in!' she screams.

It makes no difference. The girls are locked in battle, oblivious to the danger. Neither heeds her warning and, one last time, Lauren's slippers betray her. She loses her footing on the slick surface of the boards, her feet sliding out from under her, and she teeters on the edge. For a second, she sees Taisie above her and reaches out, but her hands catch only air. Then she is toppling backwards, Hollie flailing by her side.

She falls too fast to take a breath. She plunges into the sea below, the ice cold forcing all the air from her lungs. Water closes over her head, plunging her into silent darkness, enveloping her in a world of pain. The cold burns, pins and needles piercing her skin as her body convulses.

She forces herself to open her eyes, straining to see upwards. Out of reach, blurry tendrils of weak sunlight filter through the surface. She tries to kick towards them, but her legs have lost all power. The heavy wool of her robe clings to her, tangling round her knees, dragging at her ankles. Her hands grasp impotently at the cloud of cloth, but there is too much. It is pulling her under. She tugs again at her habit, but can't release herself. Her legs and hands flail hopelessly. The light recedes as she descends. She is sinking. Cold is wrapping itself around her like a deathly shroud.

For a millisecond, it is almost a relief. She feels a zen-like calm. It is quiet here. Peaceful. A release from the horrors above.

Then a shaft of panic shoots through her brain. Is this how she will die? Sinking into oblivion without protest, simply giving up?

Every nerve on high alert, she fights the feeling of surrender. She will not let herself die like this. Making one last effort to haul the robes off her legs, she kicks as hard as she can. She feels herself rising a little, and kicks again, channelling all the strength she can muster. Is she moving? The light seems a little closer. One more kick – she forces her arms through the water, shoulders straining. Just one more . . .

And then she breaks through the surface, swallowing a mouthful of ice-cold brine. She chokes as she tries to gasp air deep into her burning lungs. Fighting to tread water, she manages to raise herself up enough to get her bearings, and is alarmed to see that the current has dragged her away from the safety of the jetty. Worse, only one figure stands there peering into the sea below. Taisie.

Hollie is in the water, her wavy hair streaming out from her head like seaweed, her face sinking again and again under the surface.

There are twenty metres between them. Lauren's instincts tell her to start swimming towards her, to help her. But a deep buried memory from years of sailing, capsizing in freezing temperatures, stops her. She knows what is happening to her body. This is cold-water shock, and it could kill her. Her body has gone into overdrive, the blood rushing to her heart and lungs to try to save her. She needs to control her breathing, stop gasping, inhale air, not water, before she does anything else. If she tries to swim now, out of breath and panicking, she could die, and quickly. Be calm, she thinks. I must be calm if I want to survive.

Ninety seconds is all she needs. She knows she needs to float to live.

She tries to manoeuvre herself on to her back, desperate to shrug off the heavy layers of fabric, twisting in the water to rid herself of them but failing. She is being dragged down again. As she squirms, she catches a fleeting glimpse of the top of Hollie's head. She is frantically thrashing her arms, trying to get back to the jetty, but the current has a hold of her, and is sweeping her mercilessly in the opposite direction.

Lauren tries to shout. 'Stop. Stop moving! Keep still!' But her words are faint, she cannot find the breath for them, and Hollie is splashing and screaming too loud to hear them anyway.

A flash of colour pierces the grey of water and sky. She sees that Taisie, on the jetty above, has unhooked the bright orange life ring from its pole and is clutching it with both hands. She staggers under it as it catches the wind, the rope tangling round her ankles.

'Taisie!' Lauren tries to scream again, unsure whether Taisie has seen her.

She sees Taisie's head swing back and forth, her focus shifting between herself and Hollie. She has one safety ring. One chance. A clear choice. She can only save one person. Will it be her childhood friend, the one who has ferociously tried to protect her? Or will it be Lauren, who now knows all their secrets?

Hollie has seen her too. Her movements become more frantic. She is trying desperately to wave at Taisie but is pushing herself under with every stroke. Lauren feels strangely calm. It's clear to her that Taisie will save her friend, whatever she has done, and maybe, if she does, they will both get away with murder. No one but Lauren will ever know the truth about what happened on this strange, isolated island.

Watching Taisie prepare to throw the ring to Hollie, Lauren floats, letting the water embrace her. In this temperature she knows she doesn't have long to live. With a heavy heart she resigns herself to her fate, and it is almost with a languid sense of peace that she watches Taisie prepare to hurl the life ring to Hollie.

She sees her swing her arm back, take aim and is on the point of letting go when, mid-throw, she stops. And pivots.

Lauren is sliding towards unconsciousness. She feels comfortingly warm now. But at the very edges of her senses, she becomes aware of two things: a flash of orange flying through the sky towards her, and, in the background, the distant thrum of diesel engines.

Chapter Forty

Time morphs, changing shape, speeding up, then slowing down.

There is nothing but a sequence of sensations, interspersed with the intermittent blackness of the void. The stiffness of her fingers grasping for the life ring. The drag of the waves. The bitterness of the saltwater sluicing into her nose and mouth. The pull of the rope on the ring, fighting against the current. The scrape of pebbles against her back. The glare of the sky. The roughness of the sand.

And then a hand, slapping her cheek over and over.

'Wake up! Wake up! Come on! Come back!'

A dark shape above her. Another.

Hands grabbing at her, pulling at wet wool that refuses to give up its grip on her body.

The scour of acid in her throat as she coughs up bile and salt water.

'Lauren. Come on! Come back! I know you can hear me.'

Then pain, as the sensation of defrosting begins to penetrate the numbness of her extremities.

The spasms of her muscles as they remember how to shiver.

The release of closing her eyes. The rage at the voice that will not stop calling her.

Gradually, she realises she is lying on her side on hard wet sand. She can feel the scratchy fibres of a coarse woollen blanket thrown over her.

A strange voice is talking. 'Keep still, love, you're going to be OK.' A new voice, kind. One she doesn't recognise.

Her eyelids flutter and focus on a sturdy pair of black lace-up boots.

Boots. Not slippers.

She is crying, finally giving in to her emotions, streams of tears join the salty water on her face. Someone has come for them. The relief is like a wave of warmth surging through her body. But it is short-lived. In its wake comes a rush of memories that immediately set her body trembling again.

She turns her head to the side, looking along the beach. Twenty yards away, Taisie is sitting hunched on a tarpaulin, a fluorescent orange sheet pulled around her shoulders. The murmur of Taisie's voice reaches her, interspersed with questions from the people who surround her, sharp and insistent.

Further down the beach, an unmoving mound on the sand. A figure stretched out under another orange blanket. Covered, but for a tendril of sodden curly dark hair.

Hollie.

Lauren closes her eyes.

Chapter Forty-one

It is later, that is all she knows.

She is on a stretcher, a dry blanket has been placed gently over her. And there is someone beside her, a vast and reassuring presence. Mac.

'Lauren! Jesus, Lauren. Thank God. Are you awake?'

In response, she uses her elbow to push herself up to a half-sitting position and looks around. The normally empty beach is transformed. Three boats – one rigged up with cameras like the one that brought them over on the first day, the other two the startling red of the coastguard – are pulled up on the shore. Knots of figures, each sporting a lifejacket, huddle together up and down the beach. Some of them bend over Taisie, still sitting, defeated, huddled into herself.

Lauren looks at Mac. 'What happened?'

'You're OK, hen. You're safe. It's over.'

She almost laughs. Over? What does that mean? Then she looks at his face, the concern etched across it, and she sees he has tears in his eyes.

'But what happened? Who are they? Those people?'

'That's Production, isn't it? At last,' he says bitterly. 'Finally got to us. About an hour ago. And then called the coastguard when they saw what had been going on here. The police are on their way, apparently. Flavour of the month, we are. Not that I'm that popular with them right now.' There's a grim furrow to his brow.

'How do you mean?' asks Lauren.

'Had a bit of a barney with them to stop them filming,' says Mac, nodding towards the equipment that is lying unused in the boat. 'Pretty much had to wrestle the bloody cameras out of their hands.' It's clear this is not an exaggeration. 'Bastards,' he adds.

'And the police?' asks Lauren quietly.

Mac nods towards Taisie. 'For her,' he says briefly. Then he takes a deep breath. 'But she told us what happened. I just . . . I can't take it in. Any of it really. The thing with Nate . . . her *dad*? I mean . . .' He trails off. 'You know that bit, right?'

She nods.

'And you know about . . . about how he died? And about Hollie? That it was her who . . .' He puts his hands up to his eyes, turning away from Lauren for a second.

'Yes. I know. But . . . but where is she now? I thought I saw her . . .' There is nothing beyond where Taisie sits crouched on the sand.

'They've taken her on to the lifeboat,' he says quietly. 'On a stretcher.' He confirms what she had feared. 'I'm sorry, Lauren. She didn't make it.'

Lauren lies back down again, trying to take in what he has told her, that another of their number is dead. Further down the beach, people come and go. To her amazement, she sees Frank and Kez, huddled miserably on the edge of the jetty. Mac sees the direction of her gaze.

'Oh, yeah – think they thought they'd film a grand reunion; brought those two back for it. That turned out well, didn't it?'

Lauren allows her mind to drift, finding that it returns again and again to Taisie's story. Image after image of Hollie flash in front of her eyes. Taisie accompanying her in almost every one, like two sides of a coin. Irrelevant details keep drifting into her brain: Taisie's eyes; her voice as she sobbed. Those moments on the jetty, the whirlwind of kicking legs and flailing arms. The boards suddenly disappearing under her feet. The fall.

She keeps coming back to that scene. A tiny snippet of recollection, a minute detail, which she knows is important, lies just outside the frame. It is tugging at the edge of her subconscious, trying to find a way in.

She becomes aware that another boat has moored. When she levers herself up to look, she sees the navy and white of the police with their bulky stab vests, officers already disgorged and gathering round Taisie, who wearily looks up at them and offers her story all over again.

Lauren listens to the rise and fall of her voice, at times subdued, at others high and hysterical as the questions come at her. Fragments of what she says drift over on the wind.

'. . . he just came at me. He was so angry . . . and then he fell . . . it was an accident. I tried to save him . . . I didn't know what to do . . . I told her, she said she'd take care of it, that I didn't need to worry . . . I knew as soon as I saw him what she had done . . . when she saw us on the jetty . . . guessed I'd told Lauren everything. I knew we were both in danger . . . you don't know what she was like, but she was my friend . . . my *best* friend . . .'

And, then in a high-pitched wail: 'I was going to throw it to Hollie. I was. But then I remembered how she pulled Lauren in. She pulled her, on purpose. I saw her do it. I had to save Lauren. I couldn't let Hollie kill her too.'

This last sentence is loud enough to make Lauren push herself up on to her elbows again. She looks down the beach. A hush of concern surrounds the figure in the orange blanket, the police officers, grave and methodical, the girl bending her head towards the sand. Then, as though she feels Lauren's eyes on her, Taisie raises her head and turns slowly to face Lauren, piercing her with those blue-grey eyes.

Freeze frame. Stop. Play it again.

That's it.

That was what Lauren saw as she fell. Those eyes looking into hers, their expression just as it is now. Clear. Cold. Calculating. The realisation hits her like a punch to the solar plexus. She wasn't pulled in like Taisie said, she was pushed. And it wasn't just her who was pushed, it was Hollie too. Muddled images, out of context, tumble through her mind. A hand on her chest. The lightest of pressures, just enough to shift her centre of gravity. Her hands grasping upwards, clawing at nothing, because Taisie stepped backwards, away from her, and put her hands down by her sides. Hollie falling beside her, her expression a mask of horror.

Lauren feels as though she's been winded. She fights to think. The breeze has swung round in the other direction, carrying Taisie's voice away from her, dulling it to an unintelligible murmur. Mac is still quiet beside her, unaware of Lauren's sudden focus. In just a moment, everything has been turned upside down.

What if? What if Hollie wasn't running down the pier to attack them, but to save Lauren? What if, in that moment when Taisie moved towards her to embrace her, Hollie thought she was going to push Lauren in? It was Taisie she went straight for, who she punched first. Not Lauren. Taisie. What if Hollie was trying to keep Taisie away from Lauren. 'Stop. Stop!' she had yelled. In the confusion Lauren thought she was telling Taisie to stop talking, stop spilling their secrets. But what if that wasn't it? What if Hollie knew that Lauren was in mortal danger? That Taisie was behind it all, that she had killed both Nate and Nico, and would stop at nothing to prevent the truth coming out?

What if Hollie's face was contorted not in fury, but in fear? Fear that her friend might be about to kill again.

Chapter Forty-two

Lauren tries to recalibrate everything she has learned and what she knows to be true. Nate was Taisie's father. Taisie, in confronting him, provoked an attack that accidentally ended in his death. That all makes sense. The image of Taisie, running headlong and desperate down that staircase in the dark, panicking, this could all be true.

But the ring. The ring that had felt so deliberately hidden. Suddenly Lauren sees it for what it was: an act borne of calculation, not panic. Not the act of someone who wanted to confess.

And after that? One thing Lauren knows for sure is that Taisie is lying about what happened on the jetty. Hollie didn't pull her in, Taisie purposefully pushed both of them. So, what else is she lying about?

Lauren goes back to the beginning. The girls with their intertwined arms, their heads bent together. It's true that Hollie was always the more outgoing of the two, but did that make her the one in control? In her mind, Lauren switches the parts of Hollie and Taisie, reversing everything she was told on the jetty.

What if was *Taisie* who forced Hollie to help her cover up what happened to Nate? What if it was her, not Hollie who insisted they should say nothing, do nothing before the rest of them found him dead? What if it was Taisie who decided to eliminate Nico, who laced his bowl with yew, then disposed of it, hiding the evidence? Was it Taisie, all along? Is she the consummate liar, and a killer?

What is Lauren's evidence, though? She thinks.

In those dark and desperate minutes when they crowded round Nate's broken body, it was Hollie, not Taisie, who was hysterical. That was not the behaviour of a cold-hearted killer. It was Taisie who first suggested that he had fallen, neatly planting the idea in all their heads. Taisie who said Nate might have wanted to take some time out, alone in the wake of Lauren's accusations. Taisie who subtly backed up Nico when he started accusing her. Right from the start, Taisie had sought to muddy the waters wherever she could. Christ, she even tried to pin Nate's death on Frank earlier. She consistently and successfully did everything she could to turn the spotlight of suspicion away from herself.

Then, when it seemed that Lauren was getting closer to the truth, Taisie told the tale as closely as she could make it fit, sacrificing her best friend in the process.

Oh God, she thinks, Hollie was running *away* from Taisie in the graveyard. Hollie was scared of *her*, not the other way around.

But why save Lauren at all? Why not let her drown with Hollie? That doesn't make sense. If they both drowned, surely, she could get away with everything scot-free?

Lauren suddenly becomes aware of Mac's voice. 'I hope those lot are going to go easy on her. Taisie, I mean. She made a lot of mistakes, but she's admitted to them. And she was a real hero, in the end. She really fought to save you. I still can't believe . . .'

He trails off, but she knows what he wants to say. He can't believe she chose Lauren over Hollie. But Lauren can.

'That it was Hollie all along, it doesn't bear thinking about. I wouldn't wish that end on anyone. But when I think of what she did. What she almost did to you.' He looks down at Lauren quickly. 'I can't even think about it. Thank God for Taisie.'

Thank God for Taisie . . . So that's how the story will play out. That's the calculation Taisie made as she stood with the life ring on the jetty. If she saved Lauren, she would have a witness and she would be a hero in the end. The victim who made the right choice. If she let Hollie drown, the only other person apart from her who knew the *whole* truth, she could guarantee her secrets would be safe for ever.

Mac is still speaking, and interrupts her thoughts. '. . . you were right all along, about the murders. I should have believed you. I'm sorry. And you were right about Nate. I don't think you'll have any trouble getting people to believe he was the monster you said he was now. That'll show that bloody boss of yours, won't it?'

Lauren almost laughs. It's true. Out of the terrible wreckage of this week, the only thing salvaged is Lauren's reputation. Nate is exposed, and Lauren is vindicated.

She lies back on her stretcher, gazing past Mac's shoulder at the sky. It is as though two separate futures are written there. She can lie here, under her warm blanket, and let it all play out as Taisie has planned.

She can see it now: there will be investigations, accompanied by acres and acres of coverage on every possible media platform. A story full of drama, with a movie-star villain and a wicked social-media princess. An avaricious blackmailer who met a terrible end, and a brave reporter who risked her life to uncover the truth. And at the centre of it all, a fragile orphan, abandoned by her father, witness to the terrible accident of his death, and controlled by her terrifyingly ambitious friend in a toxic relationship. The girl who sacrificed her best friend, choosing instead to save Lauren's life over that of a killer.

And in the process? Lauren's own reputation will be restored. Everyone who didn't believe her campaign against Nate will have to admit she was right. The last two years of her life will be justified. She will be allowed back on air, more famous than she has ever been. Both she and Taisie will emerge as survivor-victims. She will finally be allowed to make her documentary about Nate, and, given the drama of his demise and her involvement in it, she will doubtless win awards. It is a bright future, an exciting one, and it is tantalisingly within her reach.

But there is an alternative. One where Lauren breaks out of her assigned role in this fable. One where she isn't the brave reporter, but a deluded and failed journalist, trying to bring down the heroine. In this future, she can launch into another lonely, unsupported crusade. One where stories conflict and courtrooms become battlegrounds of 'she said/she said'. Where warring tribes of internet supporters, Lauren's vastly outnumbered by Taisie's online army of fans, hurl vicious insults across the void. Where her reputation ensures she never gets another reporting job again. The woman who always bears a grudge. Who went on a TV show and came back with three dead bodies behind her and yet another vendetta.

There are no winners in this scenario. Every single player loses, including the others, Jude and Jackson, even Frank and Kez, and Mac. All forever tarnished by the grisly conundrum of what happened on Eilean Manach. And where is her proof? It's just her memory of Taisie's remorseless eyes, and a tiny, destabilising push. How can she bring that to bear against the rushing tide of Taisie's story? What will it achieve, throwing that shard of information into the mix?

And then she remembers Hollie. Hollie and her beautiful smile, her easy laugh, her quiet kindness, and her misplaced loyalty to her friend. A friend who destroyed her, in the end.

Lauren tilts her head sideways, gazing down the beach one more time to look at Taisie, who lifts her head and stares directly into Lauren's eyes, defiant.

Lauren looks back upwards again, at the sky, and lets out a long, painful sigh.

'Mac,' she says. 'I've got something to tell you.'

Acknowledgements

Writing *Isolation Island* has been one of the most challenging but most enjoyable things I have ever done. I have had such fun getting to know my characters and losing myself in the strange world I have made them live in, and I couldn't have done it without the support of a huge team.

First thanks go to my brilliant editor Lucy Dauman and publicist Rosie Margesson for being so enthusiastic about my wild idea when I first pitched it to you at the Headline office in London. Your excitement and belief in it have been infectious and have carried me through. The novel is deliciously darker and sharper thanks to you, Lucy. I have loved working with you both. Thanks to Sophie Wilson for zealously picking up the manuscript for the final edit and gently encouraging me to let it go.

Federica, Alexia, Hannah, Isabel and everyone else at Headline who has got behind this book, I have been overwhelmed by your support and it has been a joy to work with you. I know you aren't meant to judge a book by the cover, but I would love it if this could be an exception; Caroline Young, you created the best jacket I could ever have imagined. A huge thanks also to the sales teams and booksellers who work so hard to bring books into readers' hands.

I owe a huge debt of gratitude to everyone who has gone out of their way to respond to my bizarre requests for information while researching the book, which have ranged from the ridiculous to the macabre.

My particular thanks go to Emily Lanigan-Palotai, Collections Manager at Chester Cathedral, who furnished me with brilliant details about how monks lived in centuries gone by, including their fluffy slippers. To the plant expert John Knox at Alnwick's Poison Garden who entertained long discussions about the pros and cons of lethal vegetation and terrible ways to die. To Gabbi Batchelor from the water safety team at the RNLI who talked me through how to survive in freezing cold water. To Helen Monk who is not just one of my most loyal friends, but also very helpfully, a GP and who was happy to answer endless gruesome medical questions from me. Thanks too to the wonderful Ella Rose-Dove for talking to me about her experience of living with a prosthetic leg.

To my sisterhood of feisty females, in no particular order: Bee, Treens, Jay, Lizzie, Kate, Steph, Claire and Jane, without you this would have been a lonely journey. Thank you for listening while I regaled you with stories about my characters as if they were real, and for volunteering to be my first readers.

To my wonderful literary agent Elly James, you are part of that sisterhood and without your calm and expert guidance there would be no Eilean Manach; thank you for always being there for me. Thanks too, to freelance editor Celia Hayley for helping me find the confidence to see my way through the early drafts.

Special thanks to Kate Mosse, the ferocious and indefatigable champion of women writers everywhere – without your encouragement I would not have dared to write a single word.

In the creation of *Isolation Island*, I owe a huge debt of thanks to everyone I have worked with on reality TV shows. The events in this book are no way a reflection of your hard work and dedication but rather, an homage to the incredible realities you create.

To my family, to David, Mia and Scarlett, your patience, which I know at times I have tested, has been admirable and much appreciated. I can't promise I won't write another book, but when you read this one, I hope all those conversations I have had about *Isolation Island* will finally make sense, and you enjoy it as much as I have enjoyed writing it.

And finally, thanks to you for spending your precious time reading it.

Louise